CARTOON NETWORK

JPA

JAM PACKED ACTION!

Dan DiDio, VP-Editorial
Ben Abernathy, Editor
Ed Roeder, Art Director
Paul Levitz, President & Publisher
Georg Brewer, VP-Design & Retail Product Development
Richard Bruning, Senior VP-Creative Director
Patrick Caldon, Senior VP-Finance & Operations
Chris Caramalis, VP-Finance
Terri Cunningham, VP-Managing Editor
Alison Gill, VP-Manufacturing
Rich Johnson, VP-Book Trade Sales
Hank Kanalz, VP-General Manager, WildStorm
Lillian Laserson, Senior VP & General Counsel
Jim Lee, Editorial Director-WildStorm
David McKillips, VP-Advertising & Custom Publishing
John Nee, VP-Business Development
Gregory Noveck, Senior VP-Creative Affairs
Cheryl Rubin, VP-Brand Management
Bob Wayne, VP-Sales & Marketing

Script Adaptations by WildStorm
Lettering and Interior Design: Comicraft
Special Thanks: Kevin Bricklin, Connie Baldwin
and Sophia Psomiadis

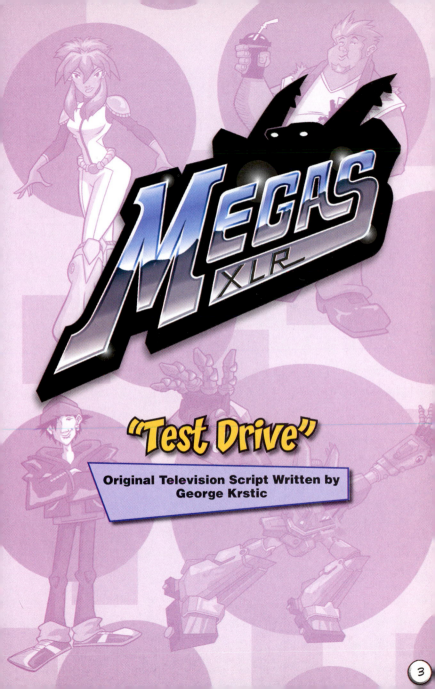

MEGAS XLR

"Test Drive"

**Original Television Script Written by
George Krstic**

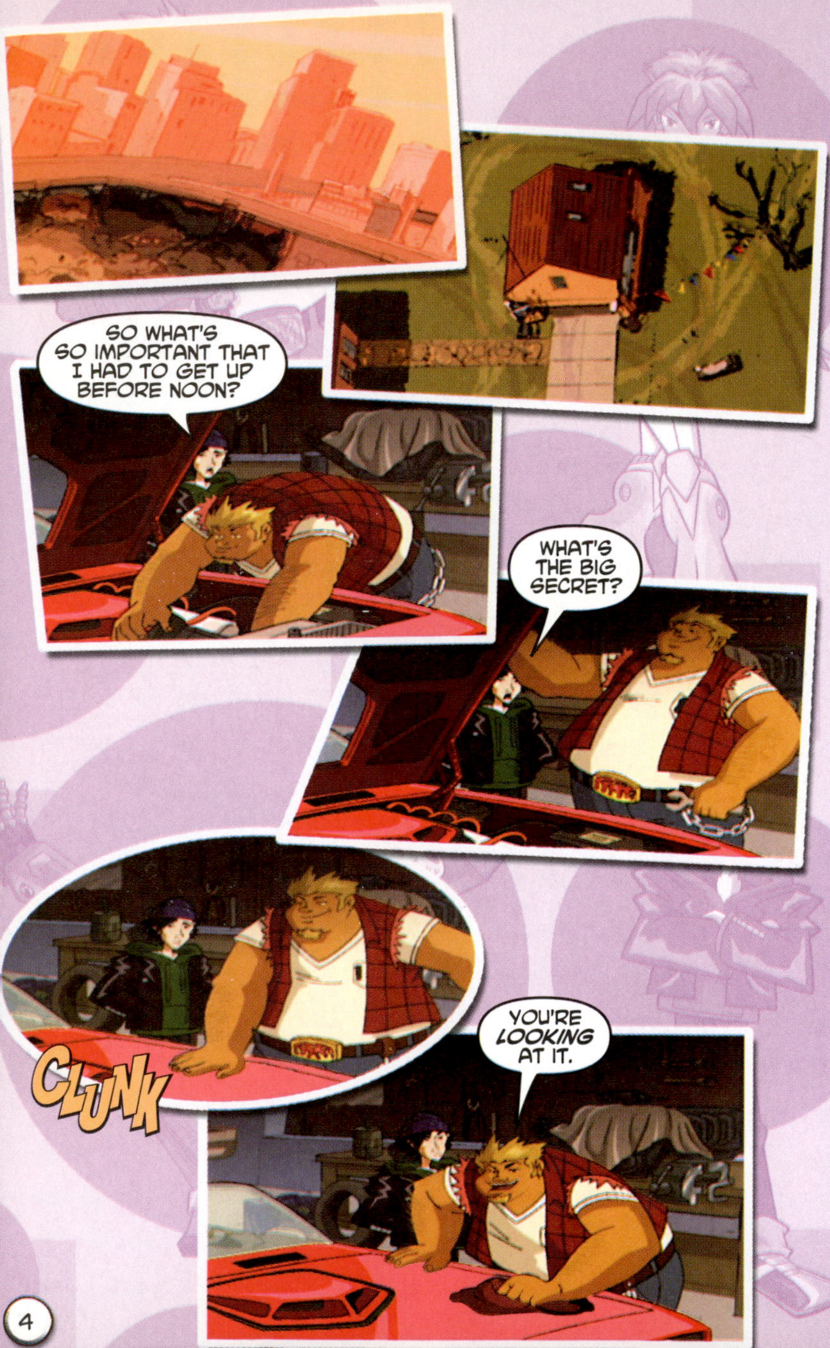
SO WHAT'S SO IMPORTANT THAT I HAD TO GET UP BEFORE NOON?
WHAT'S THE BIG SECRET?
CLUNK
YOU'RE *LOOKING* AT IT.

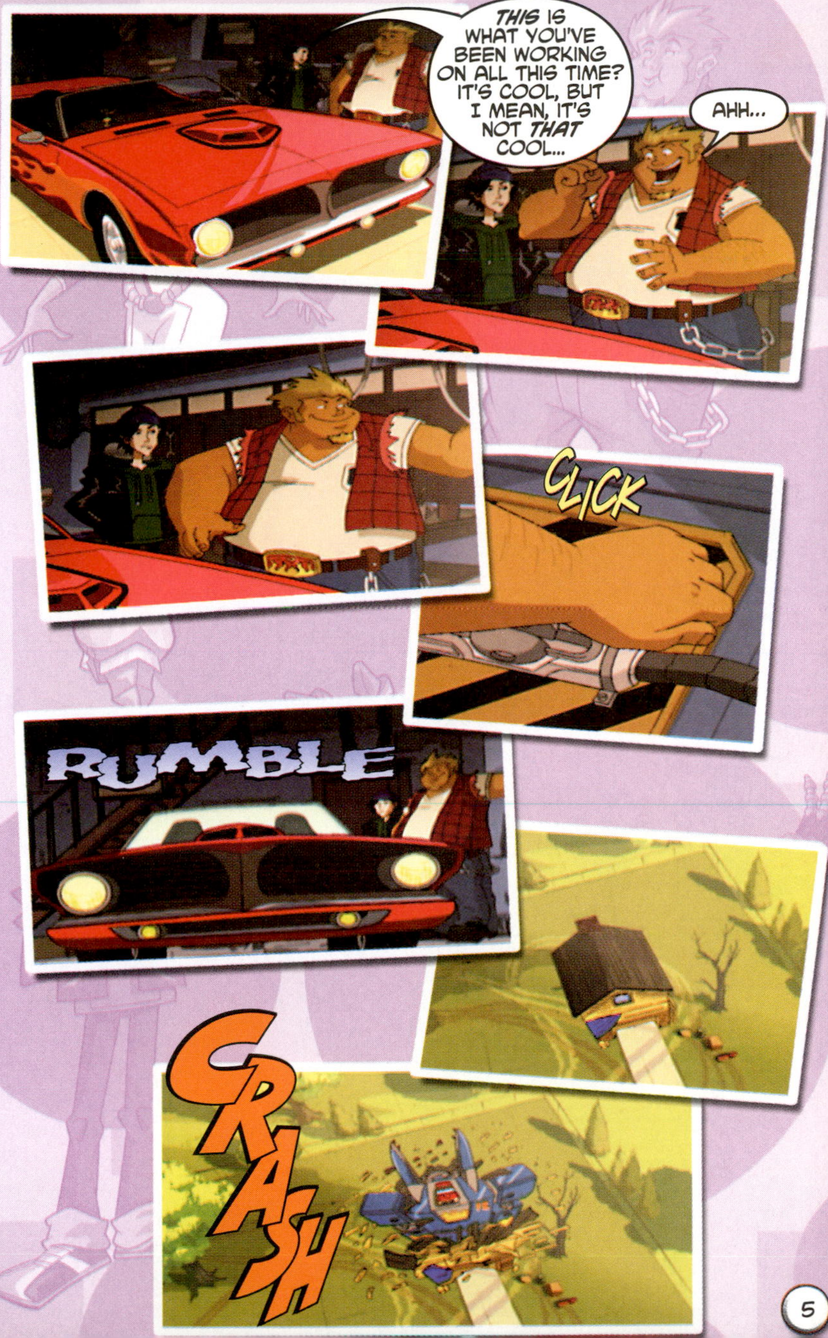
THIS IS WHAT YOU'VE BEEN WORKING ON ALL THIS TIME? IT'S COOL, BUT I MEAN, IT'S NOT *THAT* COOL...
AHH...
CLICK
RUMBLE
CRASH

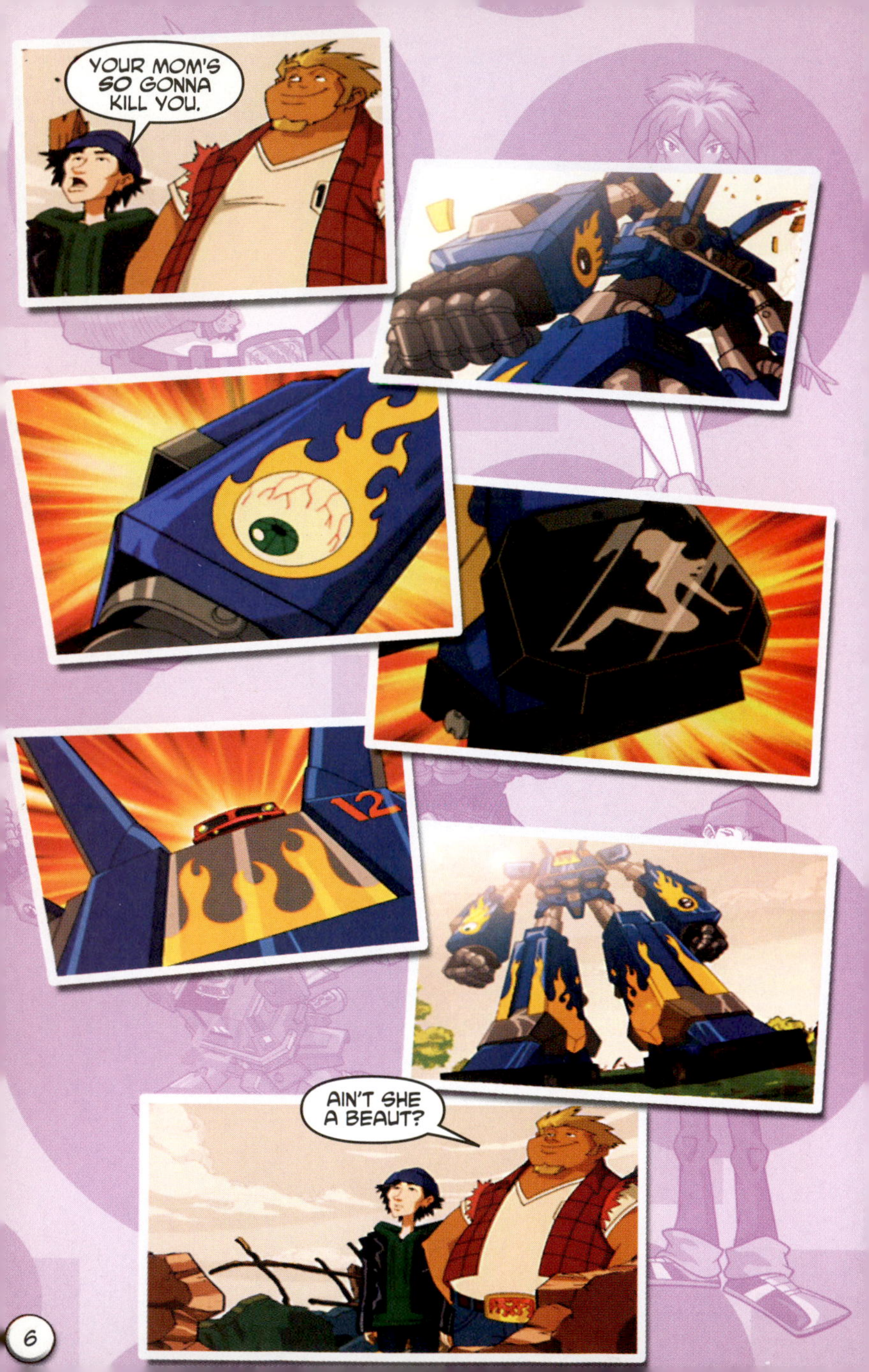
YOUR MOM'S SO GONNA KILL YOU.
12
AIN'T SHE A BEAUT?

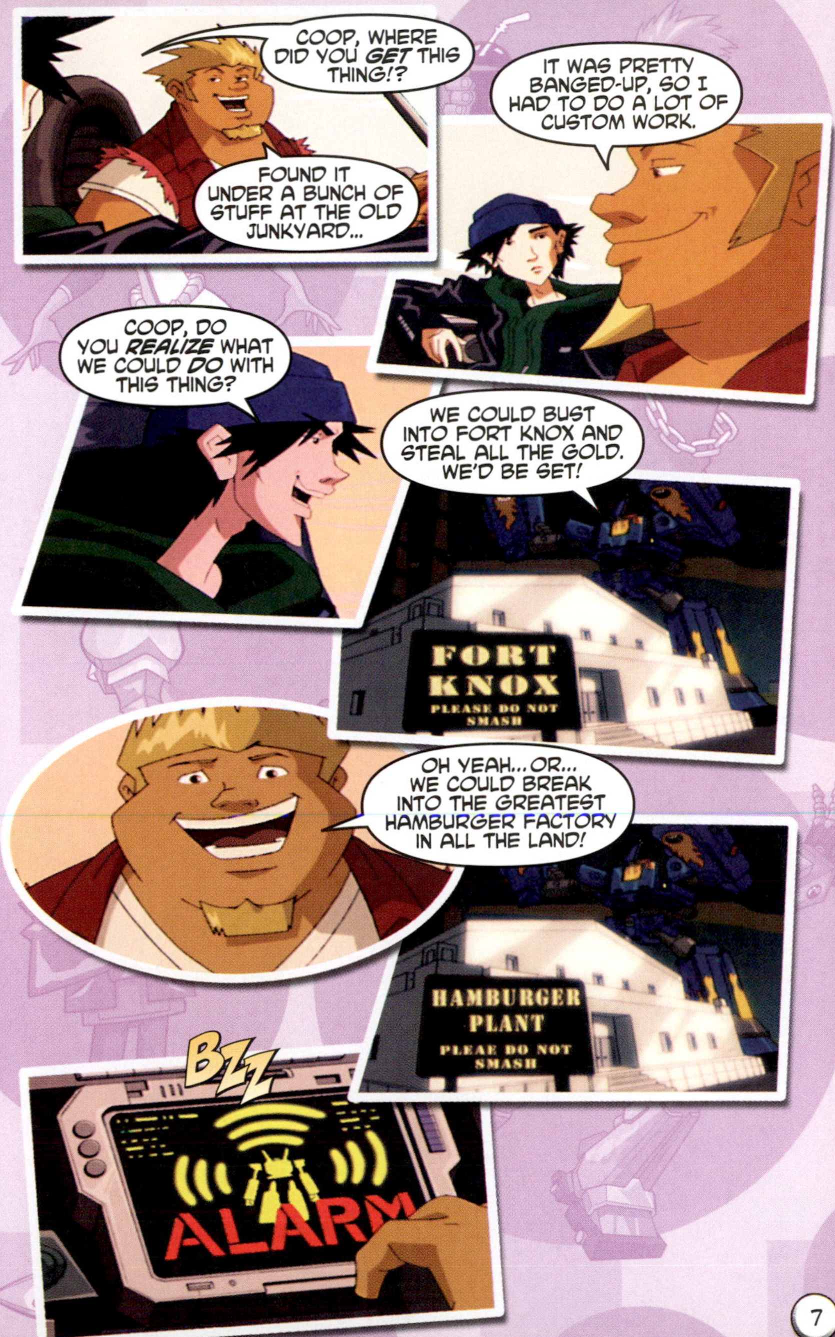
COOP, WHERE DID YOU GET THIS THING!?
FOUND IT UNDER A BUNCH OF STUFF AT THE OLD JUNKYARD...
IT WAS PRETTY BANGED-UP, SO I HAD TO DO A LOT OF CUSTOM WORK.
COOP, DO YOU REALIZE WHAT WE COULD DO WITH THIS THING?
WE COULD BUST INTO FORT KNOX AND STEAL ALL THE GOLD. WE'D BE SET!
FORT KNOX
PLEASE DO NOT SMASH
OH YEAH... OR... WE COULD BREAK INTO THE GREATEST HAMBURGER FACTORY IN ALL THE LAND!
HAMBURGER PLANT
PLEAE DO NOT SMASH
BZZ
ALARM

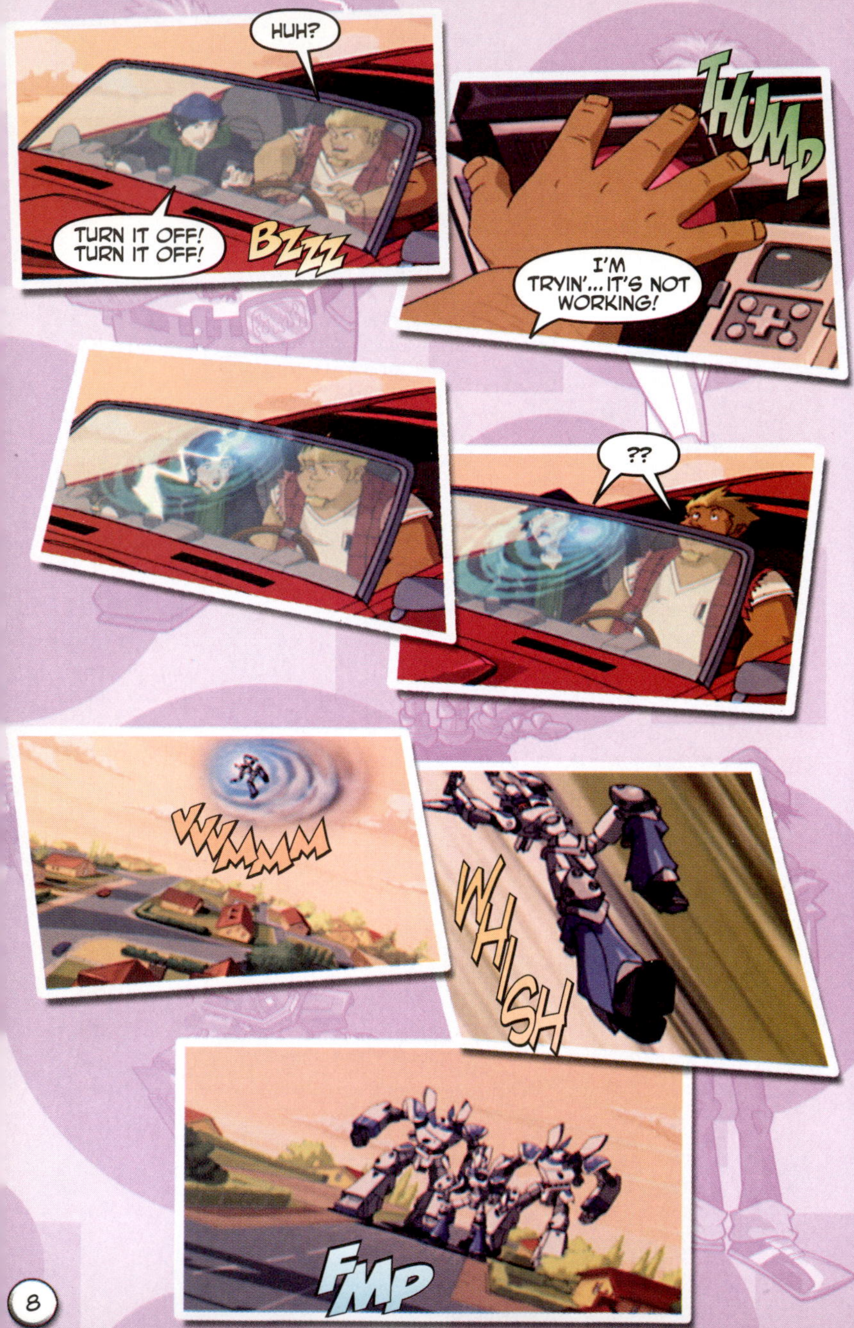
HUH?
TURN IT OFF! TURN IT OFF!
BZZZ
THUMP
I'M TRYIN'... IT'S NOT WORKING!
??
VVVMMM
WHISH
FMP

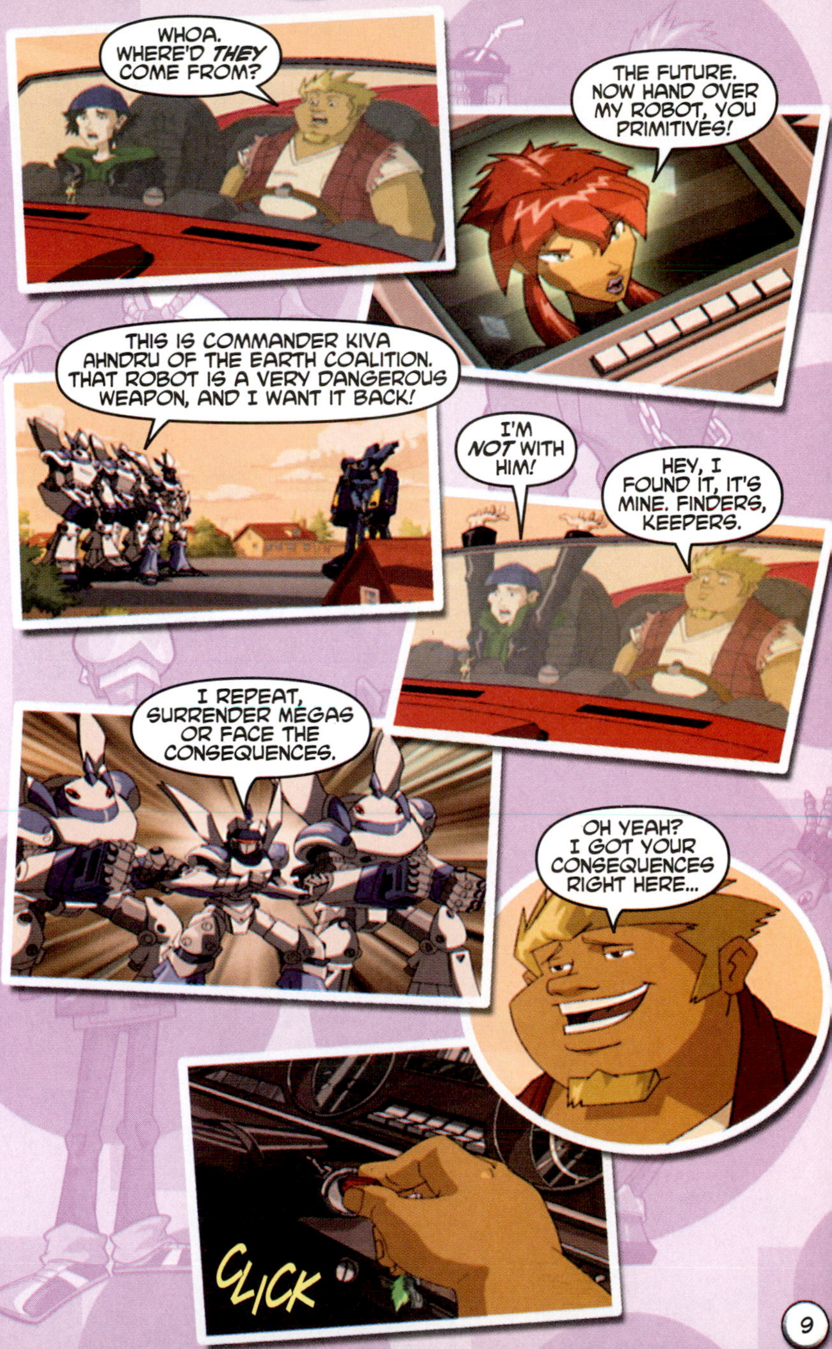
WHOA. WHERE'D *THEY* COME FROM?
THE FUTURE. NOW HAND OVER MY ROBOT, YOU PRIMITIVES!
THIS IS COMMANDER KIVA AHNDRU OF THE EARTH COALITION. THAT ROBOT IS A VERY DANGEROUS WEAPON, AND I WANT IT BACK!
I'M *NOT* WITH HIM!
HEY, I FOUND IT, IT'S MINE. FINDERS, KEEPERS.
I REPEAT, SURRENDER MEGAS OR FACE THE CONSEQUENCES.
OH YEAH? I GOT YOUR CONSEQUENCES RIGHT HERE...
CLICK

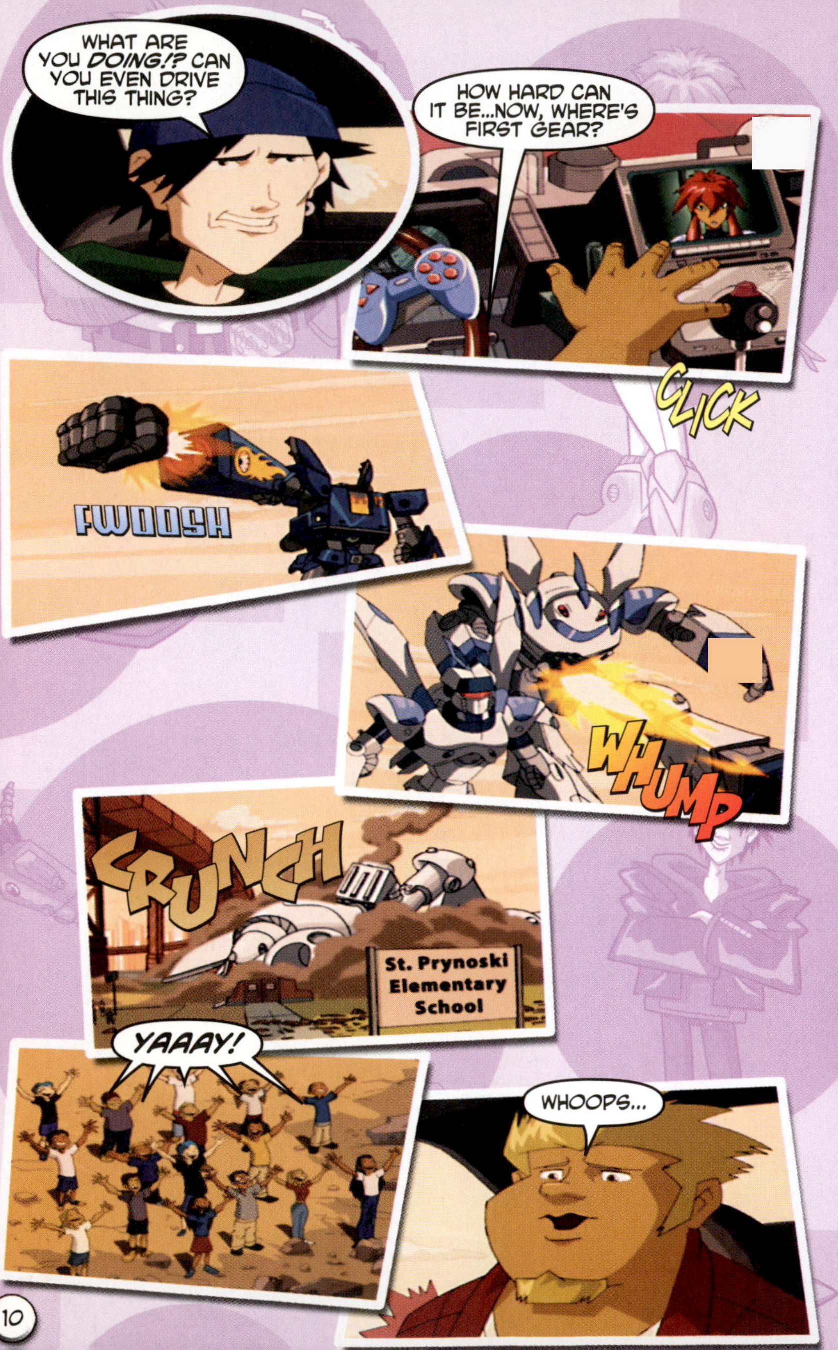
WHAT ARE YOU DOING!? CAN YOU EVEN DRIVE THIS THING?
HOW HARD CAN IT BE...NOW, WHERE'S FIRST GEAR?
CLICK
FWOOSH
WHUMP
CRUNCH
St. Prynoski Elementary School
YAAAY!
WHOOPS...

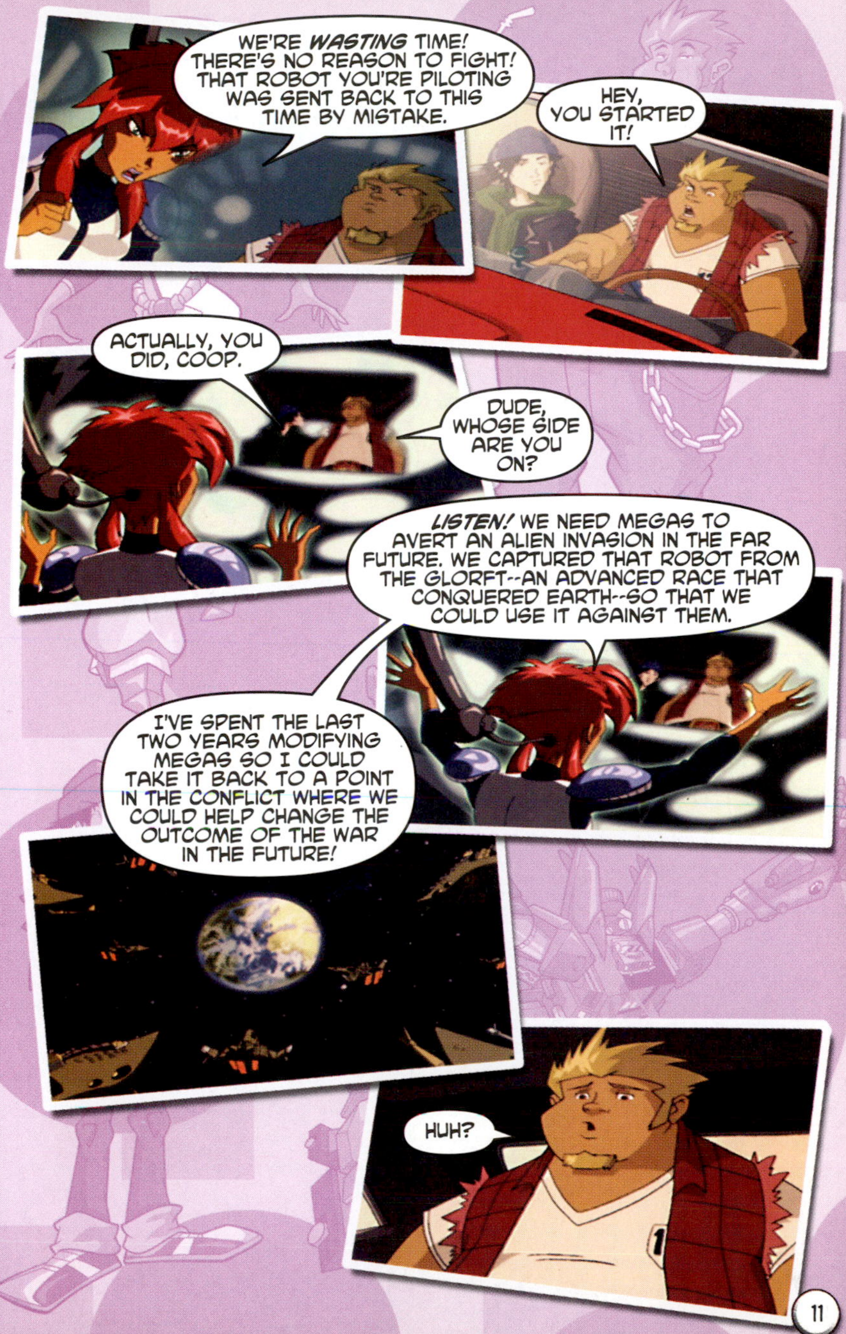

WE'RE WASTING TIME! THERE'S NO REASON TO FIGHT! THAT ROBOT YOU'RE PILOTING WAS SENT BACK TO THIS TIME BY MISTAKE.
HEY, YOU STARTED IT!
ACTUALLY, YOU DID, COOP.
DUDE, WHOSE SIDE ARE YOU ON?
LISTEN! WE NEED MEGAS TO AVERT AN ALIEN INVASION IN THE FAR FUTURE. WE CAPTURED THAT ROBOT FROM THE GLORFT--AN ADVANCED RACE THAT CONQUERED EARTH--SO THAT WE COULD USE IT AGAINST THEM.
I'VE SPENT THE LAST TWO YEARS MODIFYING MEGAS SO I COULD TAKE IT BACK TO A POINT IN THE CONFLICT WHERE WE COULD HELP CHANGE THE OUTCOME OF THE WAR IN THE FUTURE!
HUH?

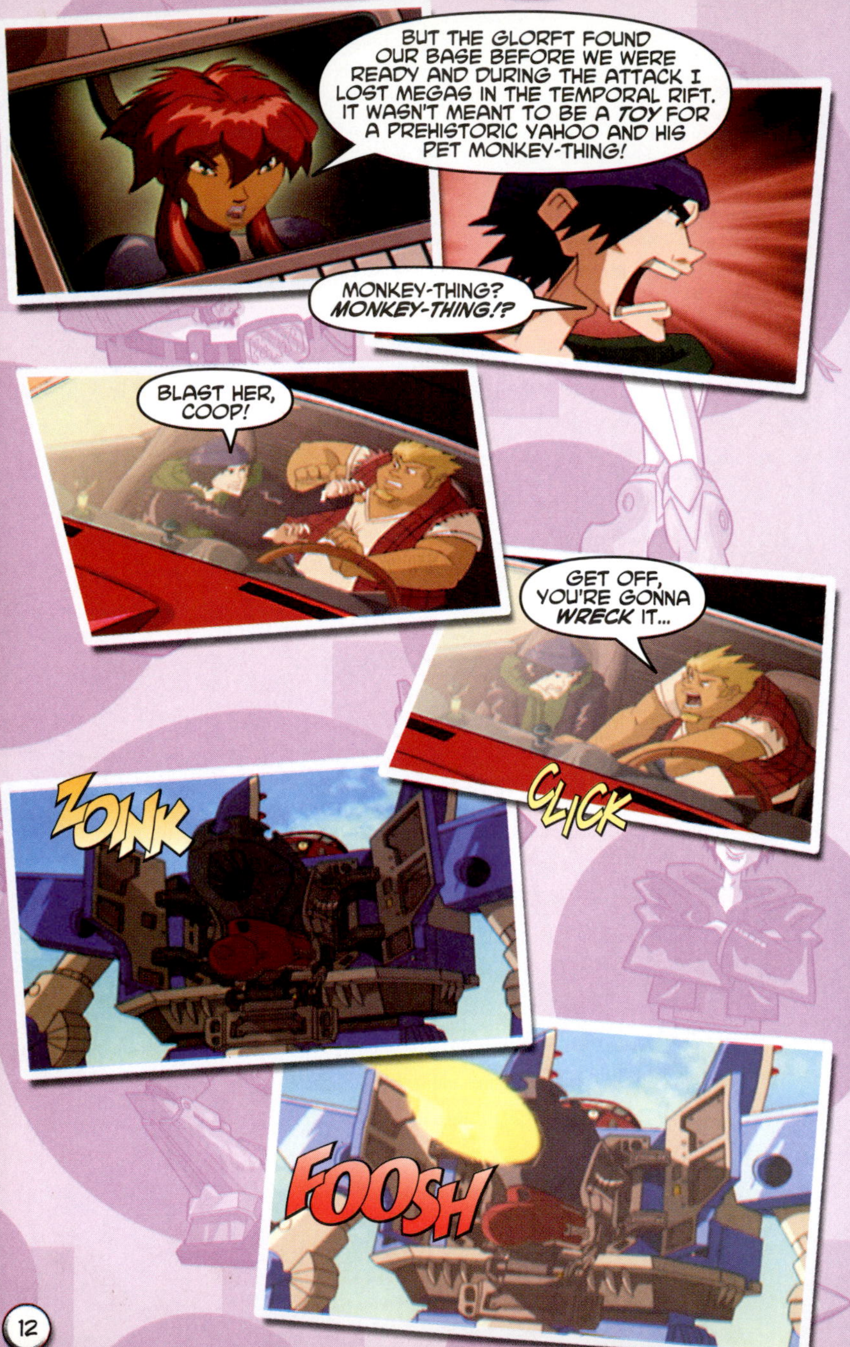
BUT THE GLORFT FOUND OUR BASE BEFORE WE WERE READY AND DURING THE ATTACK I LOST MEGAS IN THE TEMPORAL RIFT. IT WASN'T MEANT TO BE A *TOY* FOR A PREHISTORIC YAHOO AND HIS PET MONKEY-THING!
MONKEY-THING? ***MONKEY-THING!?***
BLAST HER, COOP!
GET OFF, YOU'RE GONNA ***WRECK*** IT...
CLICK
ZONK
FOOSH

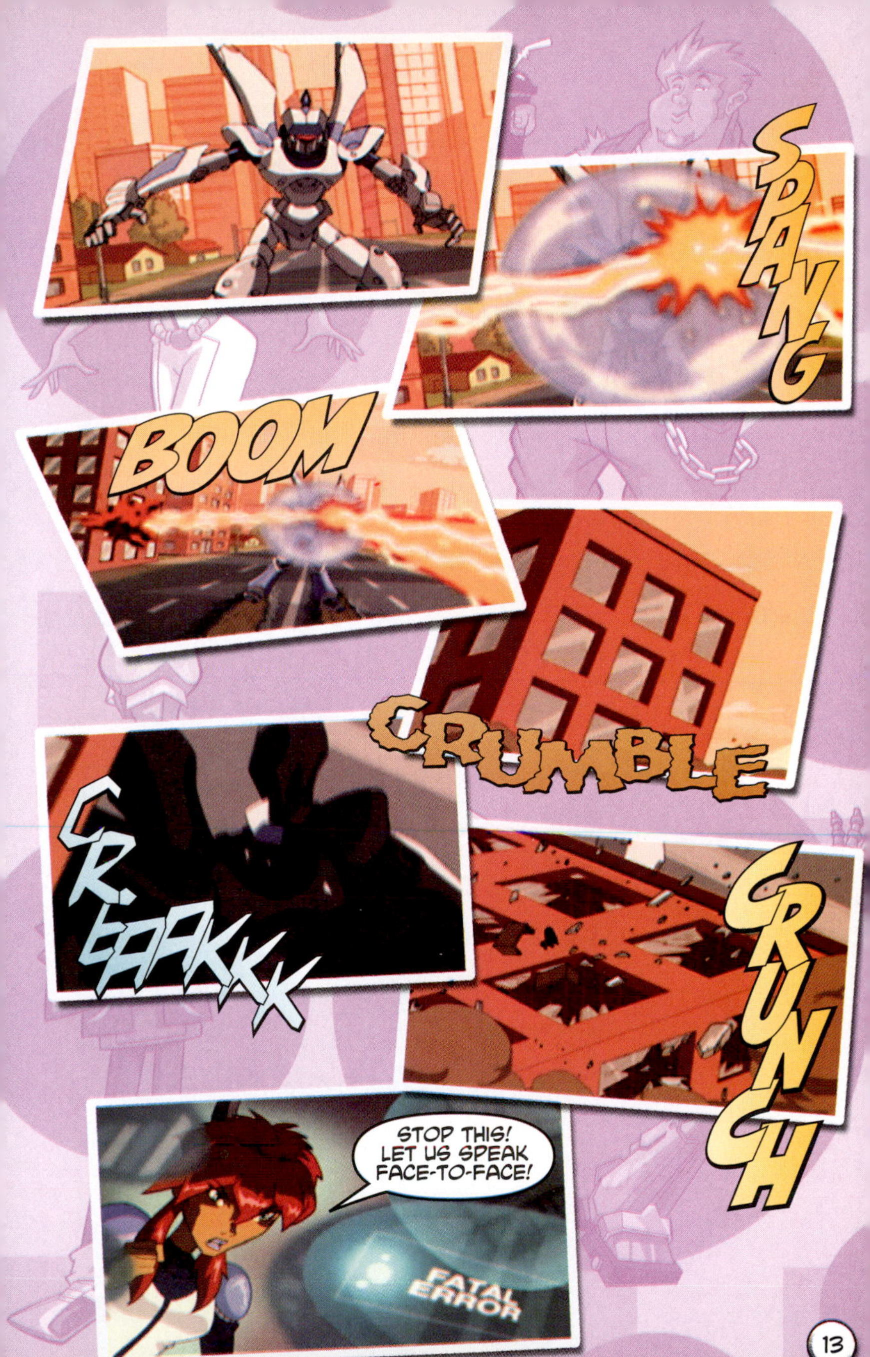

SPANG
BOOM
CRUMBLE
CRAAKKK
CRUNCH
STOP THIS! LET US SPEAK FACE-TO-FACE!
FATAL ERROR

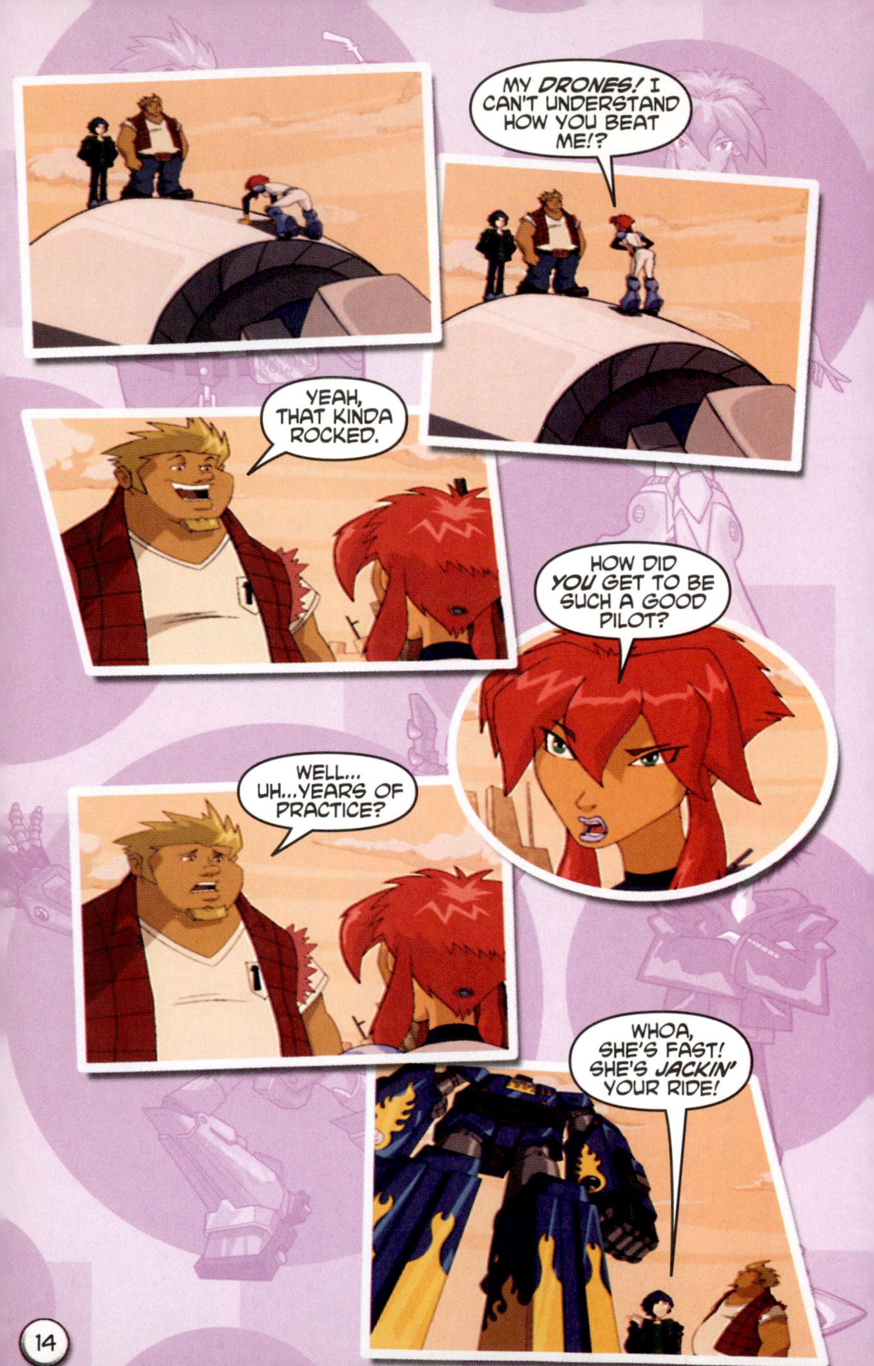
MY DRONES! I CAN'T UNDERSTAND HOW YOU BEAT ME!?
YEAH, THAT KINDA ROCKED.
HOW DID YOU GET TO BE SUCH A GOOD PILOT?
WELL... UH...YEARS OF PRACTICE?
WHOA, SHE'S FAST! SHE'S JACKIN' YOUR RIDE!

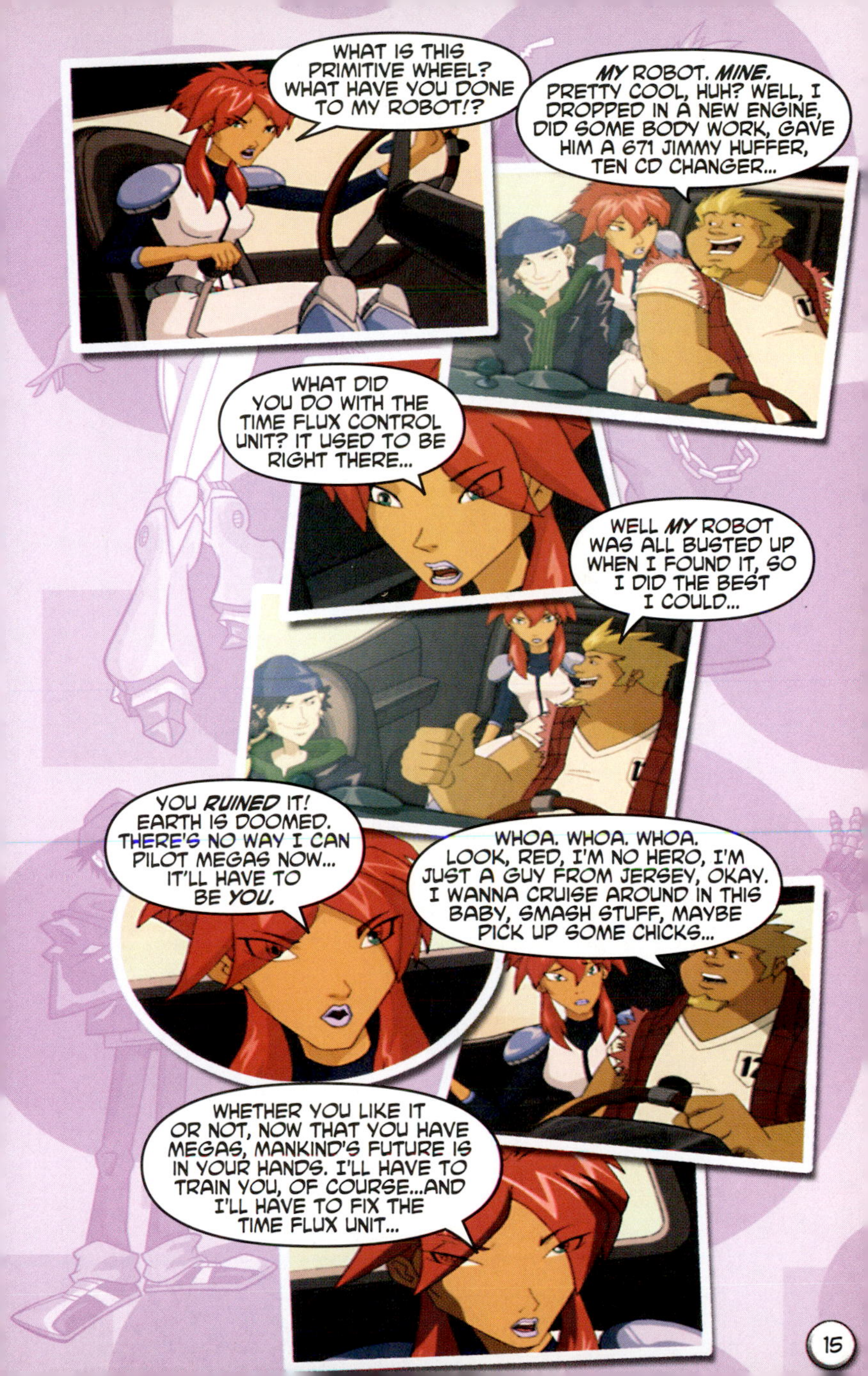
WHAT IS THIS PRIMITIVE WHEEL? WHAT HAVE YOU DONE TO MY ROBOT!?
MY ROBOT. *MINE.* PRETTY COOL, HUH? WELL, I DROPPED IN A NEW ENGINE, DID SOME BODY WORK, GAVE HIM A 671 JIMMY HUFFER, TEN CD CHANGER...
WHAT DID YOU DO WITH THE TIME FLUX CONTROL UNIT? IT USED TO BE RIGHT THERE...
WELL *MY* ROBOT WAS ALL BUSTED UP WHEN I FOUND IT, SO I DID THE BEST I COULD...
YOU *RUINED* IT! EARTH IS DOOMED. THERE'S NO WAY I CAN PILOT MEGAS NOW... IT'LL HAVE TO BE *YOU.*
WHOA. WHOA. WHOA. LOOK, RED, I'M NO HERO, I'M JUST A GUY FROM JERSEY, OKAY. I WANNA CRUISE AROUND IN THIS BABY, SMASH STUFF, MAYBE PICK UP SOME CHICKS...
WHETHER YOU LIKE IT OR NOT, NOW THAT YOU HAVE MEGAS, MANKIND'S FUTURE IS IN YOUR HANDS. I'LL HAVE TO TRAIN YOU, OF COURSE...AND I'LL HAVE TO FIX THE TIME FLUX UNIT...

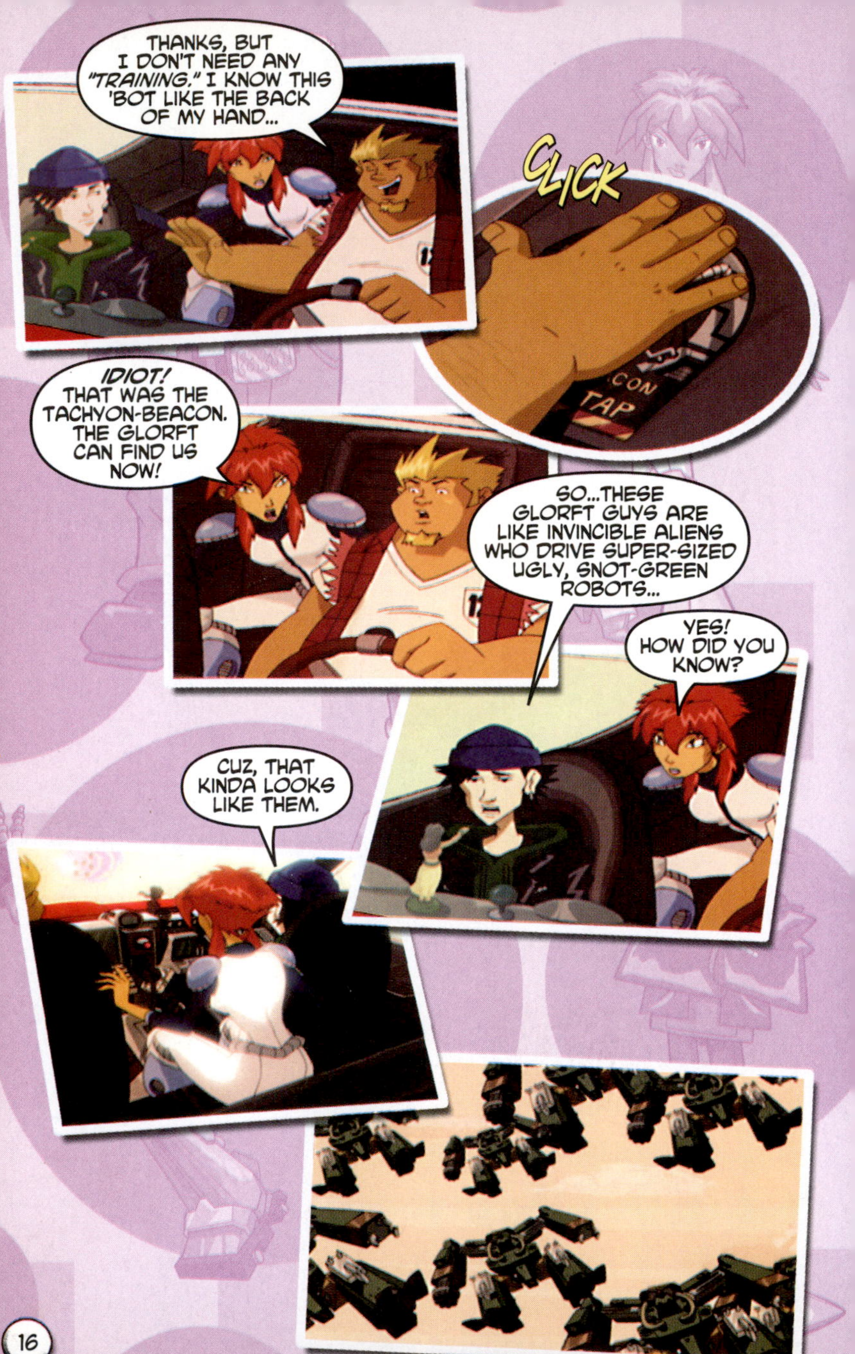
THANKS, BUT I DON'T NEED ANY "TRAINING." I KNOW THIS 'BOT LIKE THE BACK OF MY HAND...
CLICK
IDIOT! THAT WAS THE TACHYON-BEACON. THE GLORFT CAN FIND US NOW!
SO...THESE GLORFT GUYS ARE LIKE INVINCIBLE ALIENS WHO DRIVE SUPER-SIZED UGLY, SNOT-GREEN ROBOTS...
YES! HOW DID YOU KNOW?
CUZ, THAT KINDA LOOKS LIKE THEM.

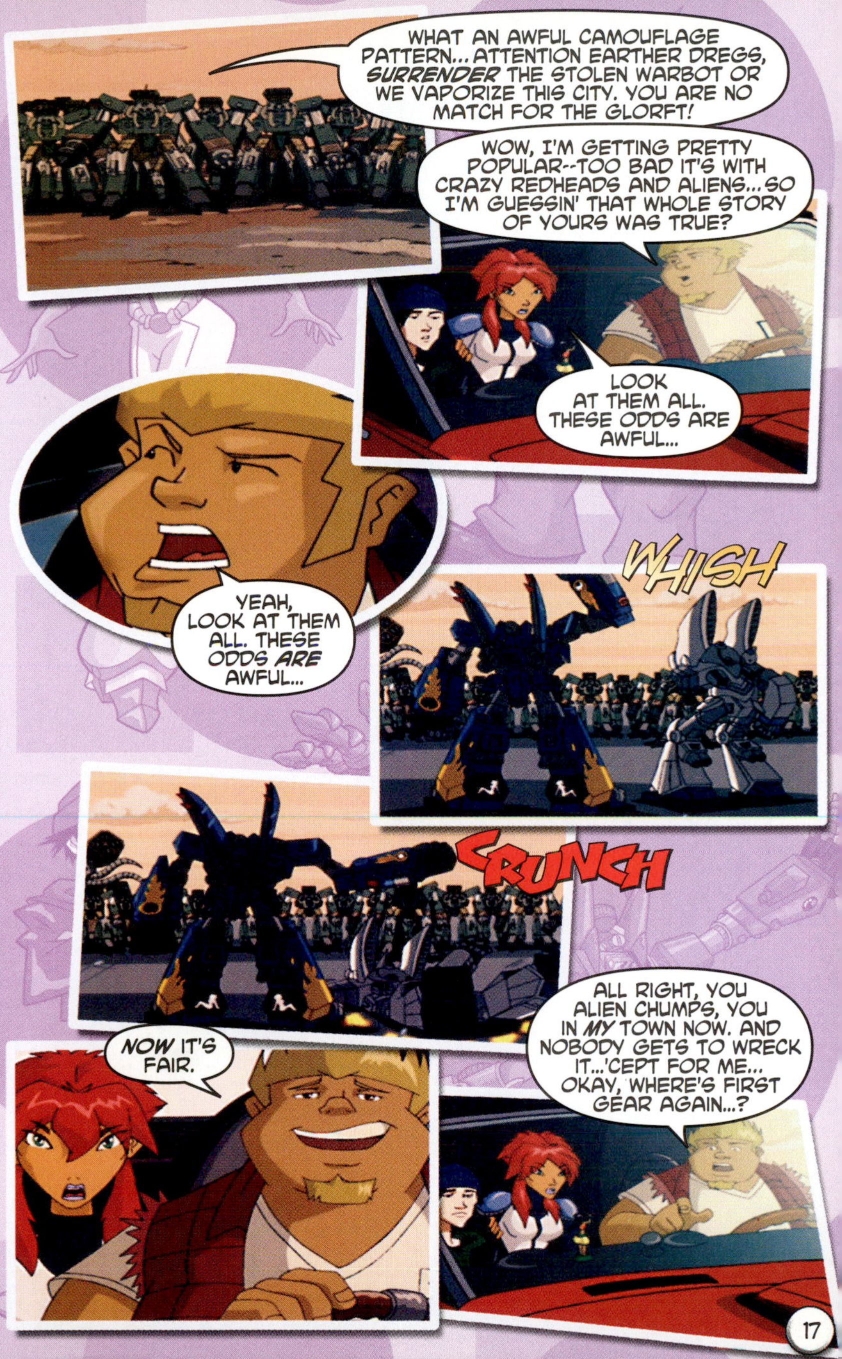

WHAT AN AWFUL CAMOUFLAGE PATTERN... ATTENTION EARTHER DREGS, SURRENDER THE STOLEN WARBOT OR WE VAPORIZE THIS CITY. YOU ARE NO MATCH FOR THE GLORFT!
WOW, I'M GETTING PRETTY POPULAR--TOO BAD IT'S WITH CRAZY REDHEADS AND ALIENS... SO I'M GUESSIN' THAT WHOLE STORY OF YOURS WAS TRUE?
LOOK AT THEM ALL. THESE ODDS ARE AWFUL...
YEAH, LOOK AT THEM ALL. THESE ODDS ARE AWFUL...
WHISH
CRUNCH
ALL RIGHT, YOU ALIEN CHUMPS, YOU IN MY TOWN NOW. AND NOBODY GETS TO WRECK IT...'CEPT FOR ME... OKAY, WHERE'S FIRST GEAR AGAIN...?
NOW IT'S FAIR.

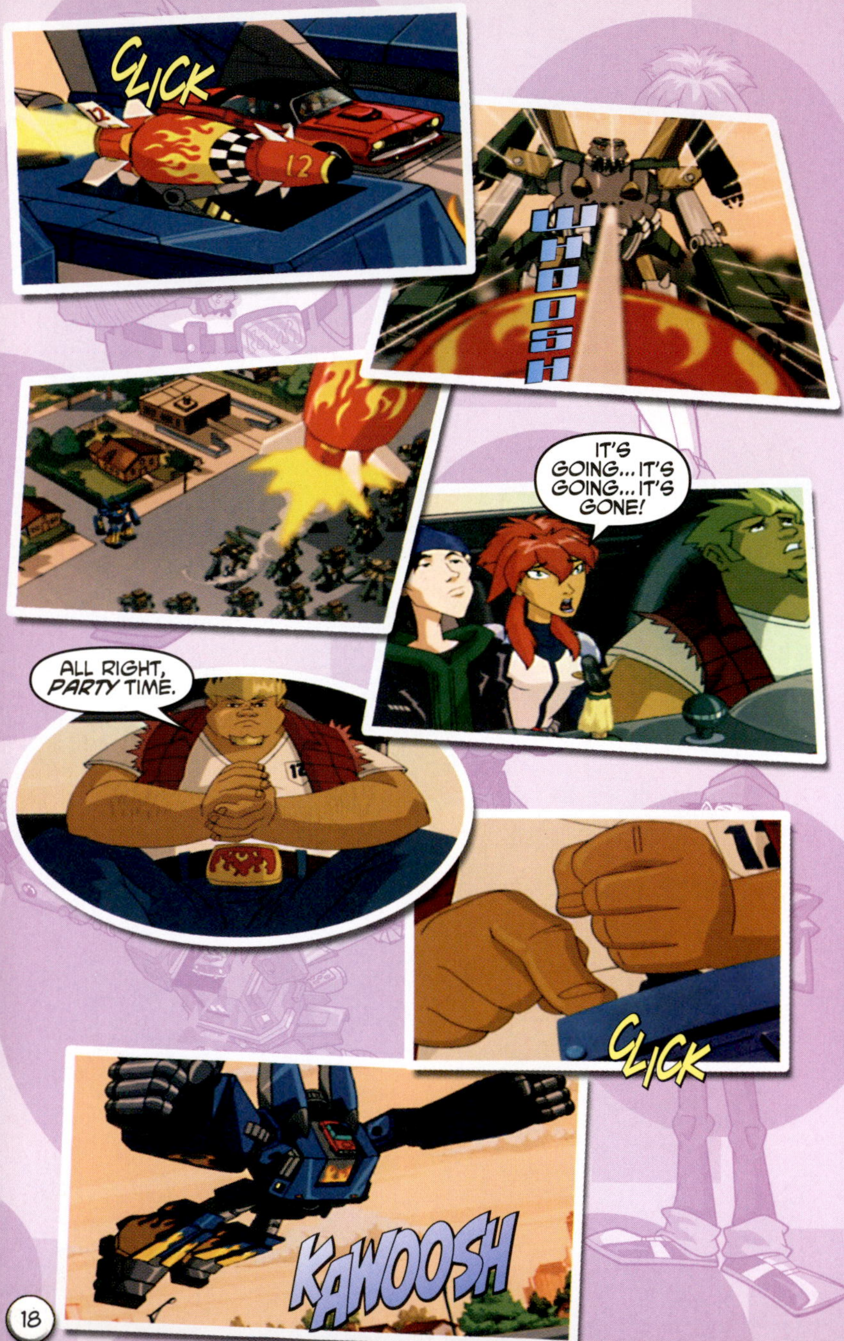
CLICK
WHOOSH
IT'S GOING... IT'S GOING... IT'S GONE!
ALL RIGHT, PARTY TIME.
CLICK
KAWOOSH

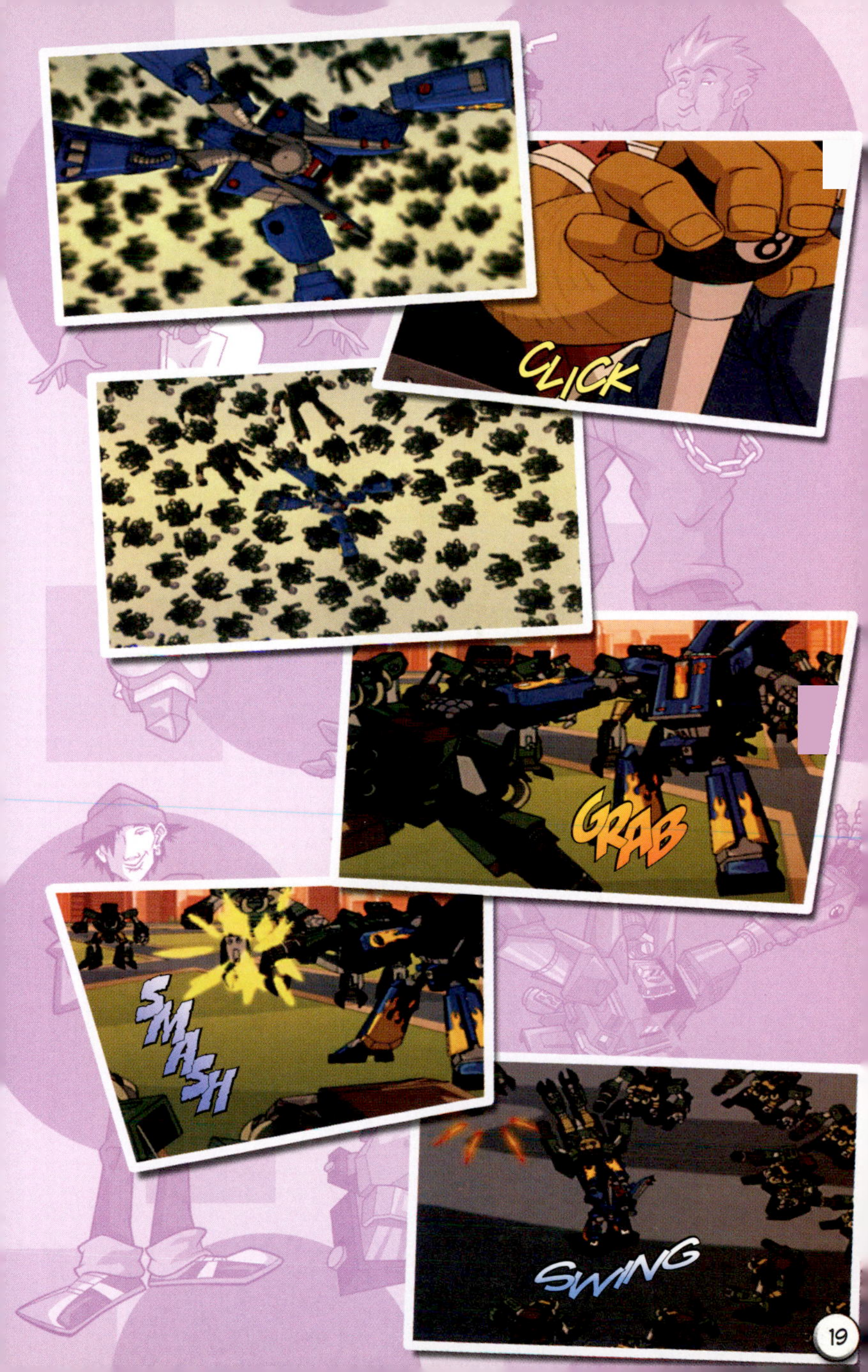
CLICK
GRAB
SMASH
SWING

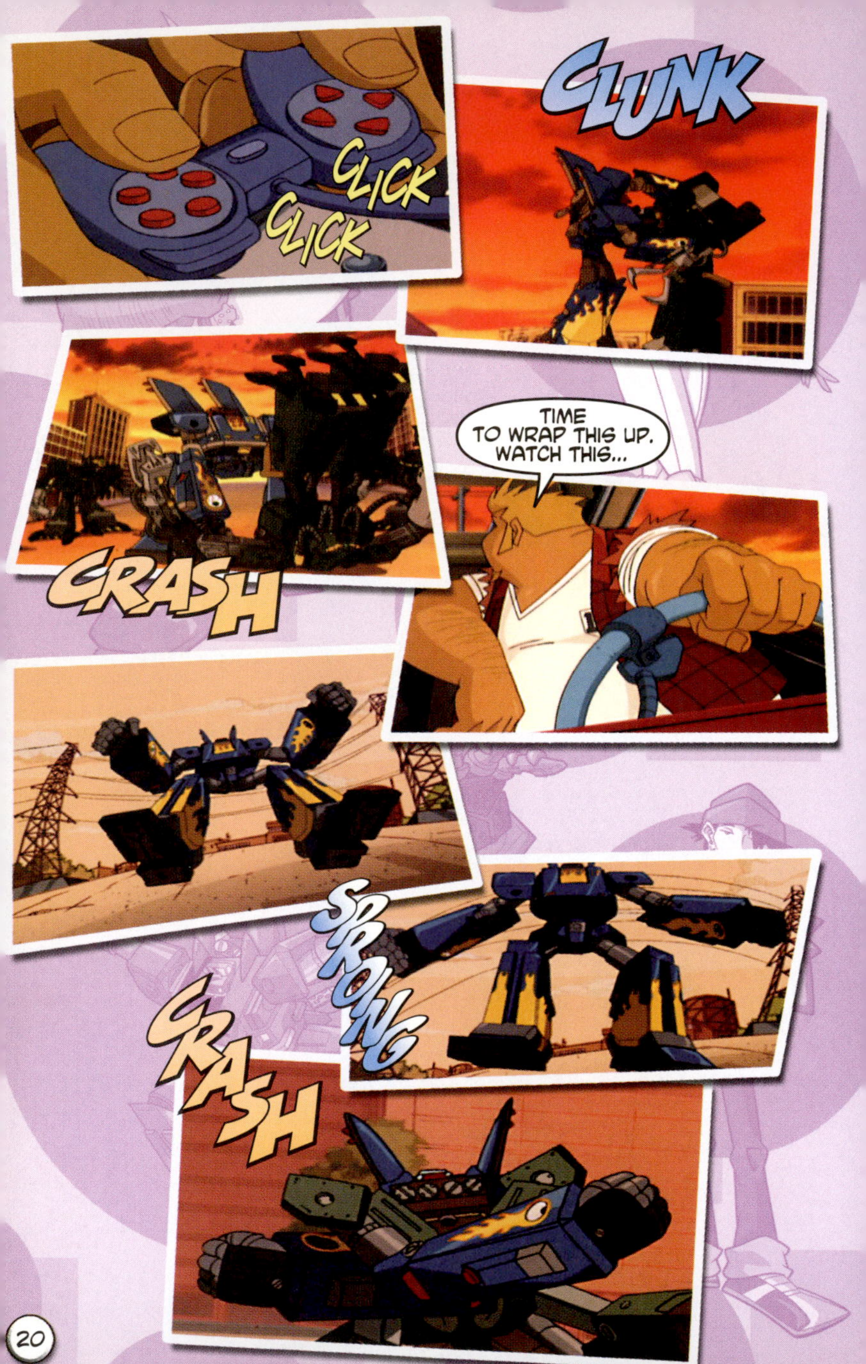
CLICK
CLICK
CLUNK
CRASH
TIME TO WRAP THIS UP. WATCH THIS...
SPRONG
CRASH

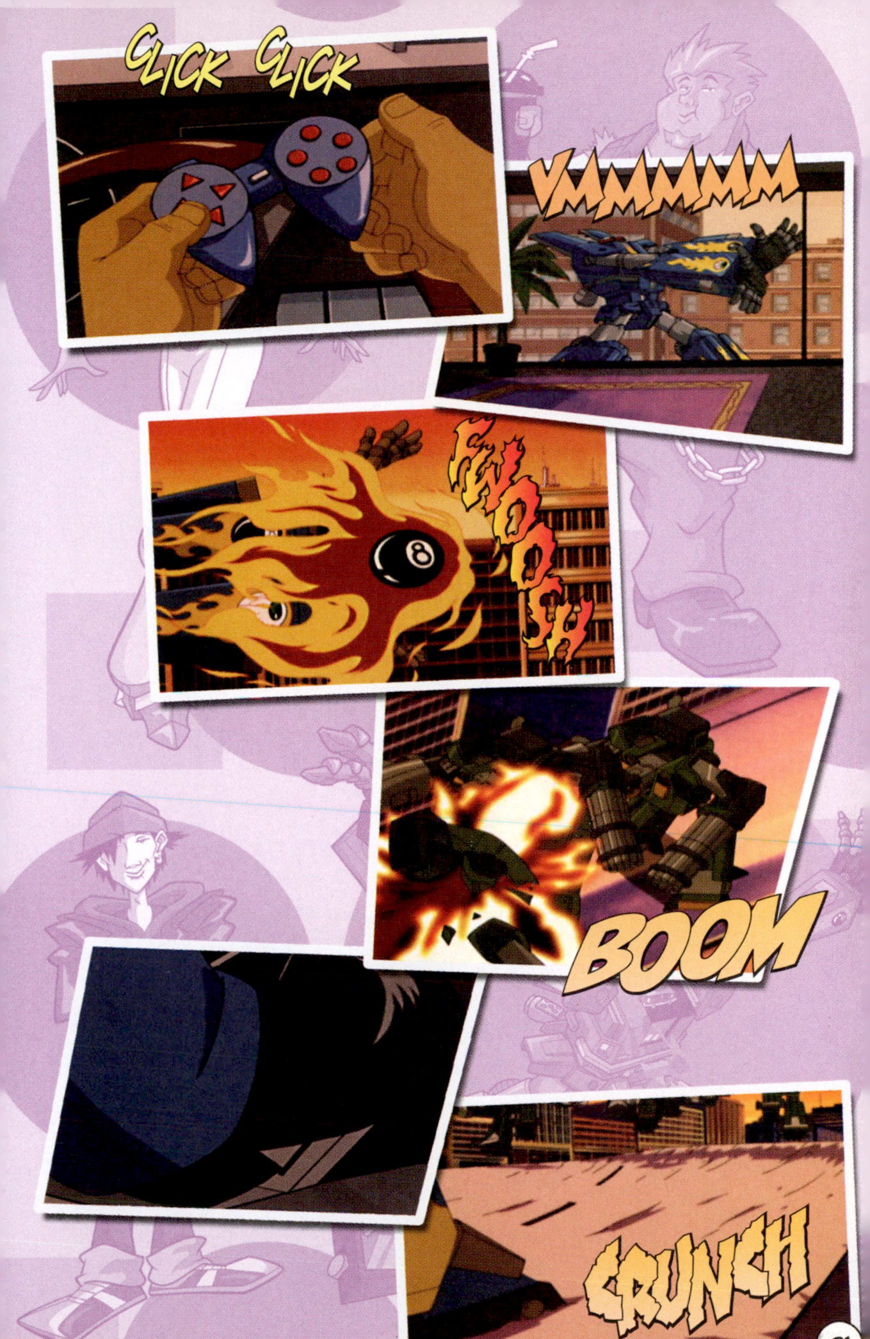
CLICK CLICK
VMMMMM
FWOOSH
BOOM
CRUNCH

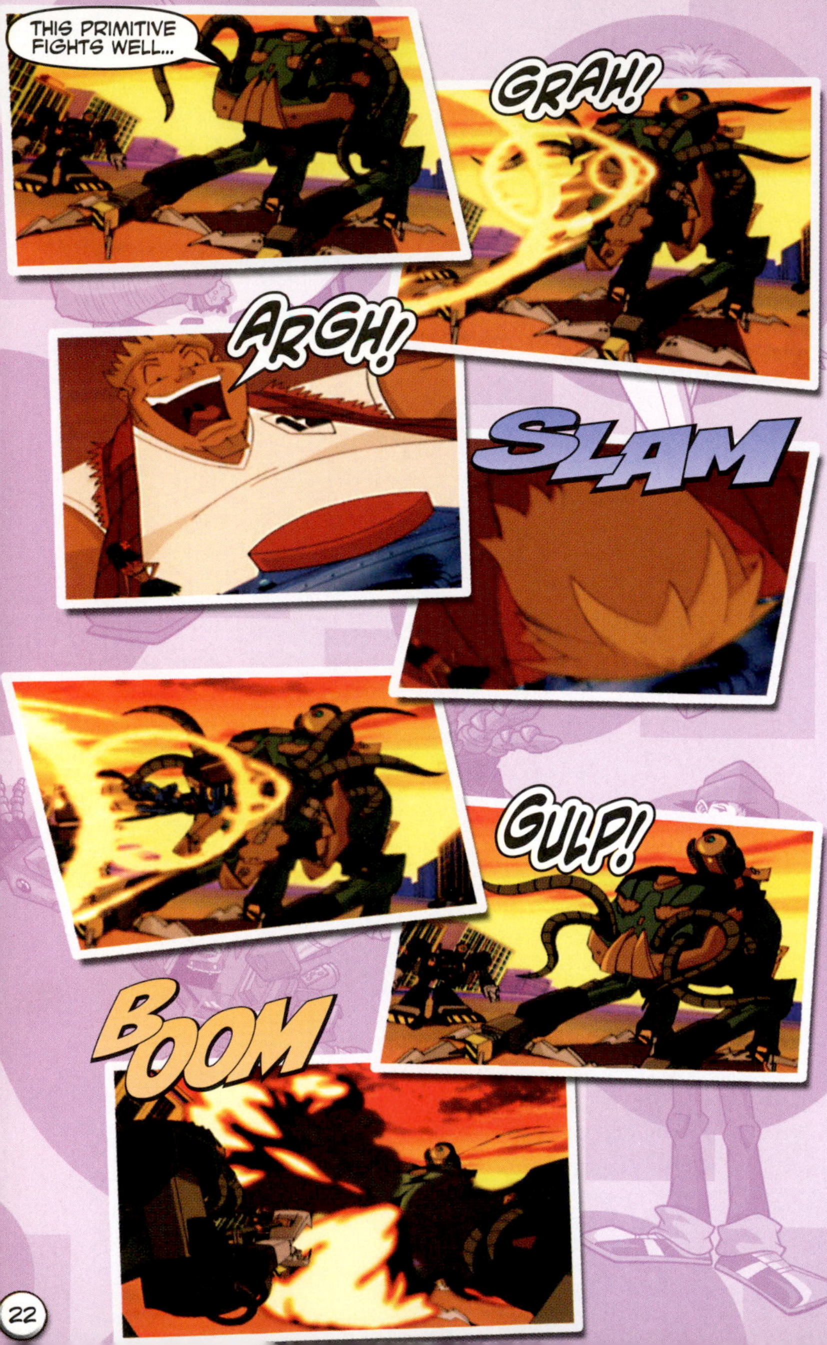
THIS PRIMITIVE FIGHTS WELL...
GRAH!
ARGH!
SLAM
GULP!
BOOM

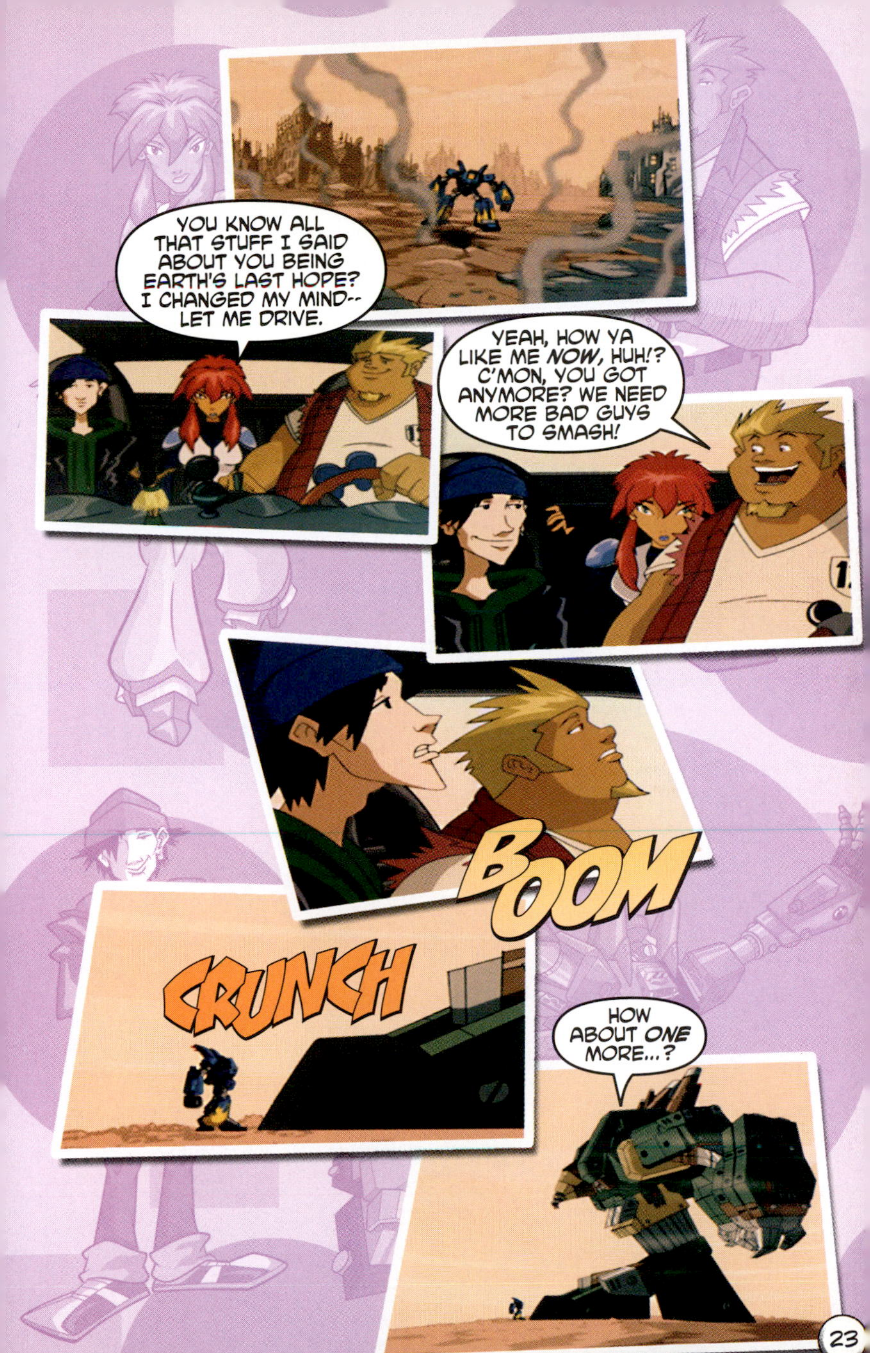

YOU KNOW ALL THAT STUFF I SAID ABOUT YOU BEING EARTH'S LAST HOPE? I CHANGED MY MIND-- LET ME DRIVE.
YEAH, HOW YA LIKE ME *NOW*, HUH!? C'MON, YOU GOT ANYMORE? WE NEED MORE BAD GUYS TO SMASH!
BOOM
CRUNCH
HOW ABOUT *ONE* MORE...?

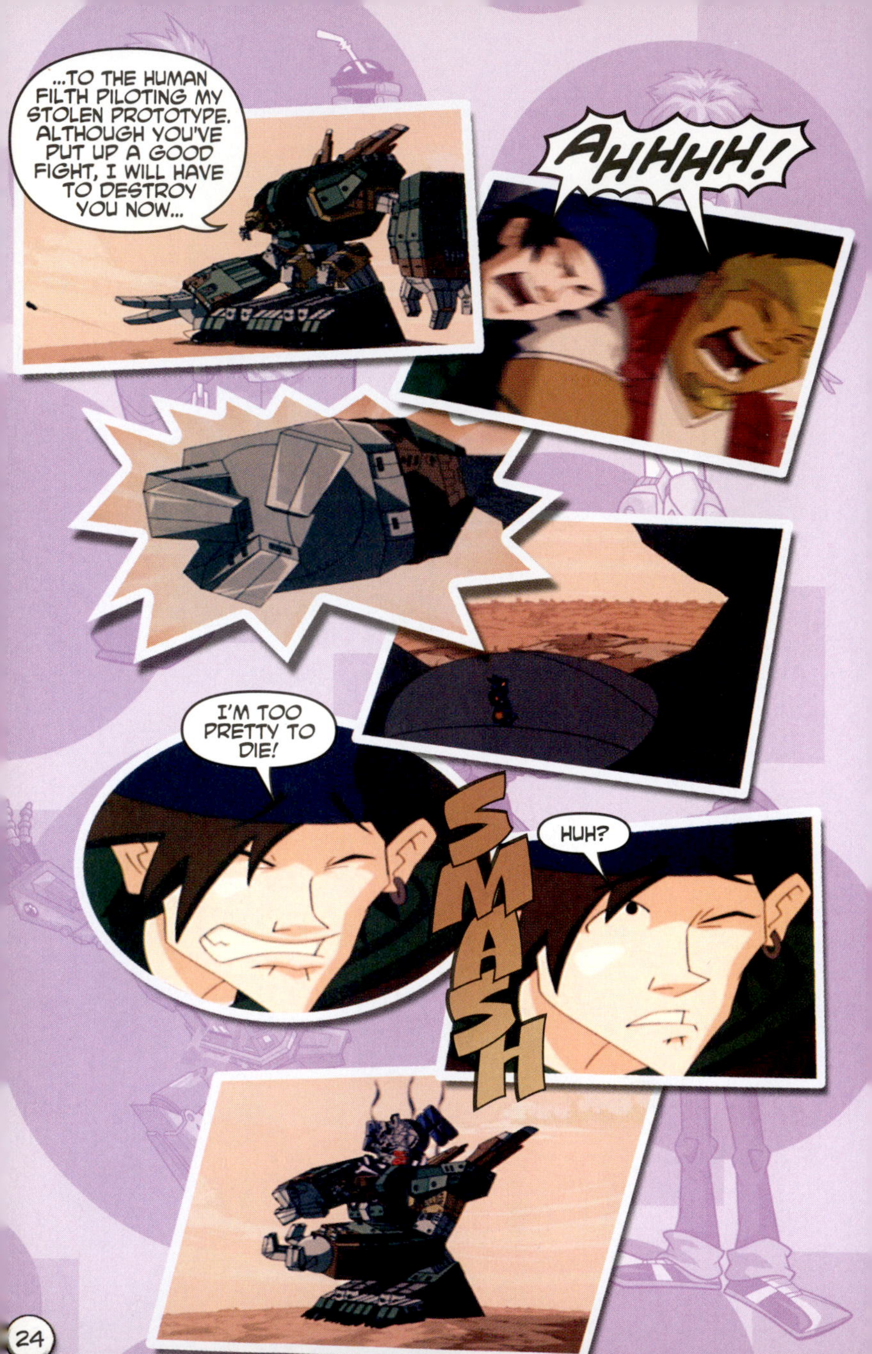
...TO THE HUMAN FILTH PILOTING MY STOLEN PROTOTYPE. ALTHOUGH YOU'VE PUT UP A GOOD FIGHT, I WILL HAVE TO DESTROY YOU NOW...
AHHHH!
I'M TOO PRETTY TO DIE!
SMASH
HUH?

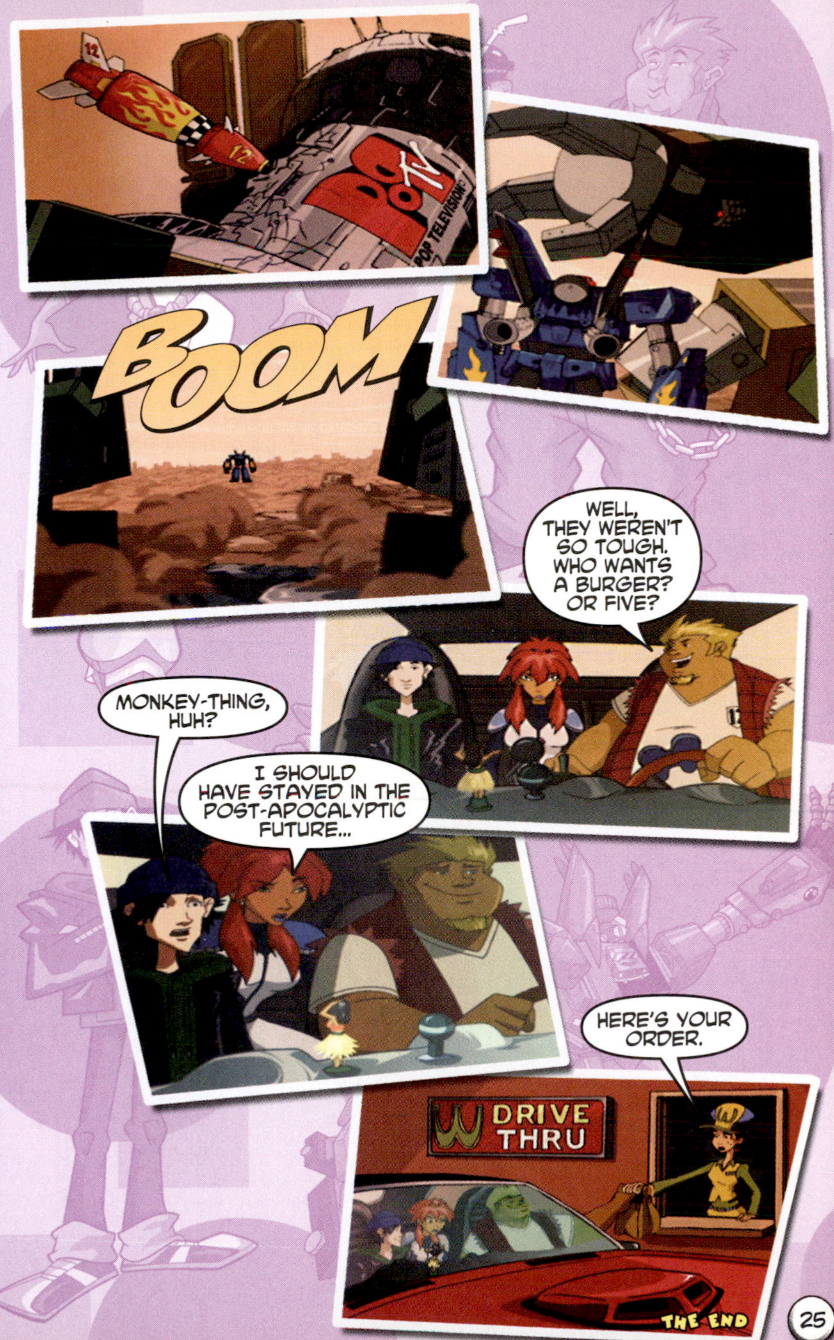
DO TV
POP TELEVISION
12
BOOM
WELL, THEY WEREN'T SO TOUGH. WHO WANTS A BURGER? OR FIVE?
MONKEY-THING, HUH?
I SHOULD HAVE STAYED IN THE POST-APOCALYPTIC FUTURE...
HERE'S YOUR ORDER.
DRIVE THRU
THE END

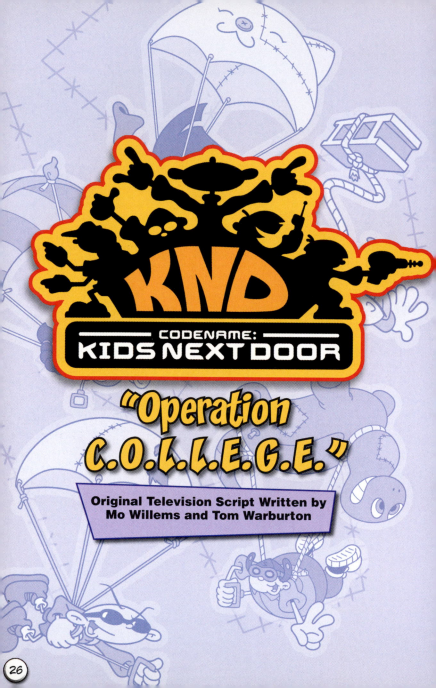

KND
CODENAME: KIDS NEXT DOOR

"Operation C.O.L.L.E.G.E."

Original Television Script Written by Mo Willems and Tom Warburton

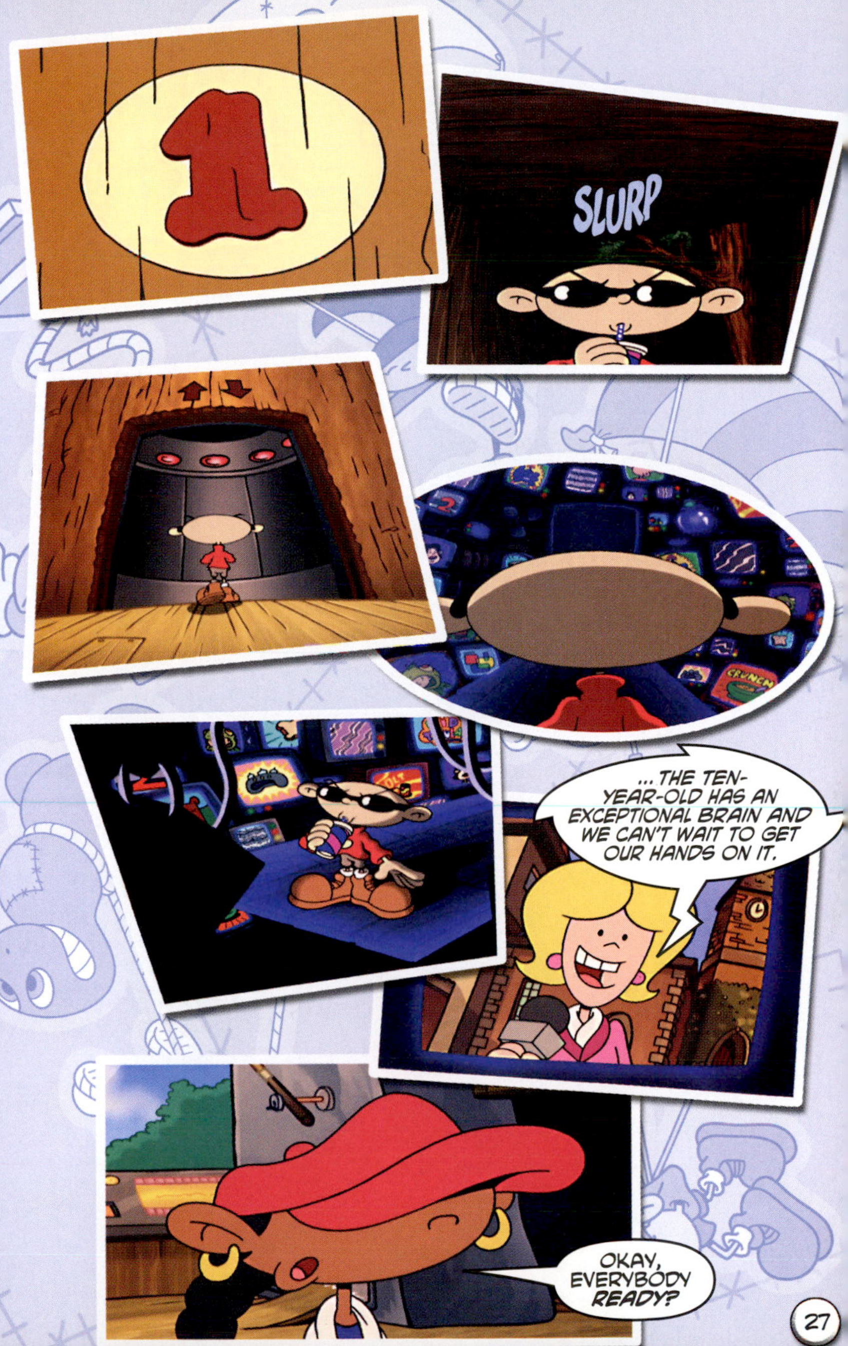

SLURP
...THE TEN-YEAR-OLD HAS AN EXCEPTIONAL BRAIN AND WE CAN'T WAIT TO GET OUR HANDS ON IT.
OKAY, EVERYBODY READY?

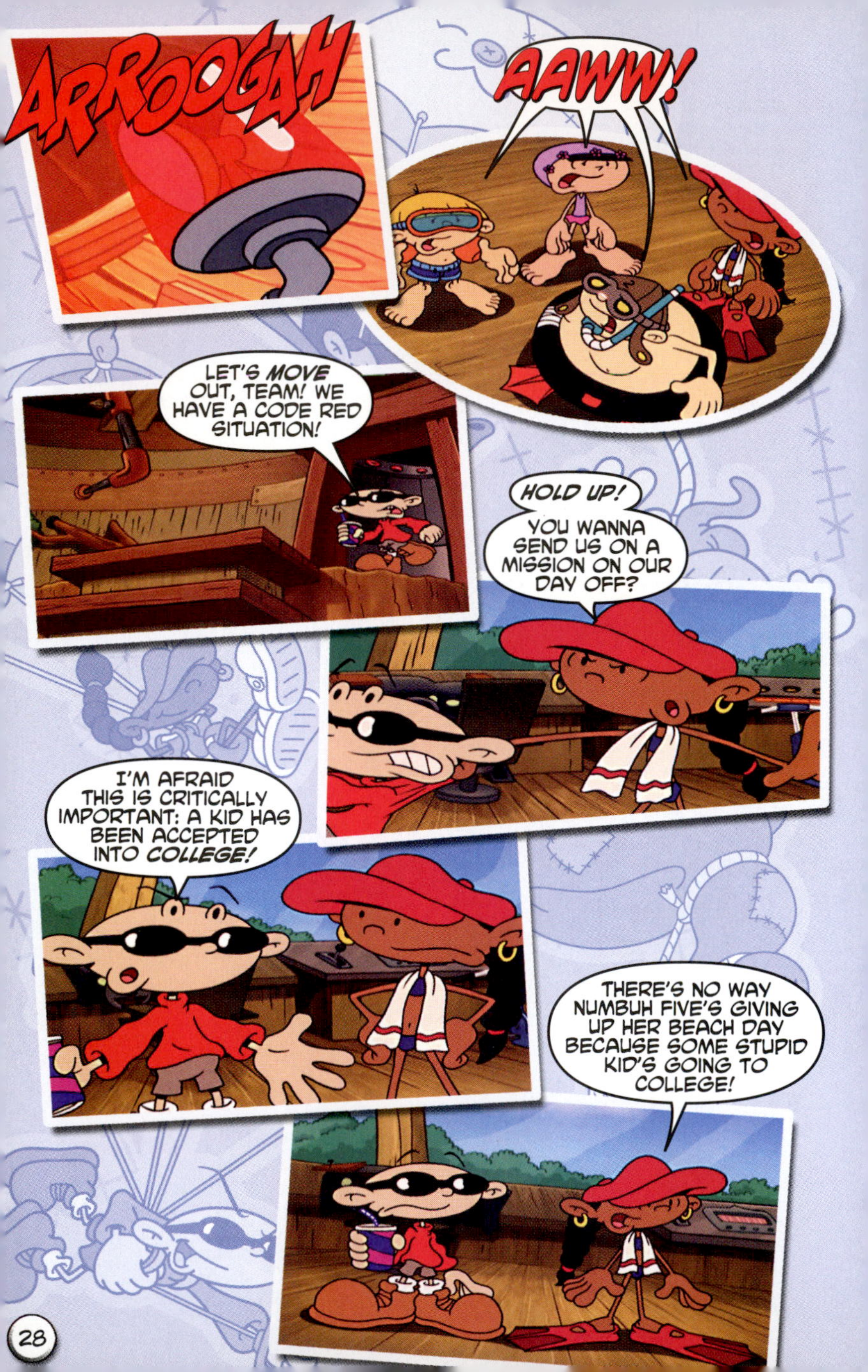
ARROOGAH
AAWW!
LET'S MOVE OUT, TEAM! WE HAVE A CODE RED SITUATION!
HOLD UP!
YOU WANNA SEND US ON A MISSION ON OUR DAY OFF?
I'M AFRAID THIS IS CRITICALLY IMPORTANT: A KID HAS BEEN ACCEPTED INTO COLLEGE!
THERE'S NO WAY NUMBUH FIVE'S GIVING UP HER BEACH DAY BECAUSE SOME STUPID KID'S GOING TO COLLEGE!

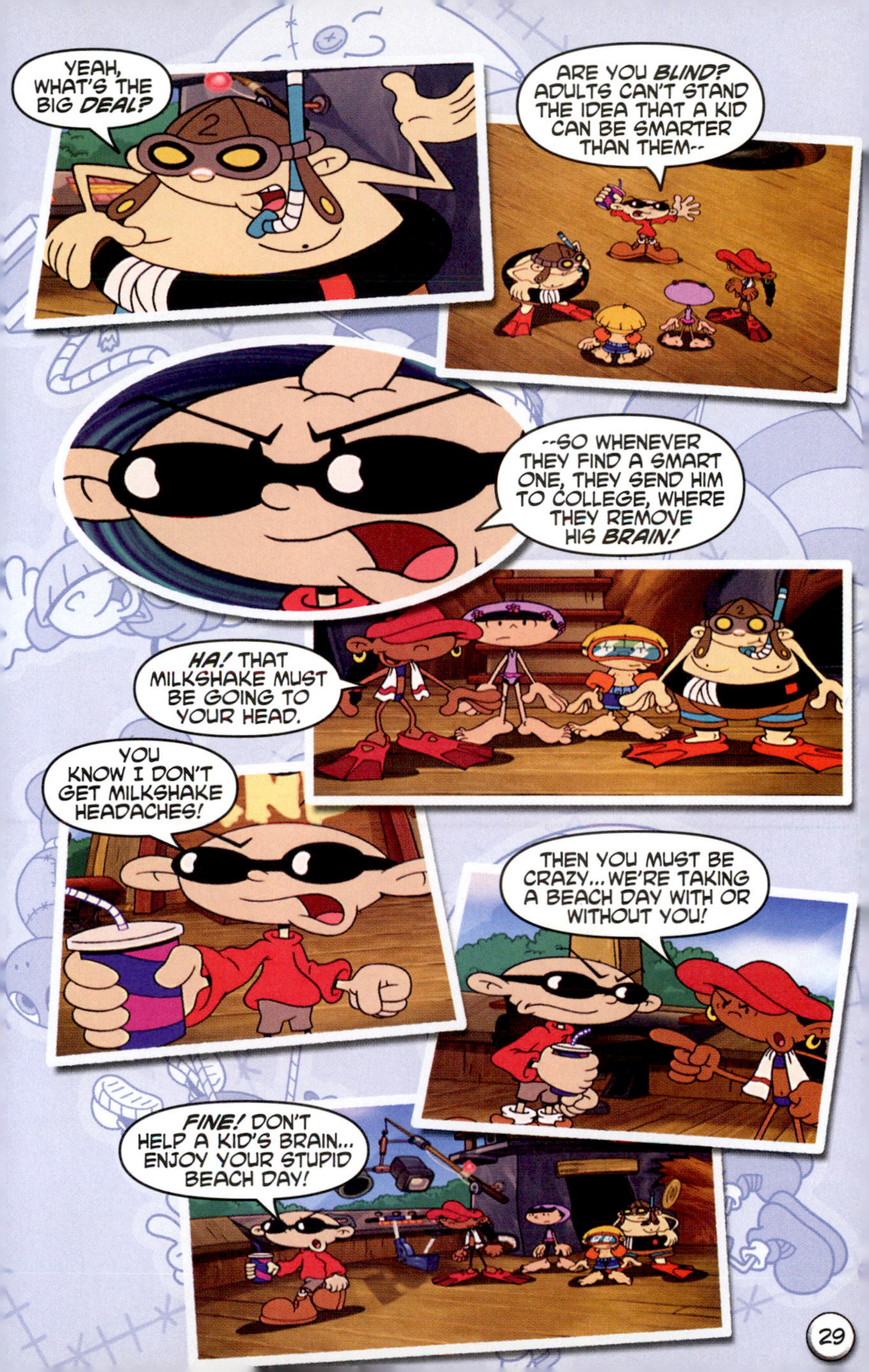
YEAH, WHAT'S THE BIG *DEAL?*
ARE YOU *BLIND?* ADULTS CAN'T STAND THE IDEA THAT A KID CAN BE SMARTER THAN THEM--
--SO WHENEVER THEY FIND A SMART ONE, THEY SEND HIM TO COLLEGE, WHERE THEY REMOVE HIS *BRAIN!*
HA! THAT MILKSHAKE MUST BE GOING TO YOUR HEAD.
YOU KNOW I DON'T GET MILKSHAKE HEADACHES!
THEN YOU MUST BE CRAZY... WE'RE TAKING A BEACH DAY WITH OR WITHOUT YOU!
FINE! DON'T HELP A KID'S BRAIN... ENJOY YOUR STUPID BEACH DAY!

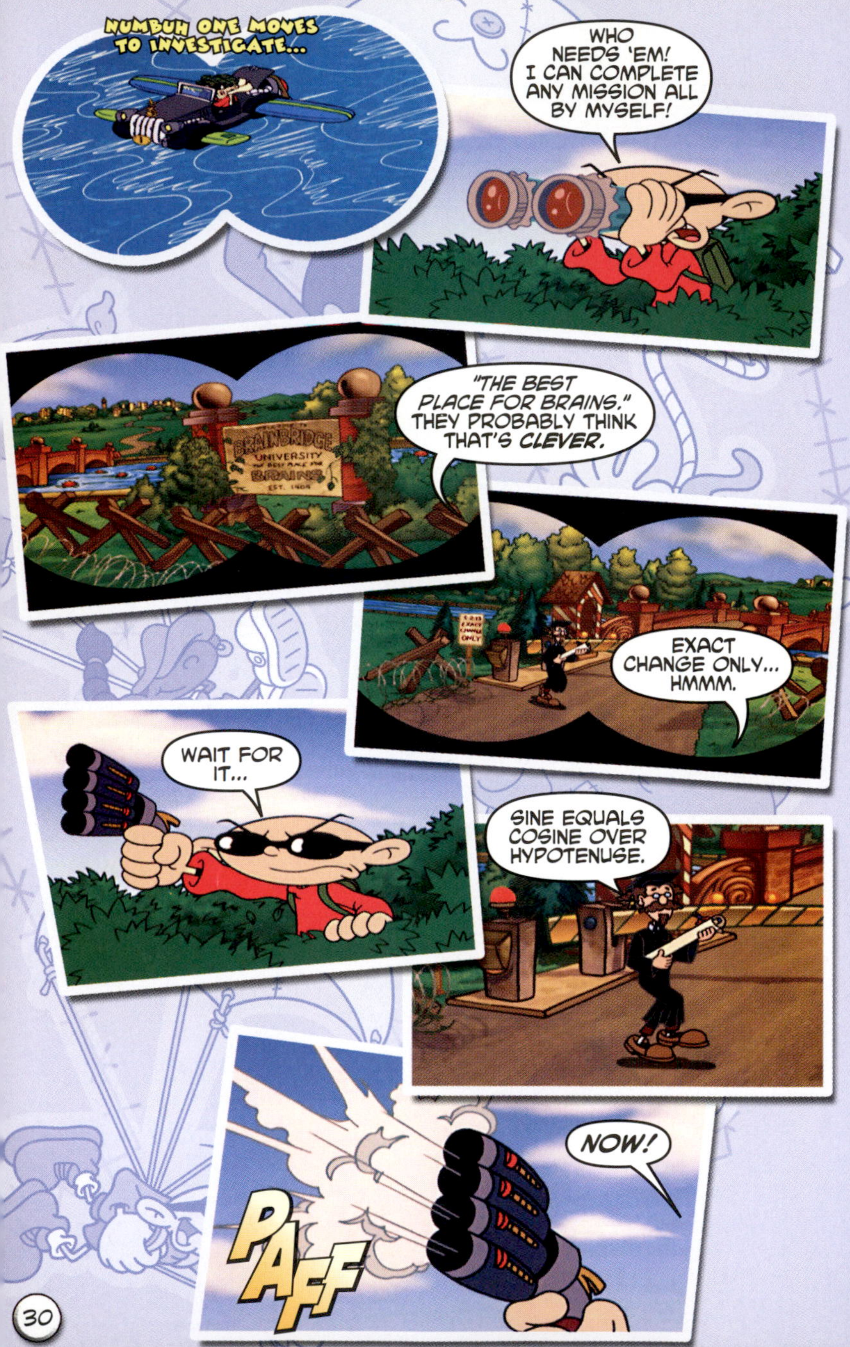
NUMBUH ONE MOVES TO INVESTIGATE...
WHO NEEDS 'EM! I CAN COMPLETE ANY MISSION ALL BY MYSELF!
BRAINBRIDGE UNIVERSITY
BRAINS
EST. 1404
"THE BEST PLACE FOR BRAINS." THEY PROBABLY THINK THAT'S *CLEVER.*
EXACT CHANGE ONLY
EXACT CHANGE ONLY... HMMM.
WAIT FOR IT...
SINE EQUALS COSINE OVER HYPOTENUSE.
NOW!
PAFF

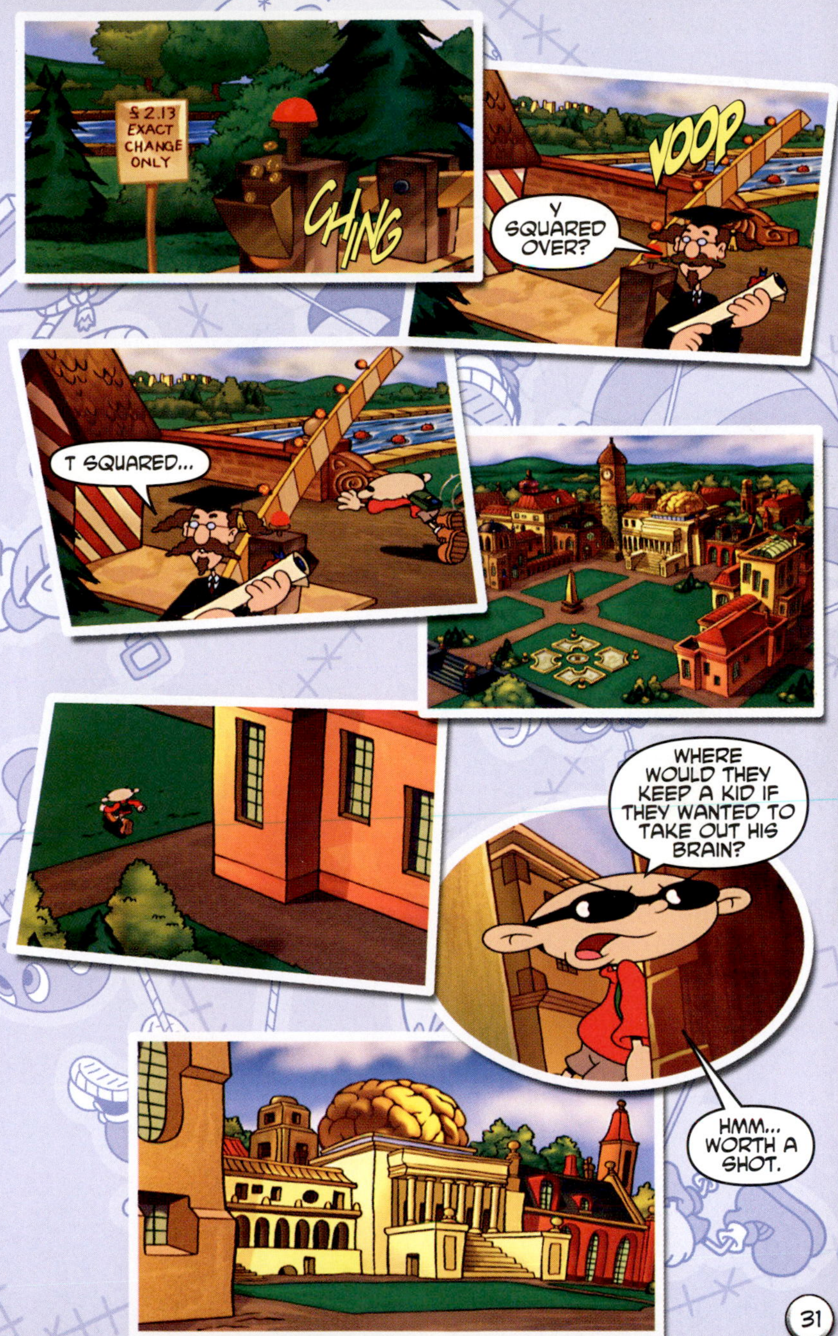
£2.13
EXACT
CHANGE
ONLY
CHING
VOOP
Y SQUARED OVER?
T SQUARED...
WHERE WOULD THEY KEEP A KID IF THEY WANTED TO TAKE OUT HIS BRAIN?
HMM... WORTH A SHOT.

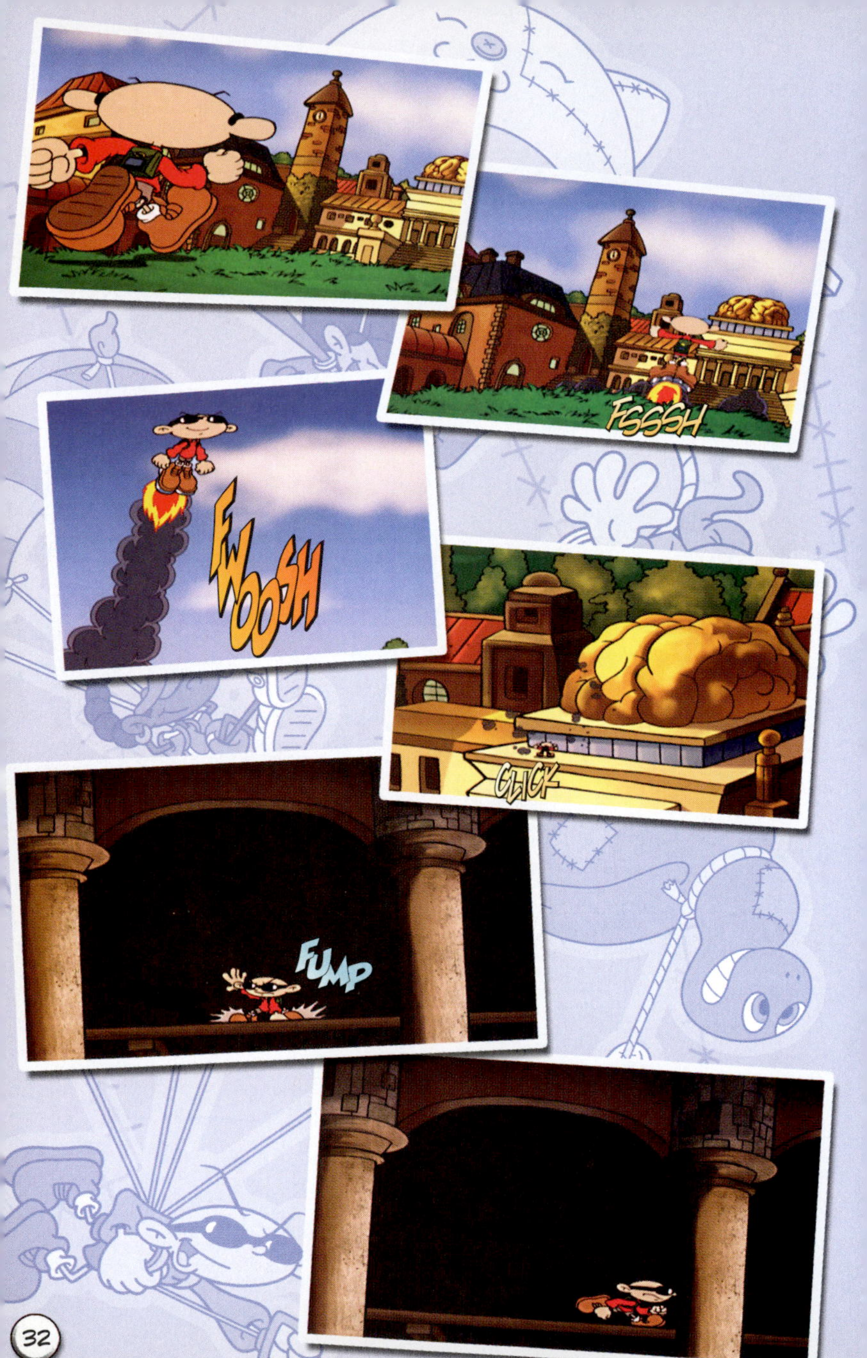
FSSSH
FWOOSH
CLICK
FUMP

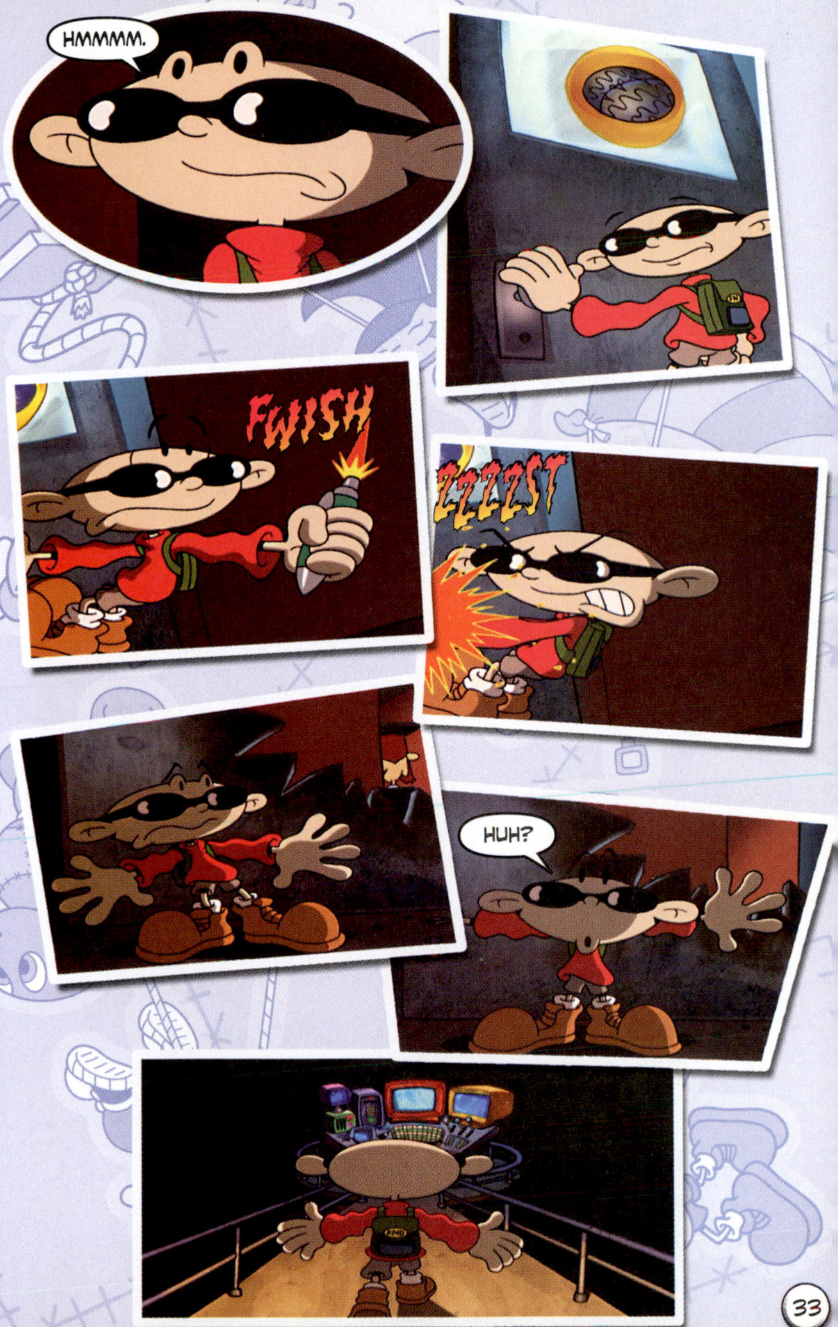
HMMMM.
FWISH
ZZZZST
HUH?

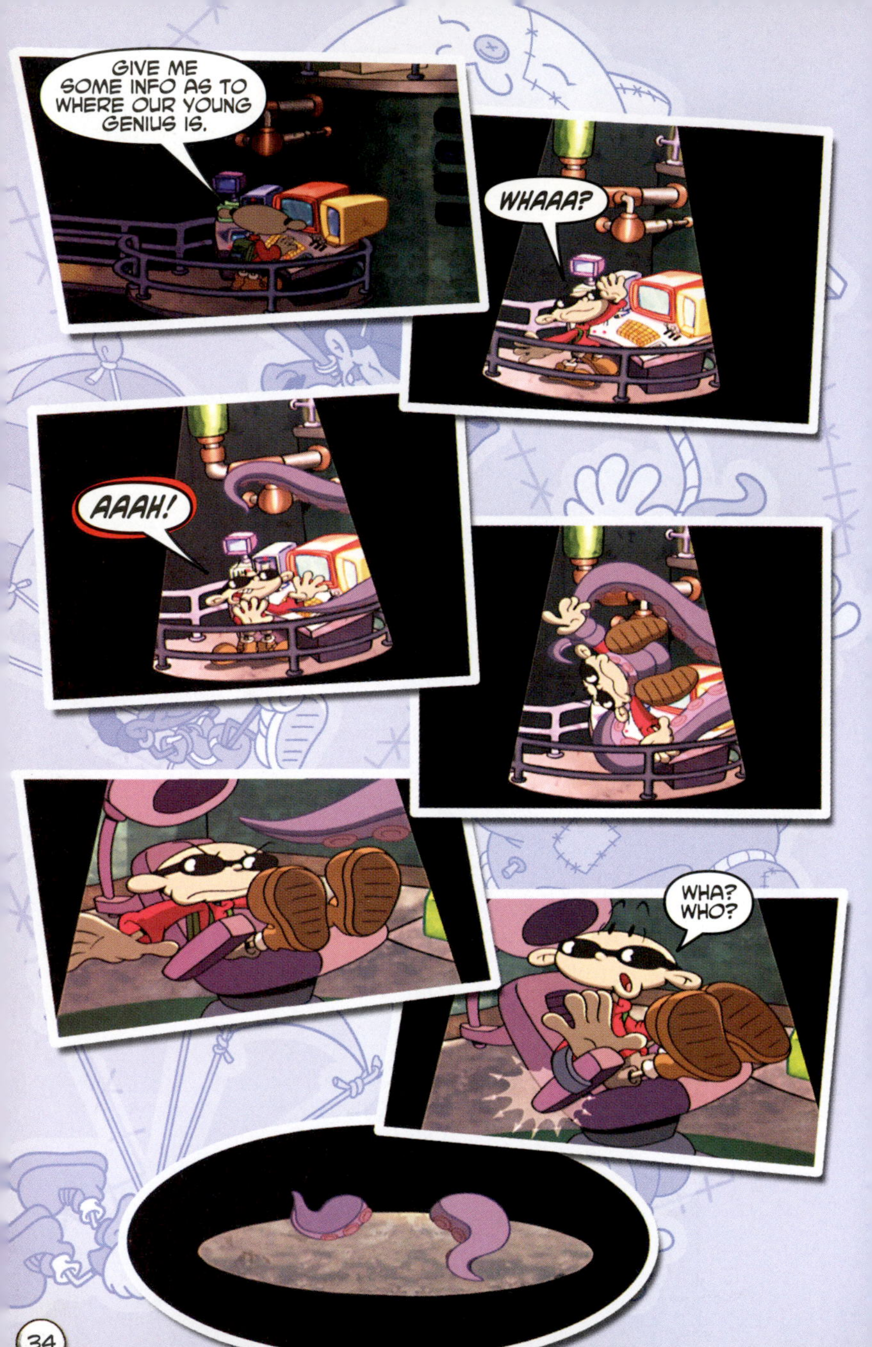
GIVE ME SOME INFO AS TO WHERE OUR YOUNG GENIUS IS.
WHAAA?
AAAH!
WHA? WHO?

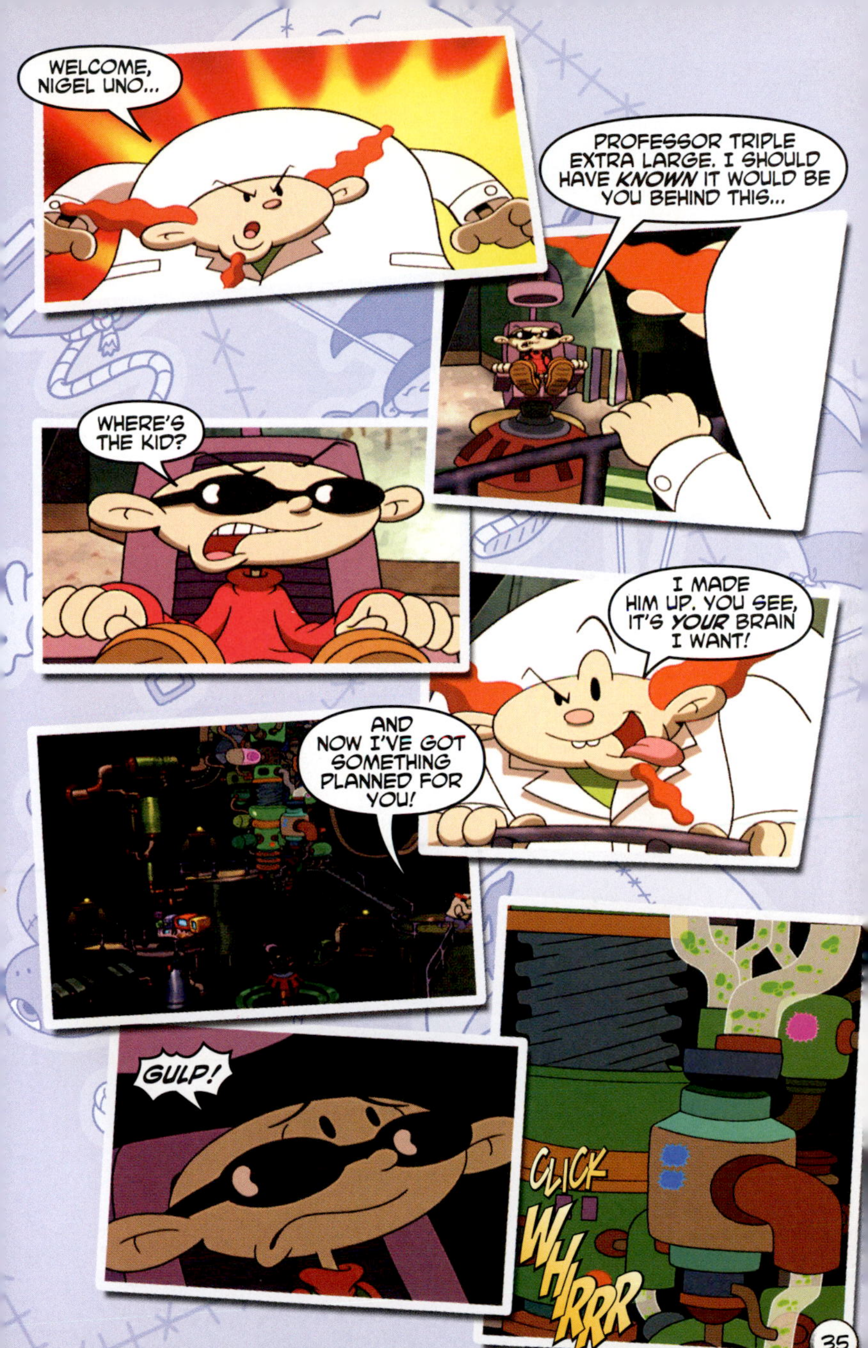
WELCOME, NIGEL UNO...
PROFESSOR TRIPLE EXTRA LARGE. I SHOULD HAVE KNOWN IT WOULD BE YOU BEHIND THIS...
WHERE'S THE KID?
I MADE HIM UP. YOU SEE, IT'S YOUR BRAIN I WANT!
AND NOW I'VE GOT SOMETHING PLANNED FOR YOU!
GULP!
CLICK
WHIRRR

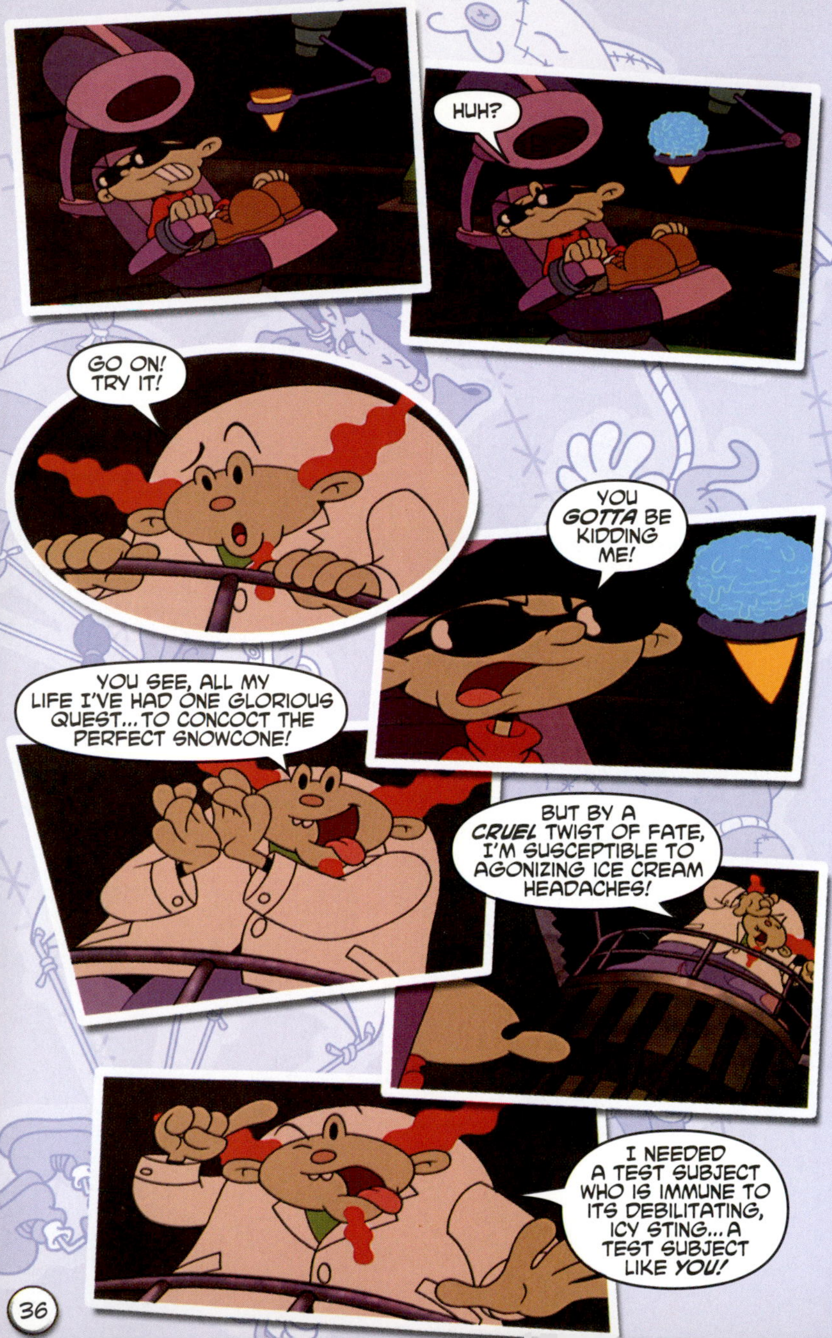
HUH?
GO ON! TRY IT!
YOU GOTTA BE KIDDING ME!
YOU SEE, ALL MY LIFE I'VE HAD ONE GLORIOUS QUEST... TO CONCOCT THE PERFECT SNOWCONE!
BUT BY A CRUEL TWIST OF FATE, I'M SUSCEPTIBLE TO AGONIZING ICE CREAM HEADACHES!
I NEEDED A TEST SUBJECT WHO IS IMMUNE TO ITS DEBILITATING, ICY STING... A TEST SUBJECT LIKE YOU!

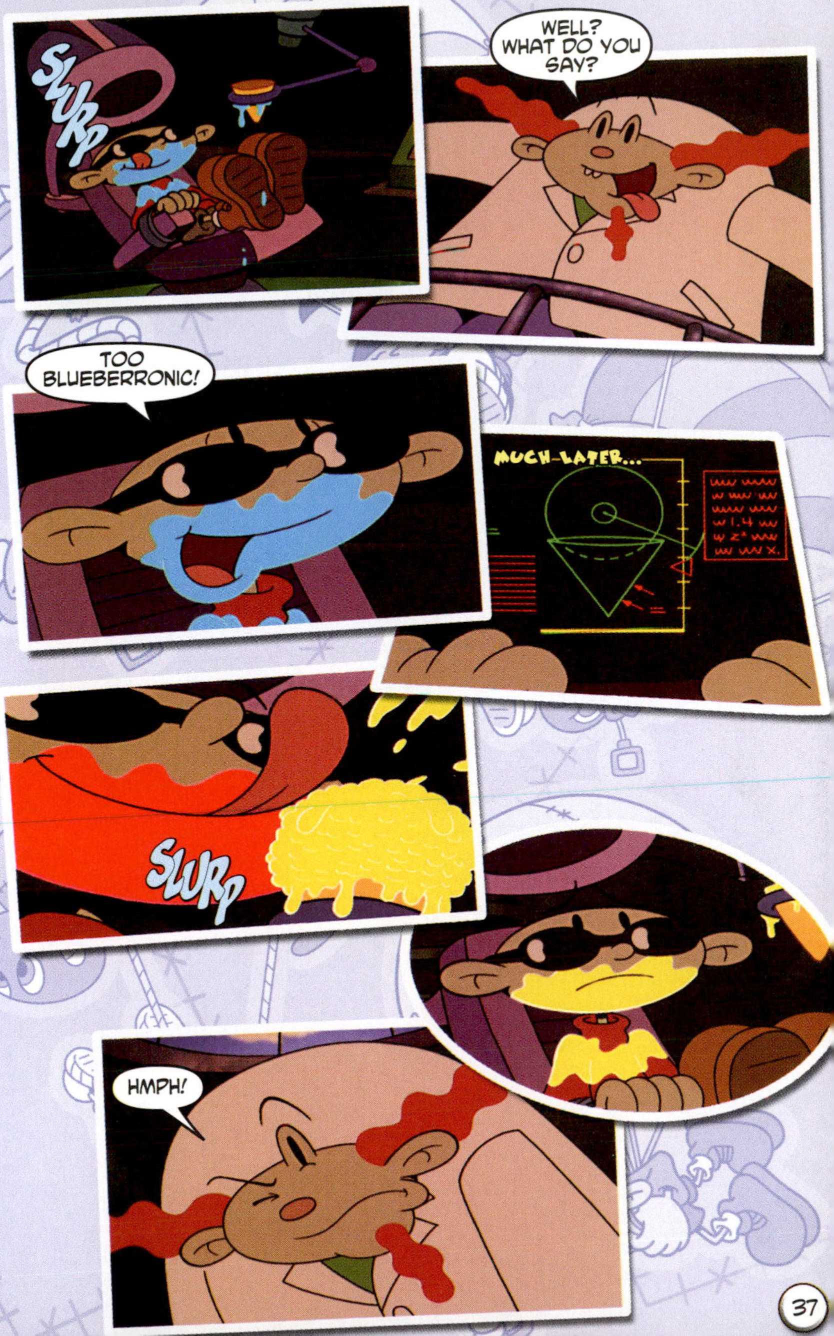
SLURP
WELL? WHAT DO YOU SAY?
TOO BLUEBERRONIC!
MUCH LATER...
SLURP
HMPH!

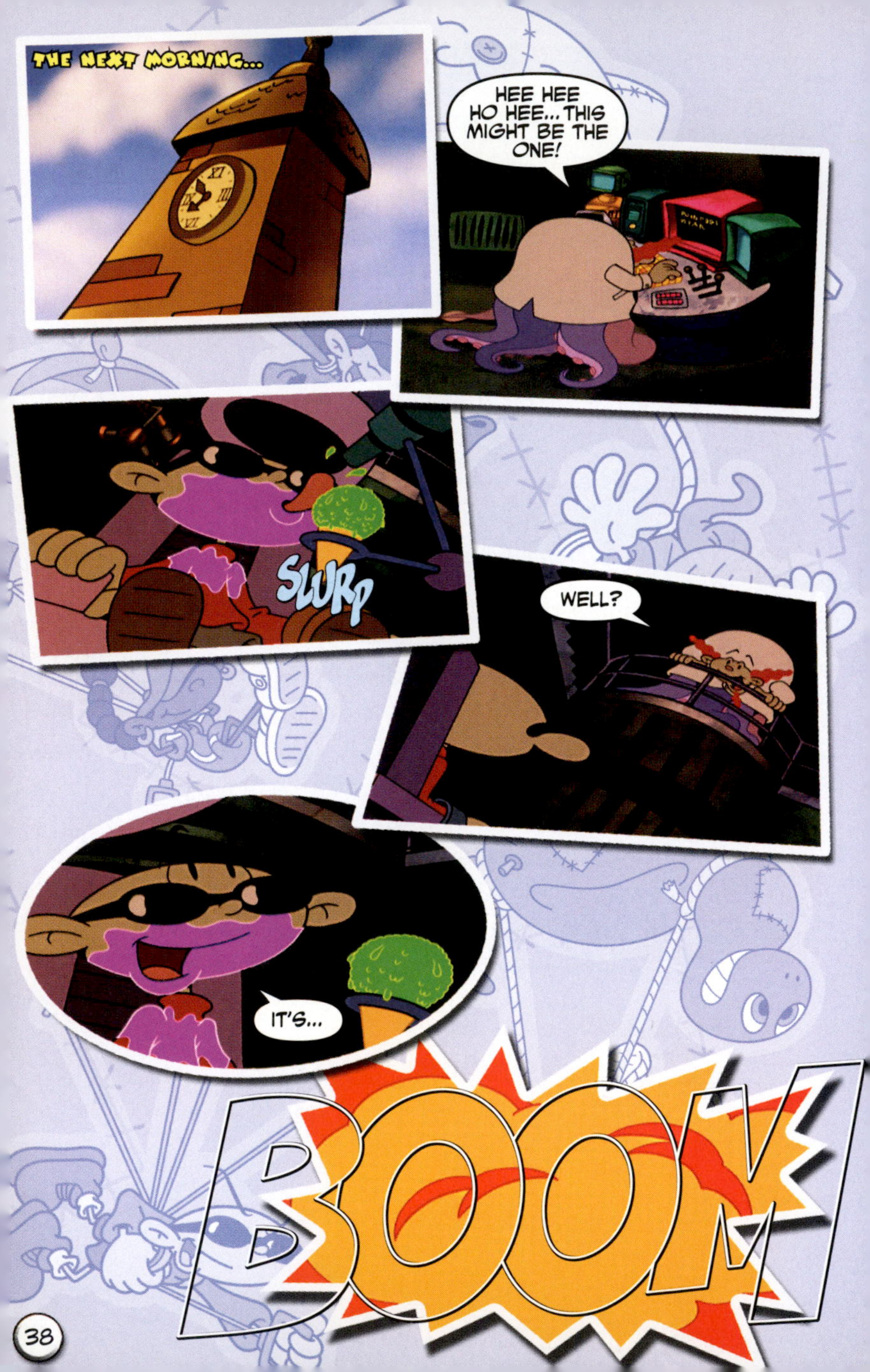
THE NEXT MORNING...
HEE HEE HO HEE... THIS MIGHT BE THE ONE!
SLURP
WELL?
IT'S...
BOOM

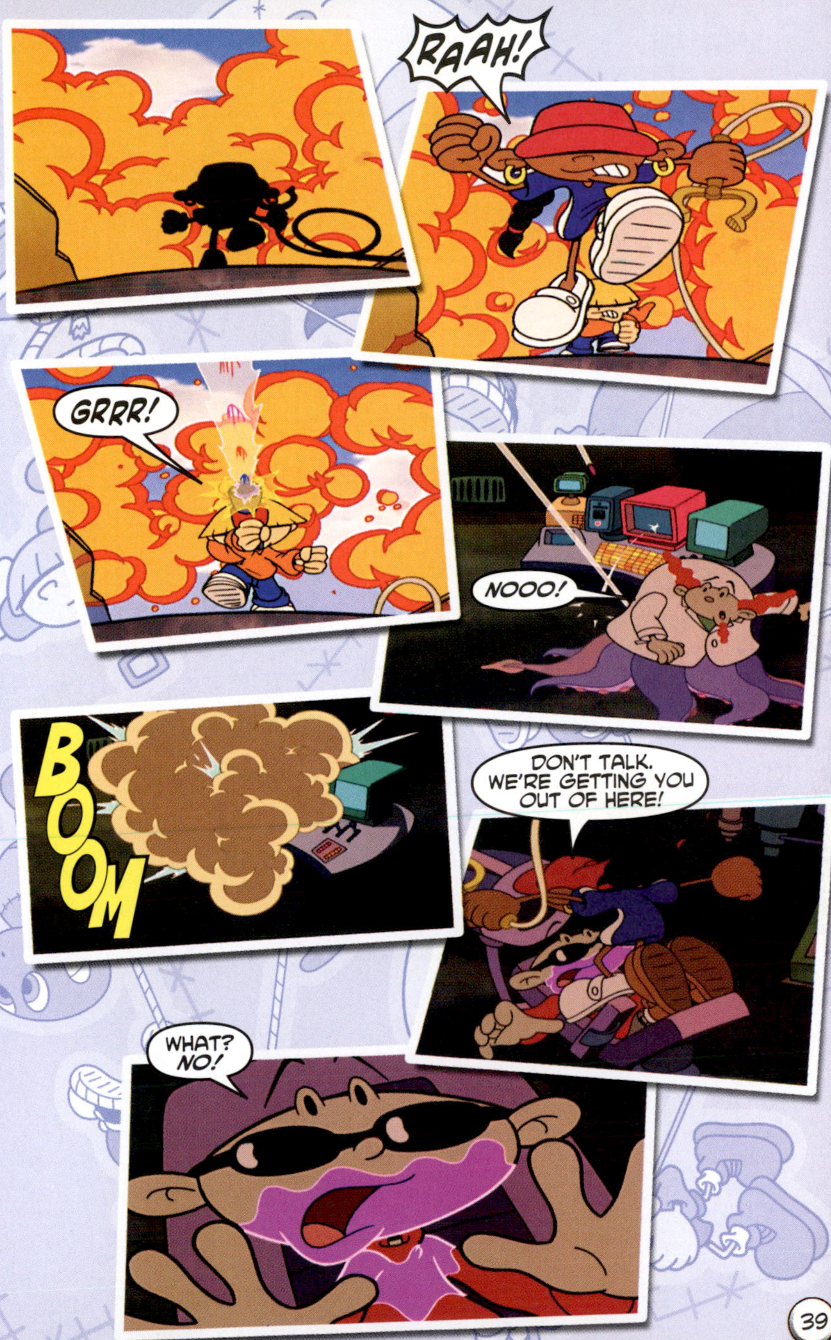
RAAH!
GRRR!
NOOO!
BOOM
DON'T TALK. WE'RE GETTING YOU OUT OF HERE!
WHAT? NO!

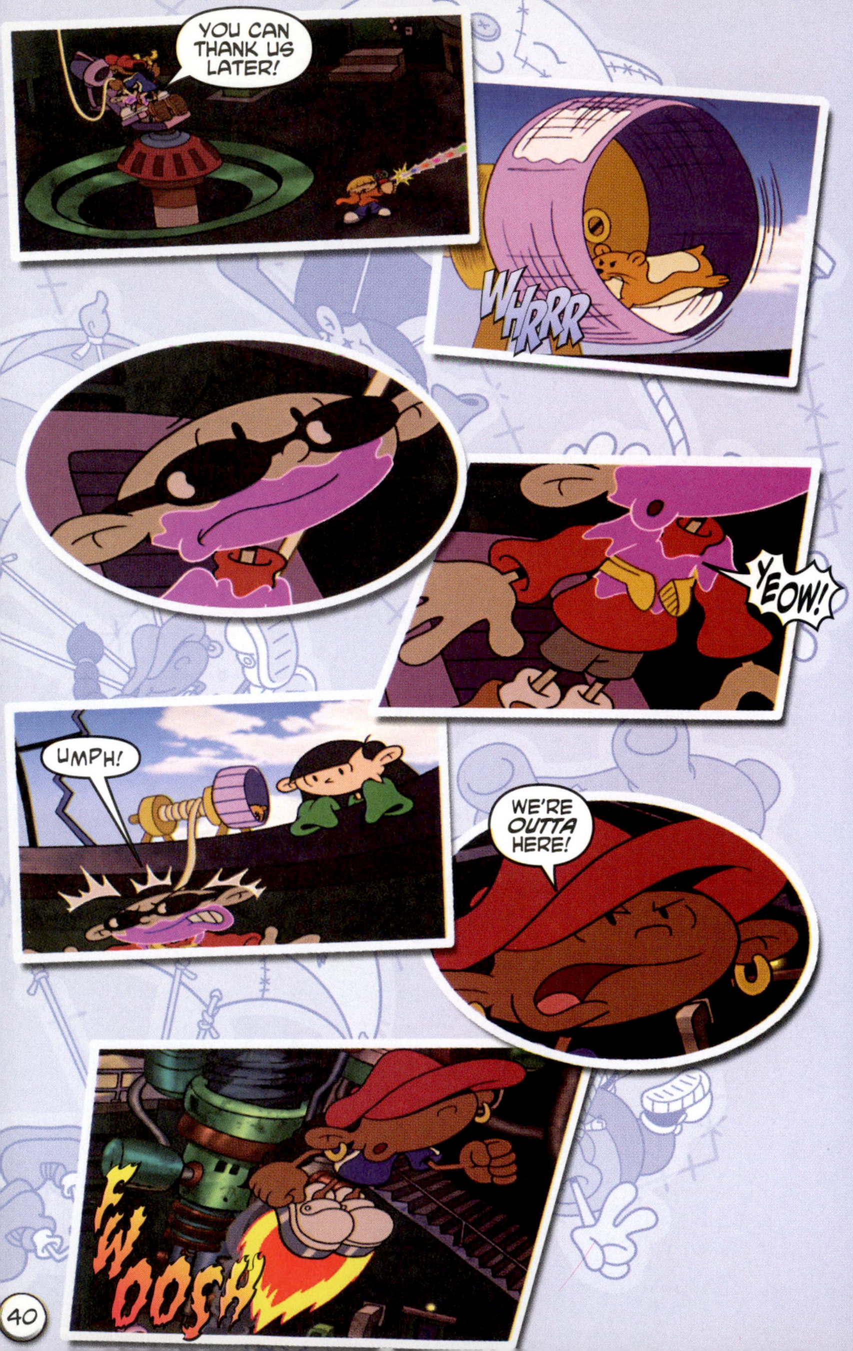
YOU CAN THANK US LATER!
WHRRR
YEOW!
UMPH!
WE'RE OUTTA HERE!
FWOOSH

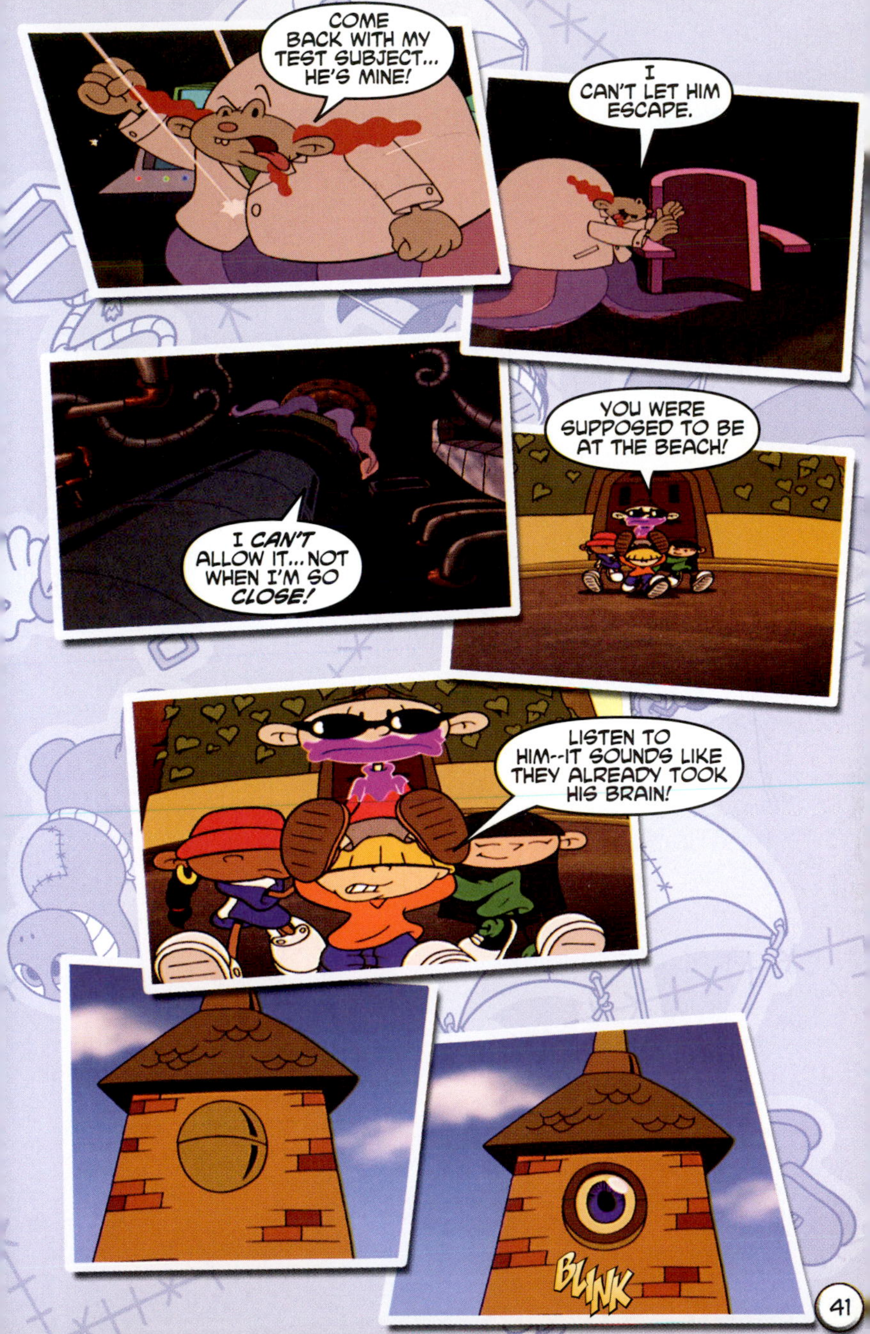
COME BACK WITH MY TEST SUBJECT... HE'S MINE!
I CAN'T LET HIM ESCAPE.
I CAN'T ALLOW IT... NOT WHEN I'M SO CLOSE!
YOU WERE SUPPOSED TO BE AT THE BEACH!
LISTEN TO HIM--IT SOUNDS LIKE THEY ALREADY TOOK HIS BRAIN!
BLINK

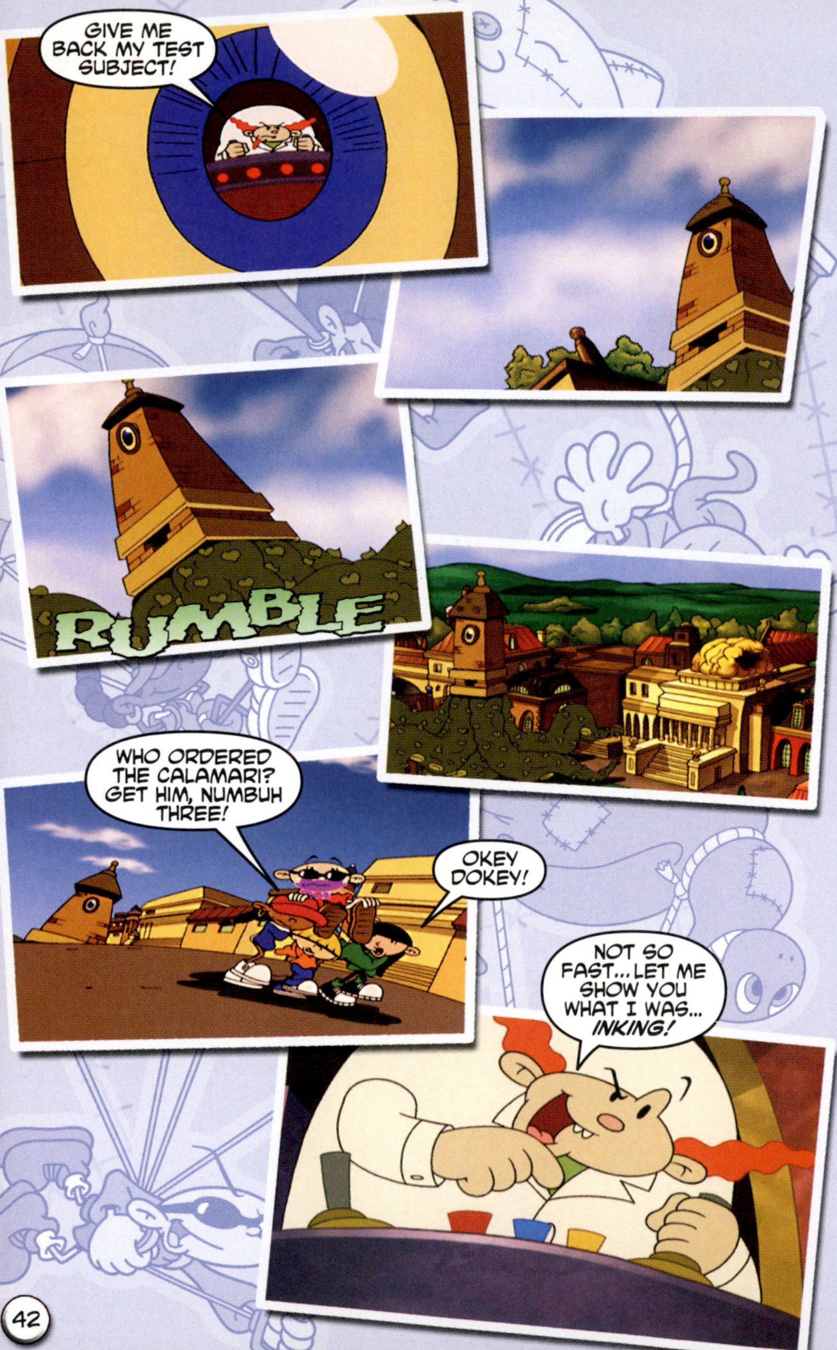
GIVE ME BACK MY TEST SUBJECT!
RUMBLE
WHO ORDERED THE CALAMARI? GET HIM, NUMBUH THREE!
OKEY DOKEY!
NOT SO FAST... LET ME SHOW YOU WHAT I WAS... *INKING!*

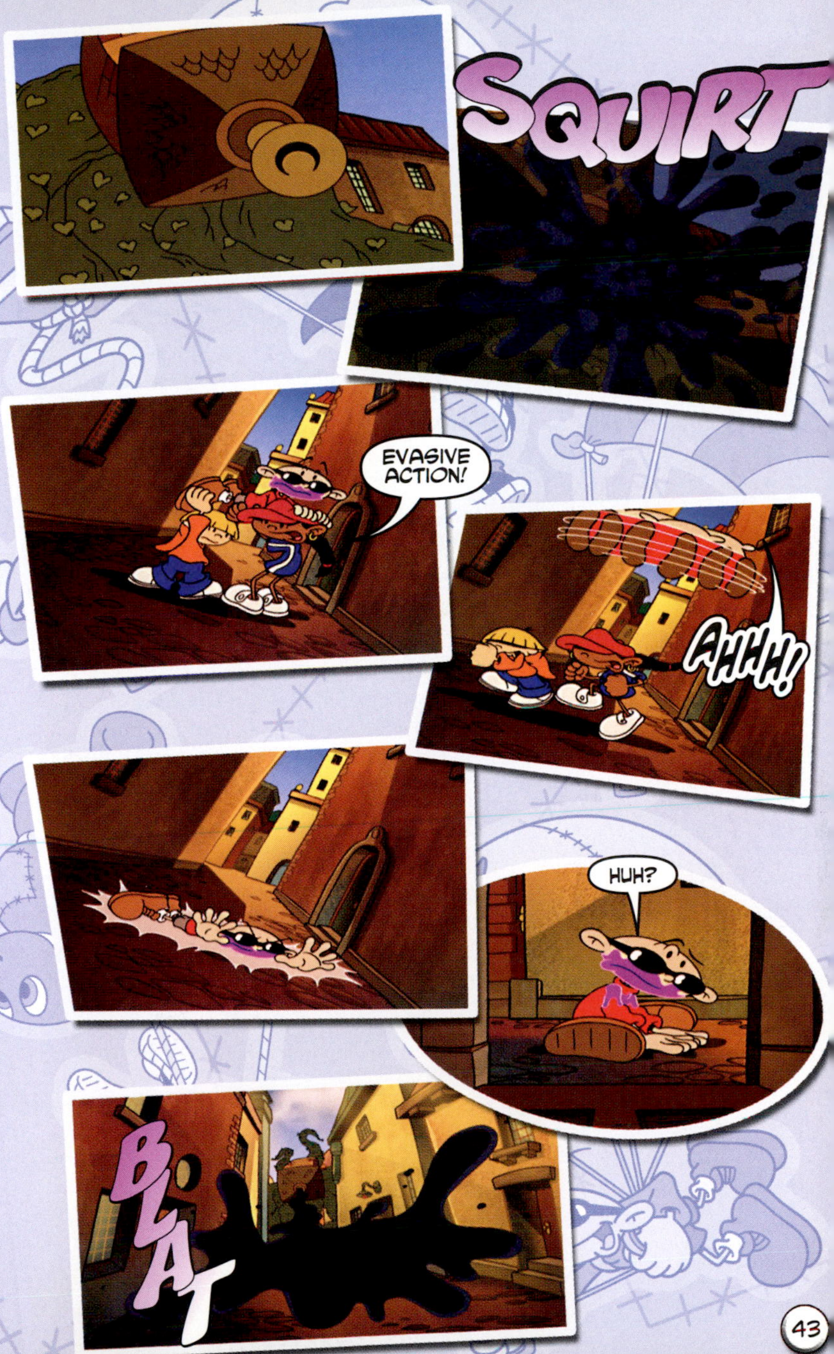
SQUIRT
EVASIVE ACTION!
AHHH!
HUH?
BLAT

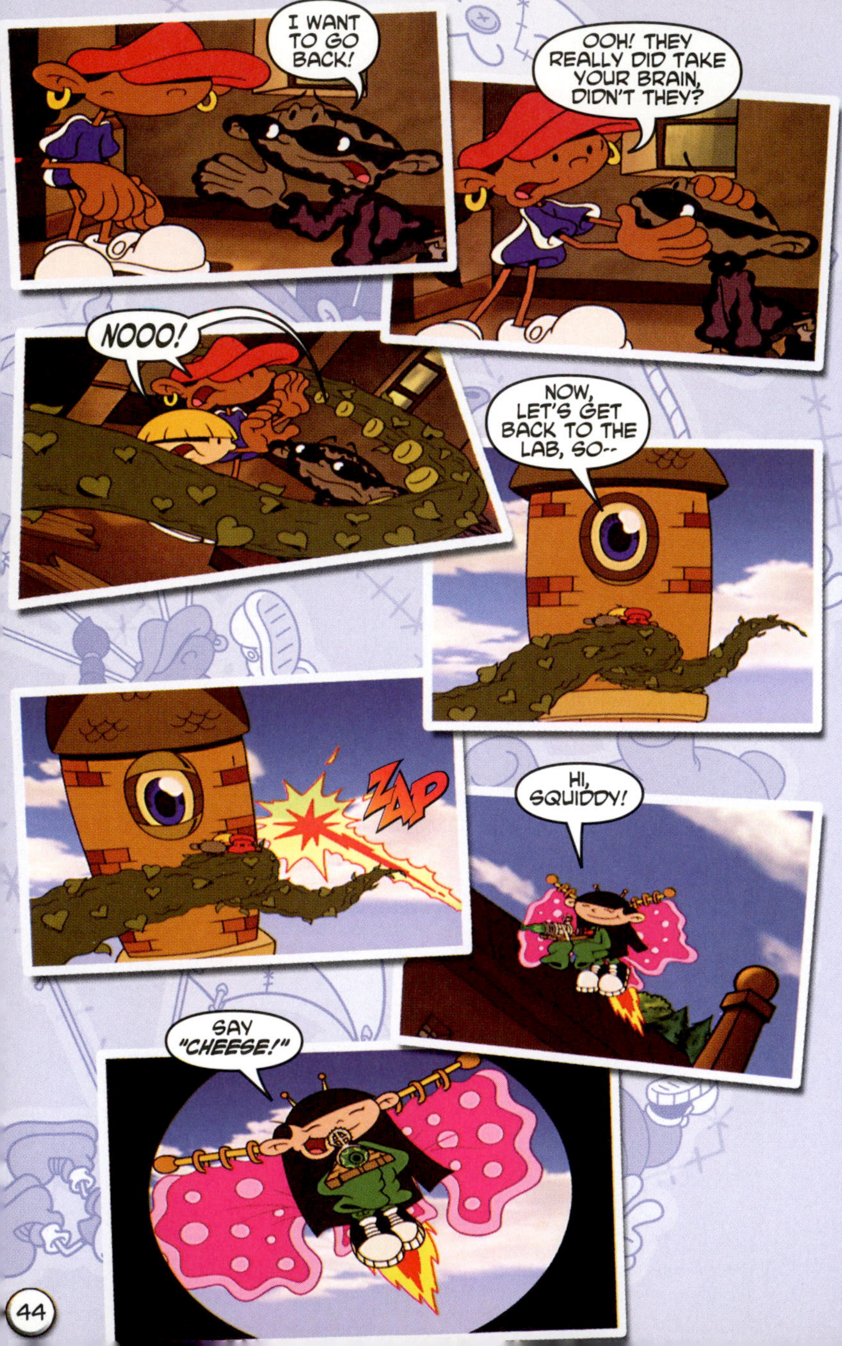
I WANT TO GO BACK!
OOH! THEY REALLY DID TAKE YOUR BRAIN, DIDN'T THEY?
NOOO!
NOW, LET'S GET BACK TO THE LAB, SO--
ZAP
HI, SQUIDDY!
SAY "CHEESE!"

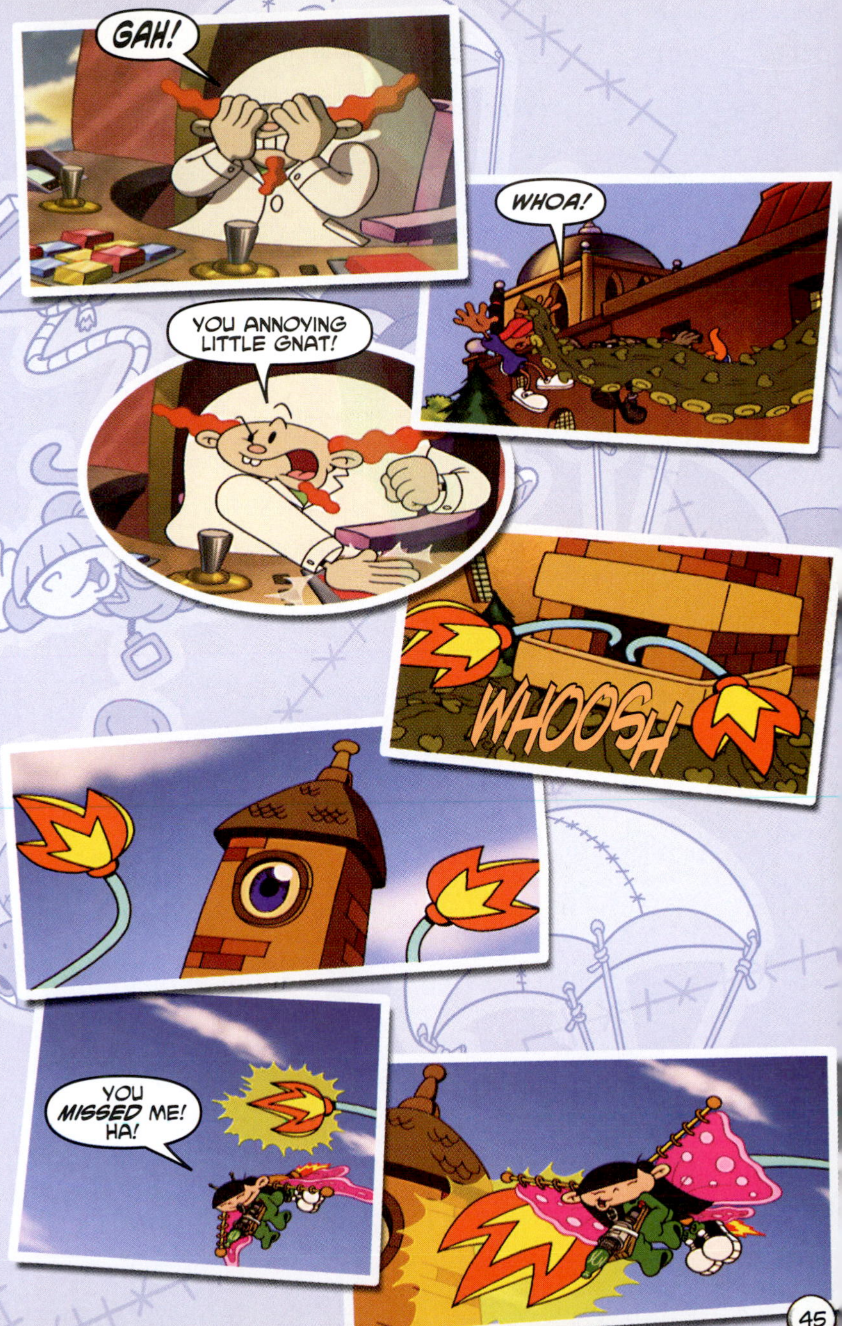
GAH!
WHOA!
YOU ANNOYING LITTLE GNAT!
WHOOSH
YOU MISSED ME! HA!

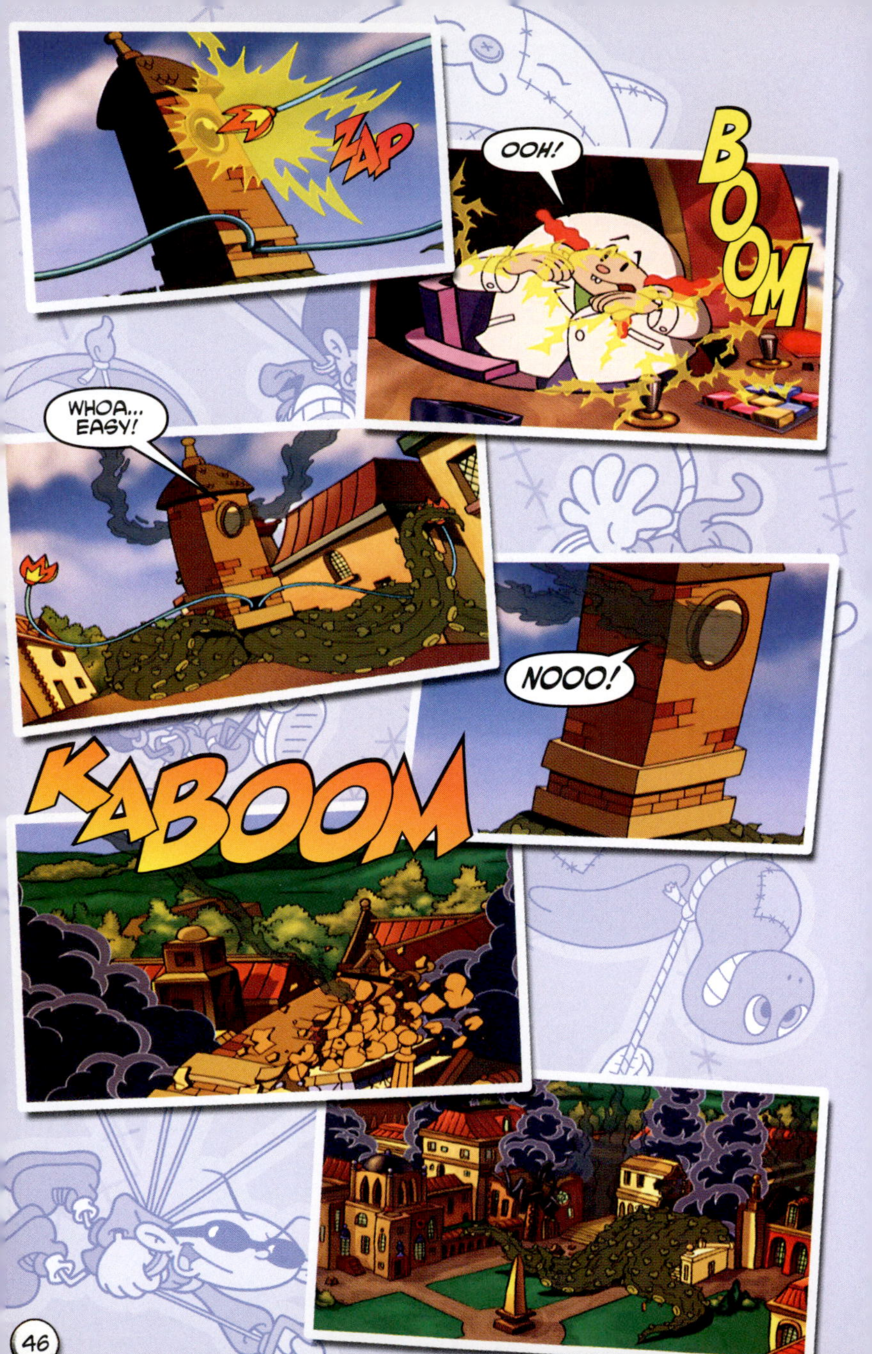
ZAP
OOH!
BOOM
WHOA... EASY!
NOOO!
KABOOM

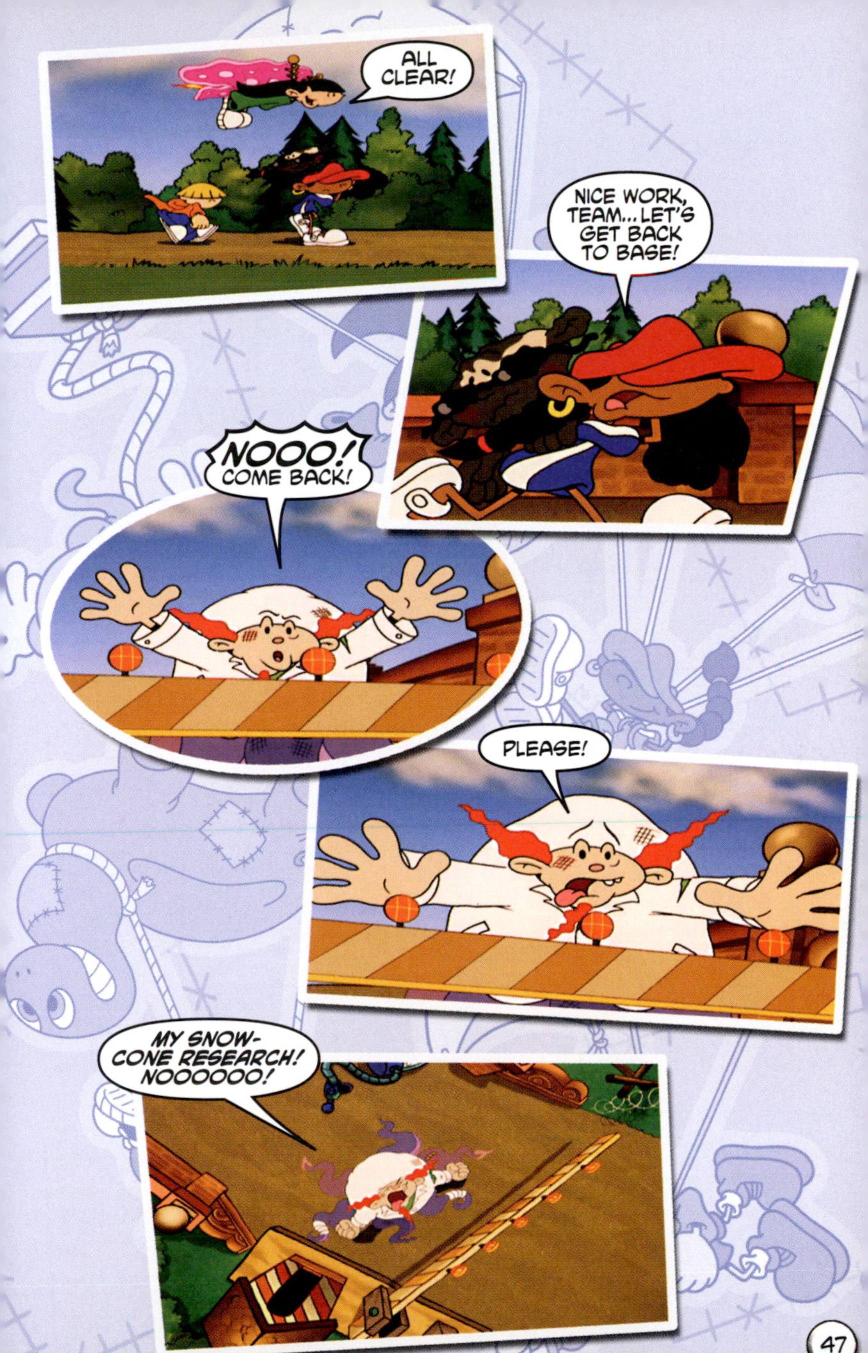
ALL CLEAR!
NICE WORK, TEAM... LET'S GET BACK TO BASE!
NOOO! COME BACK!
PLEASE!
MY SNOW-CONE RESEARCH! NOOOOOO!

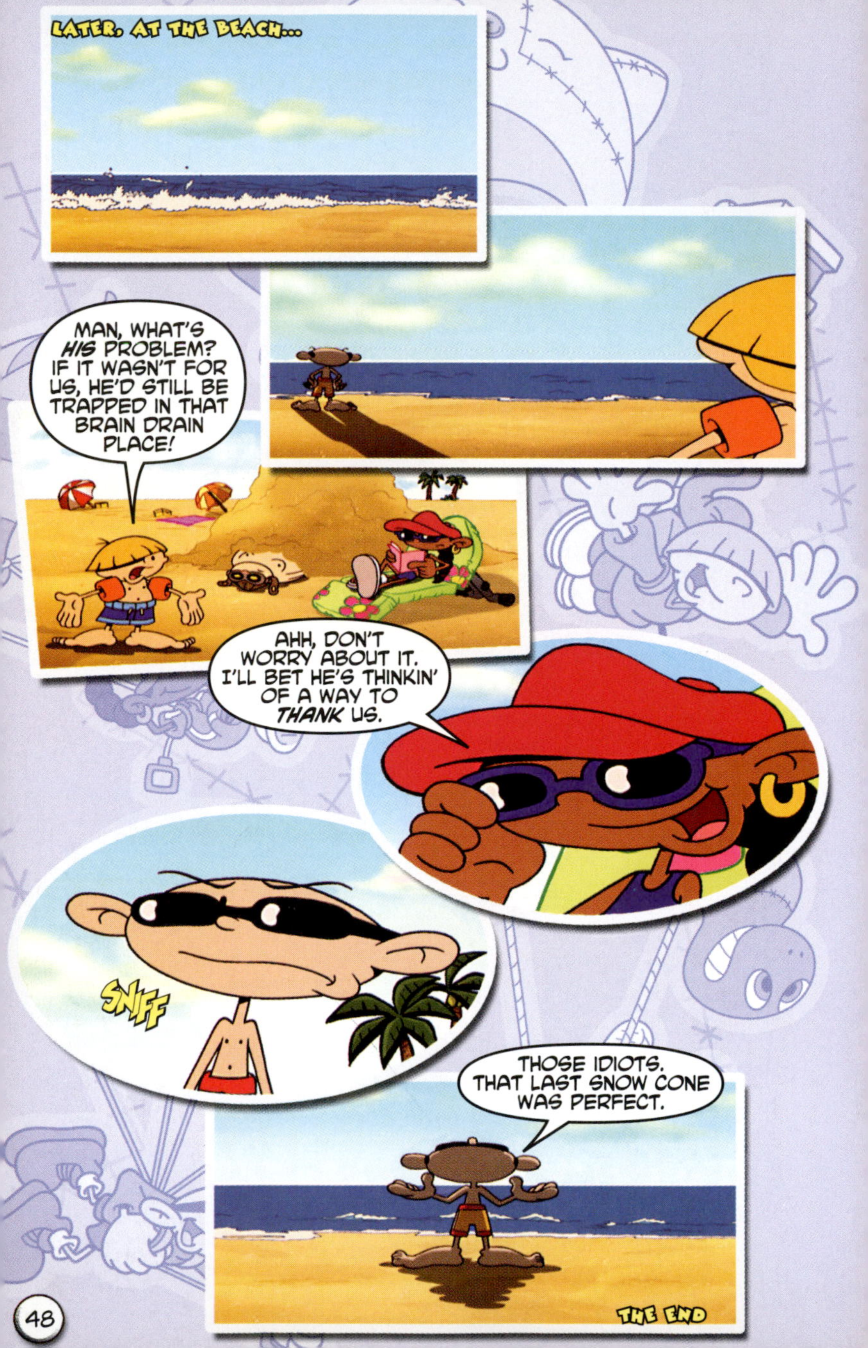

LATER, AT THE BEACH...
MAN, WHAT'S HIS PROBLEM? IF IT WASN'T FOR US, HE'D STILL BE TRAPPED IN THAT BRAIN DRAIN PLACE!
AHH, DON'T WORRY ABOUT IT. I'LL BET HE'S THINKIN' OF A WAY TO THANK US.
SNIFF
THOSE IDIOTS. THAT LAST SNOW CONE WAS PERFECT.
THE END

"Jack and the Gangsters"

Original Television Script Written by
Chris Reccardi

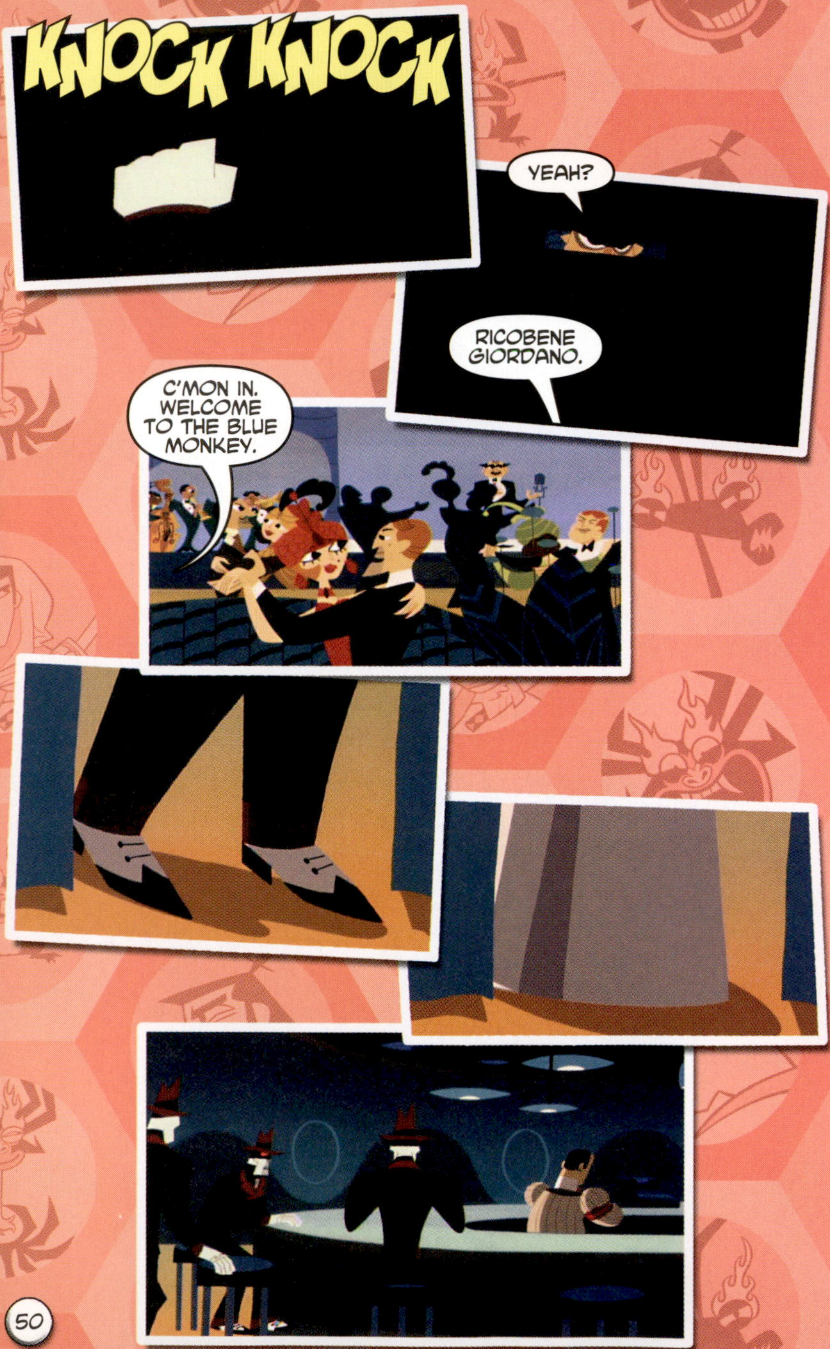
KNOCK KNOCK
YEAH?
RICOBENE GIORDANO.
C'MON IN. WELCOME TO THE BLUE MONKEY.

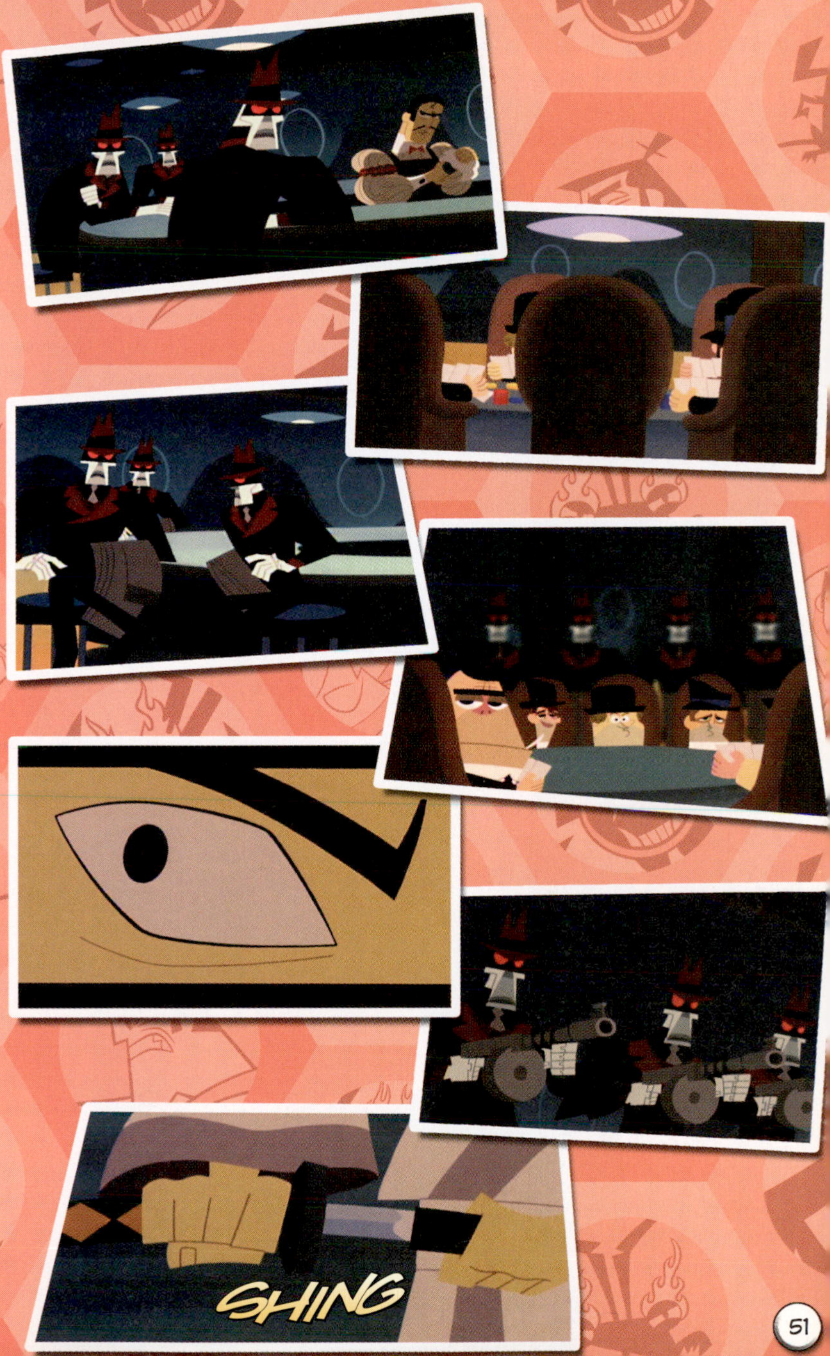
SHING

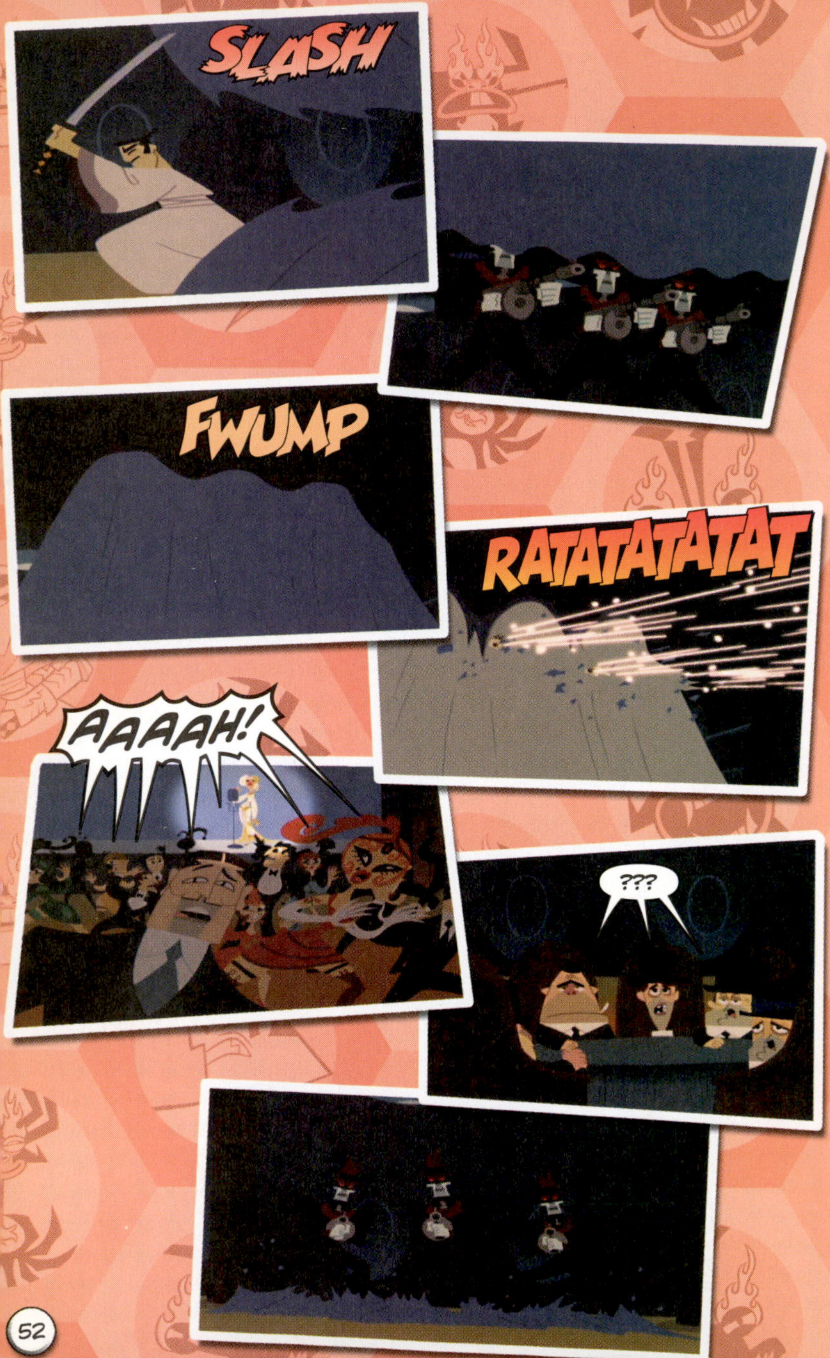
SLASH
FWUMP
RATATATATAT
AAAAAH!
???

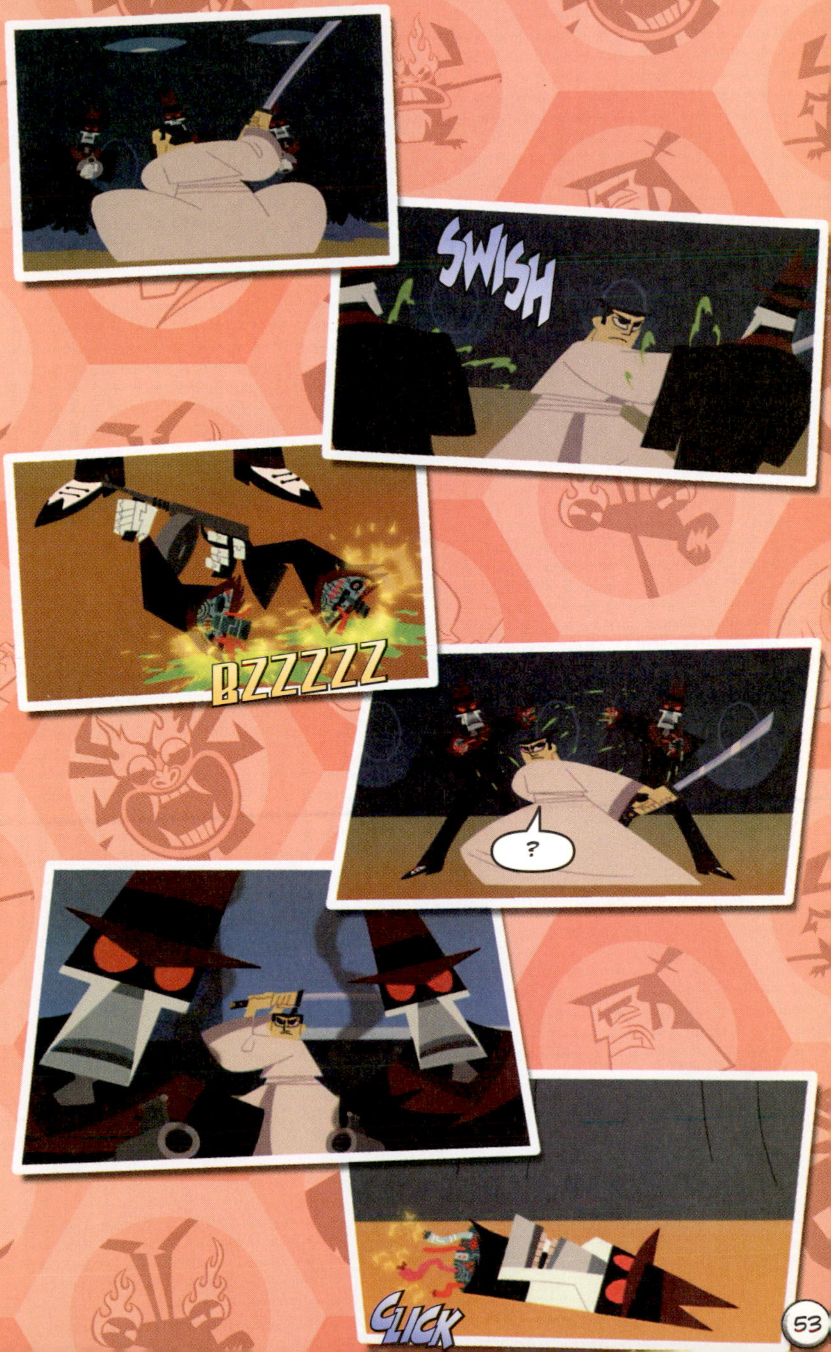
SWISH
BZZZZZ
?
CLICK

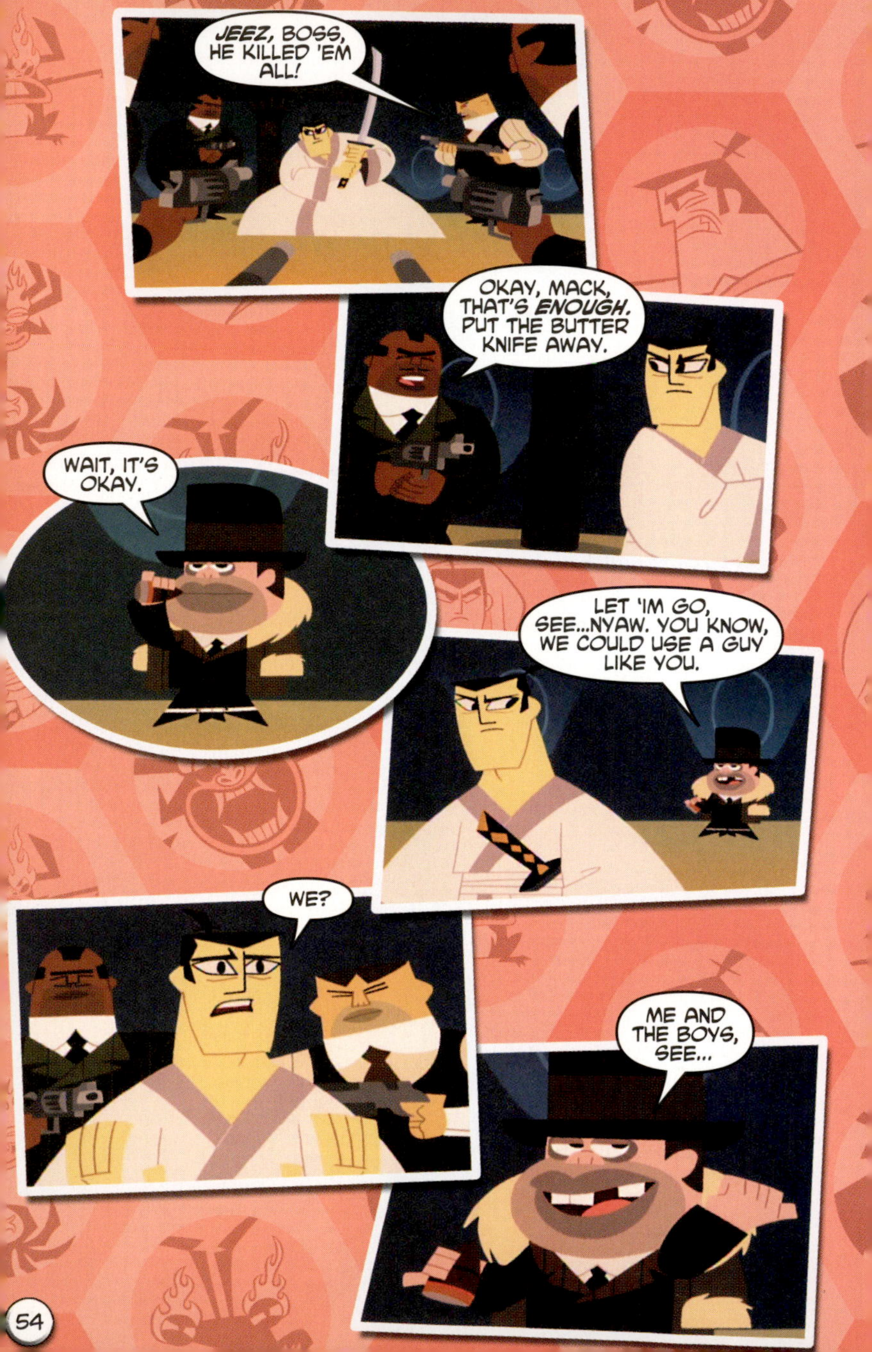
JEEZ, BOSS, HE KILLED 'EM ALL!
OKAY, MACK, THAT'S ENOUGH. PUT THE BUTTER KNIFE AWAY.
WAIT, IT'S OKAY.
LET 'IM GO, SEE...NYAW. YOU KNOW, WE COULD USE A GUY LIKE YOU.
WE?
ME AND THE BOYS, SEE...

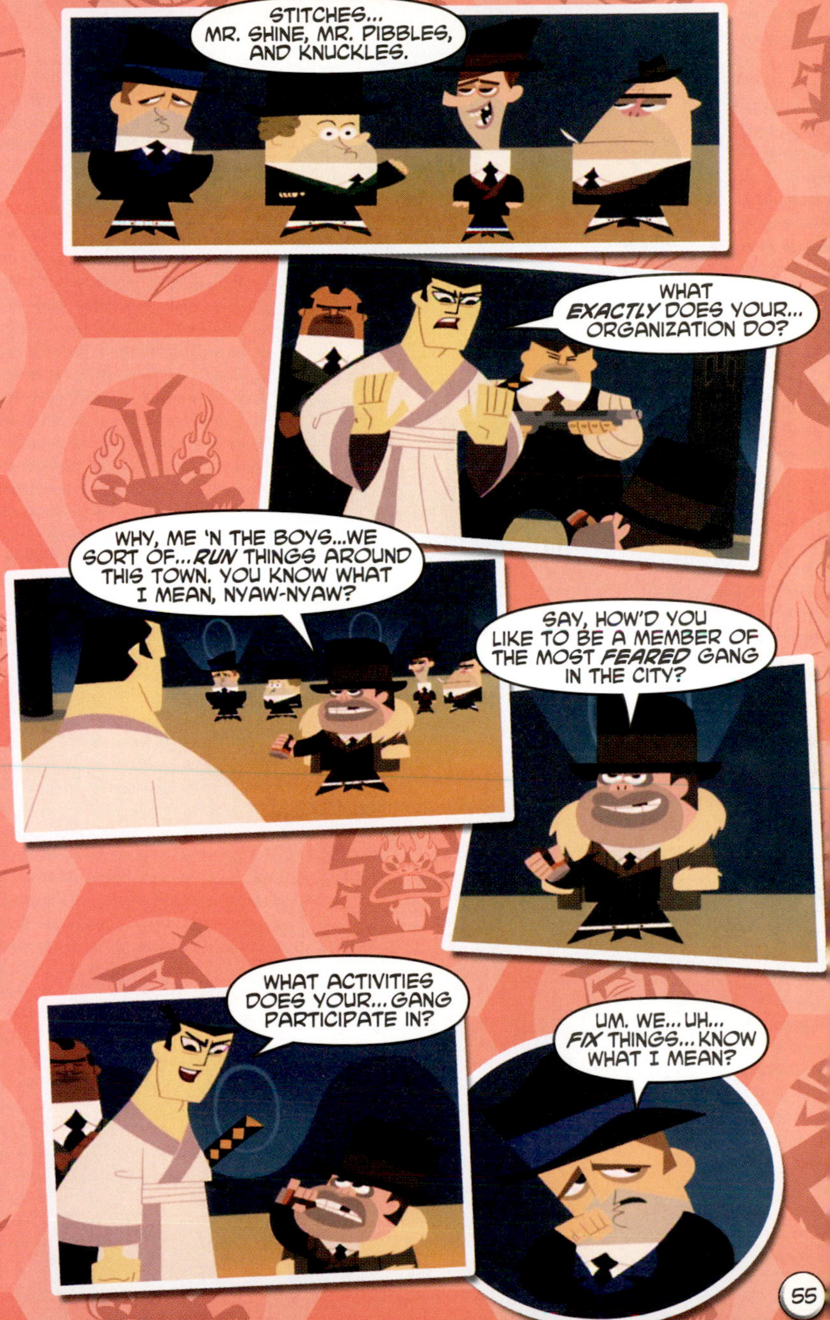
STITCHES... MR. SHINE, MR. PIBBLES, AND KNUCKLES.
WHAT *EXACTLY* DOES YOUR... ORGANIZATION DO?
WHY, ME 'N THE BOYS...WE SORT OF...*RUN* THINGS AROUND THIS TOWN. YOU KNOW WHAT I MEAN, NYAW-NYAW?
SAY, HOW'D YOU LIKE TO BE A MEMBER OF THE MOST *FEARED* GANG IN THE CITY?
WHAT ACTIVITIES DOES YOUR...GANG PARTICIPATE IN?
UM. WE...UH... *FIX* THINGS...KNOW WHAT I MEAN?

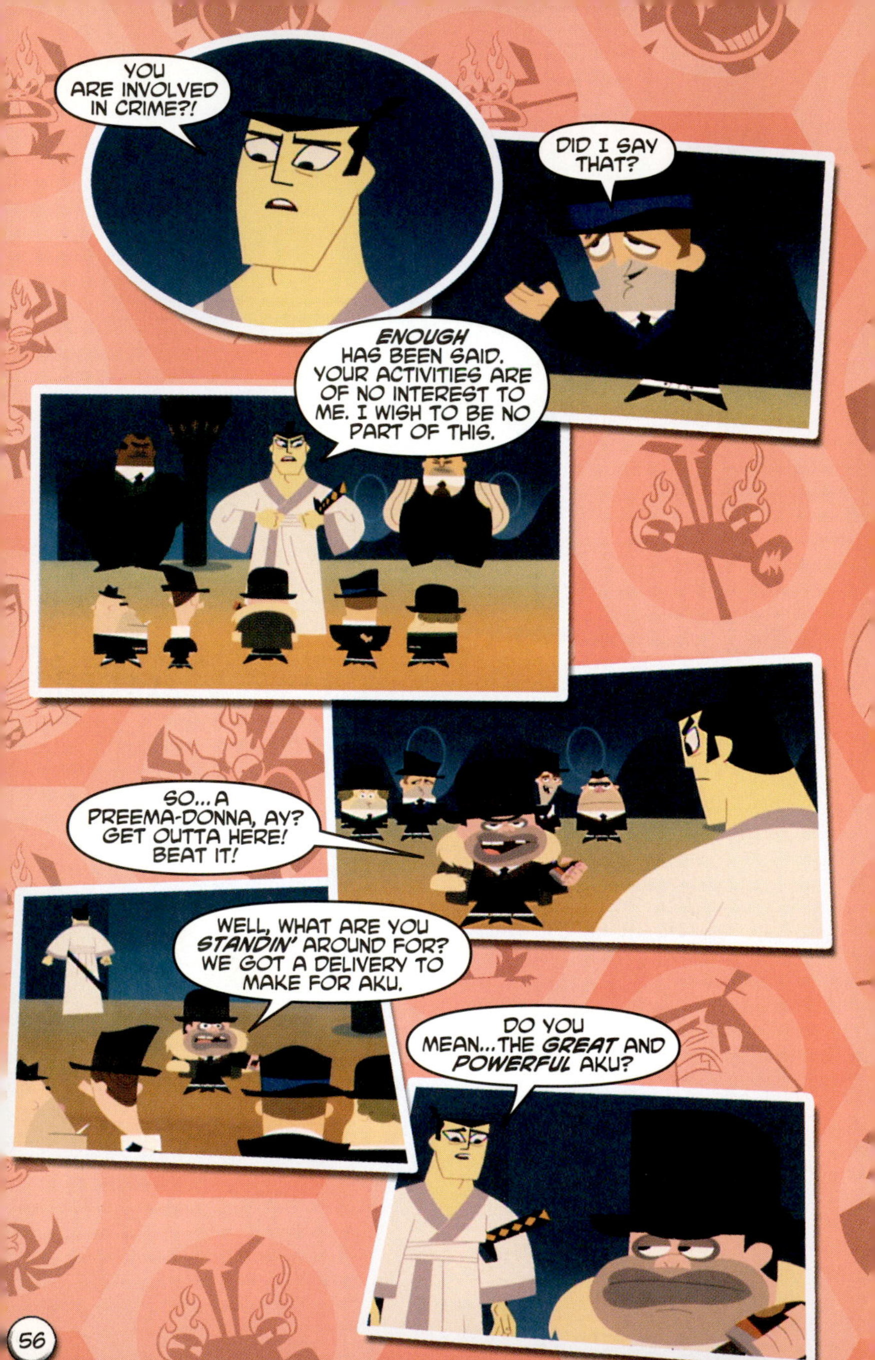
YOU ARE INVOLVED IN CRIME?!
DID I SAY THAT?
ENOUGH HAS BEEN SAID. YOUR ACTIVITIES ARE OF NO INTEREST TO ME. I WISH TO BE NO PART OF THIS.
SO... A PREEMA-DONNA, AY? GET OUTTA HERE! BEAT IT!
WELL, WHAT ARE YOU *STANDIN'* AROUND FOR? WE GOT A DELIVERY TO MAKE FOR AKU.
DO YOU MEAN... THE *GREAT* AND *POWERFUL* AKU?

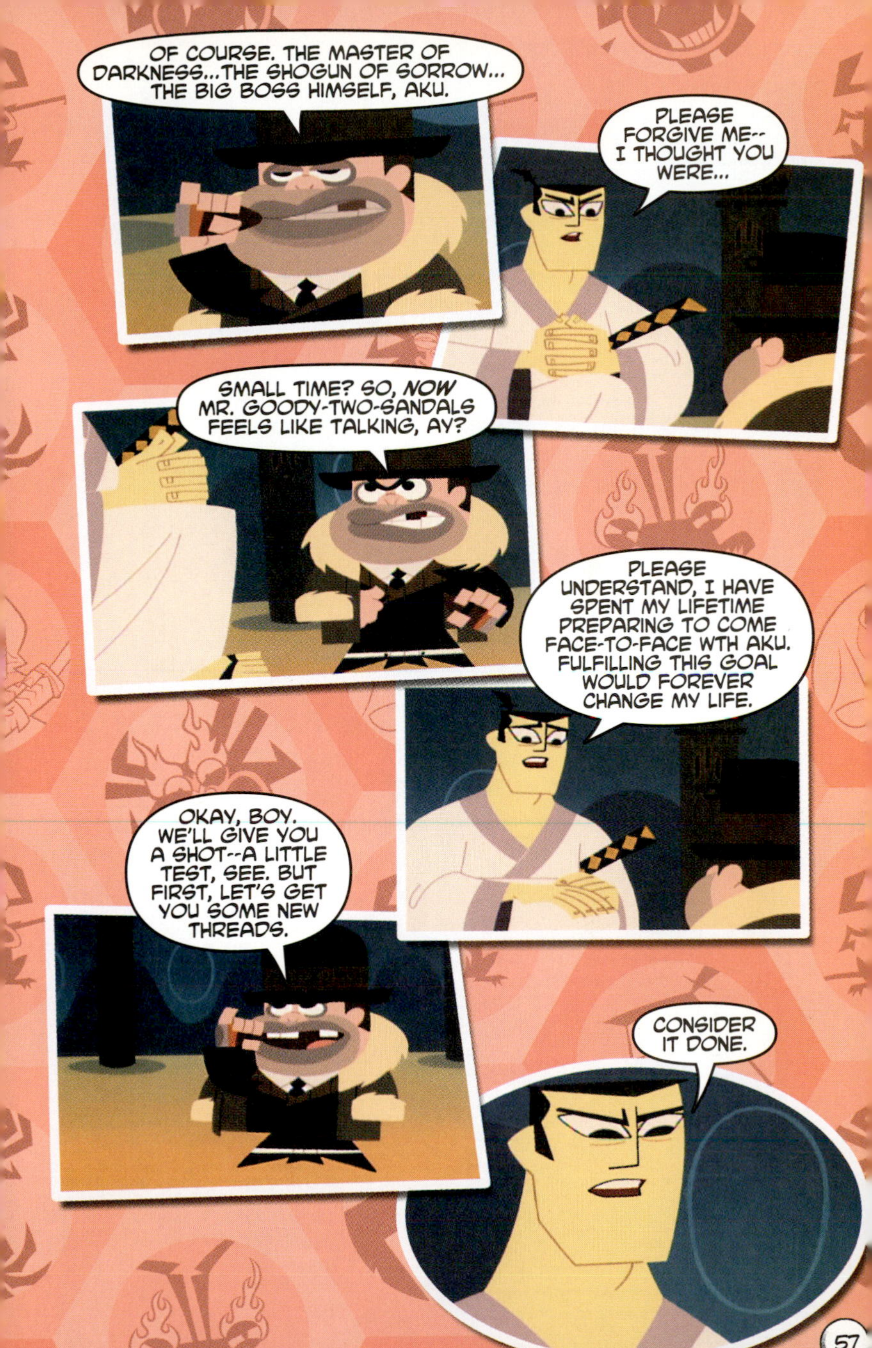
OF COURSE. THE MASTER OF DARKNESS...THE SHOGUN OF SORROW... THE BIG BOSS HIMSELF, AKU.
PLEASE FORGIVE ME-- I THOUGHT YOU WERE...
SMALL TIME? SO, NOW MR. GOODY-TWO-SANDALS FEELS LIKE TALKING, AY?
PLEASE UNDERSTAND, I HAVE SPENT MY LIFETIME PREPARING TO COME FACE-TO-FACE WTH AKU. FULFILLING THIS GOAL WOULD FOREVER CHANGE MY LIFE.
OKAY, BOY. WE'LL GIVE YOU A SHOT--A LITTLE TEST, SEE. BUT FIRST, LET'S GET YOU SOME NEW THREADS.
CONSIDER IT DONE.

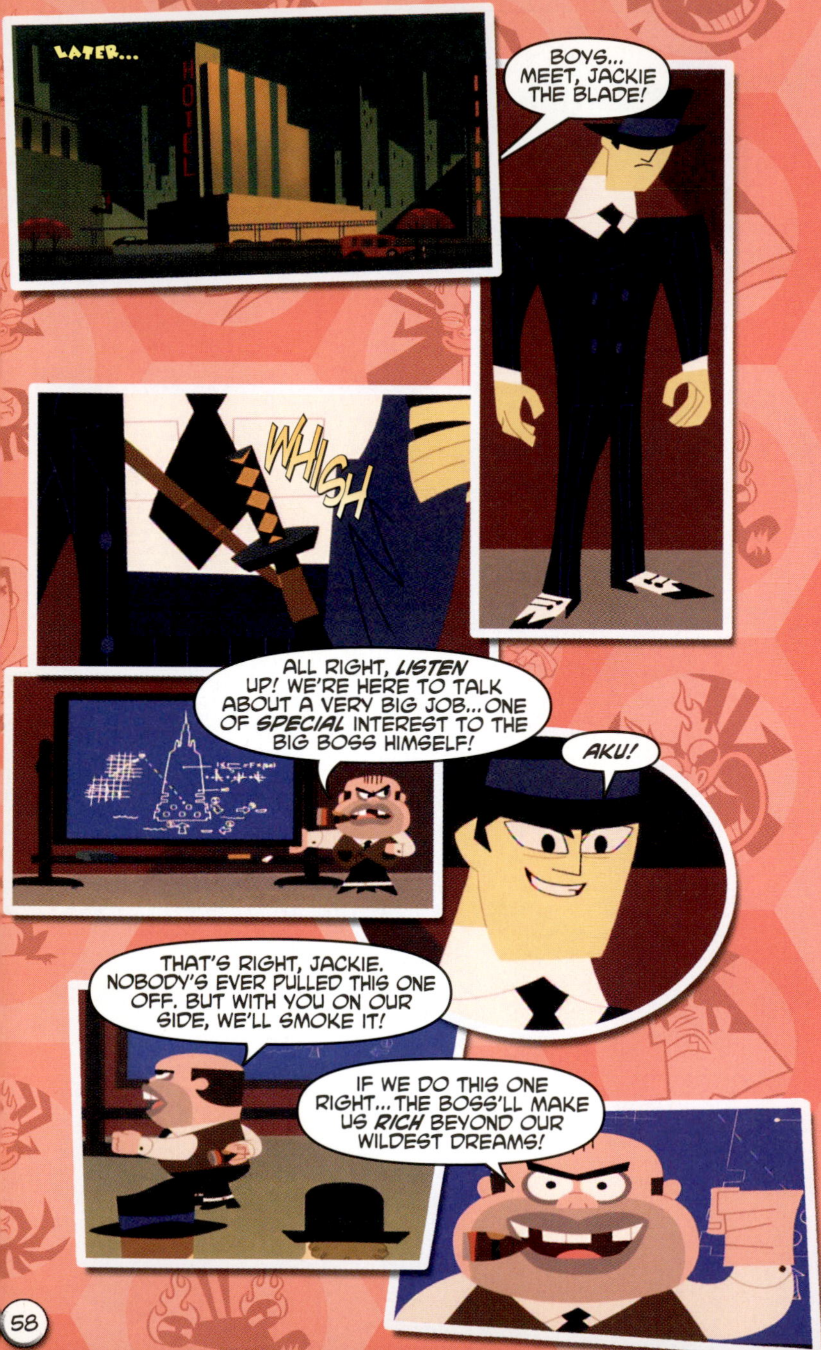
LATER...
BOYS... MEET, JACKIE THE BLADE!
WHISH
HOTEL
ALL RIGHT, LISTEN UP! WE'RE HERE TO TALK ABOUT A VERY BIG JOB... ONE OF SPECIAL INTEREST TO THE BIG BOSS HIMSELF!
AKU!
THAT'S RIGHT, JACKIE. NOBODY'S EVER PULLED THIS ONE OFF. BUT WITH YOU ON OUR SIDE, WE'LL SMOKE IT!
IF WE DO THIS ONE RIGHT... THE BOSS'LL MAKE US RICH BEYOND OUR WILDEST DREAMS!

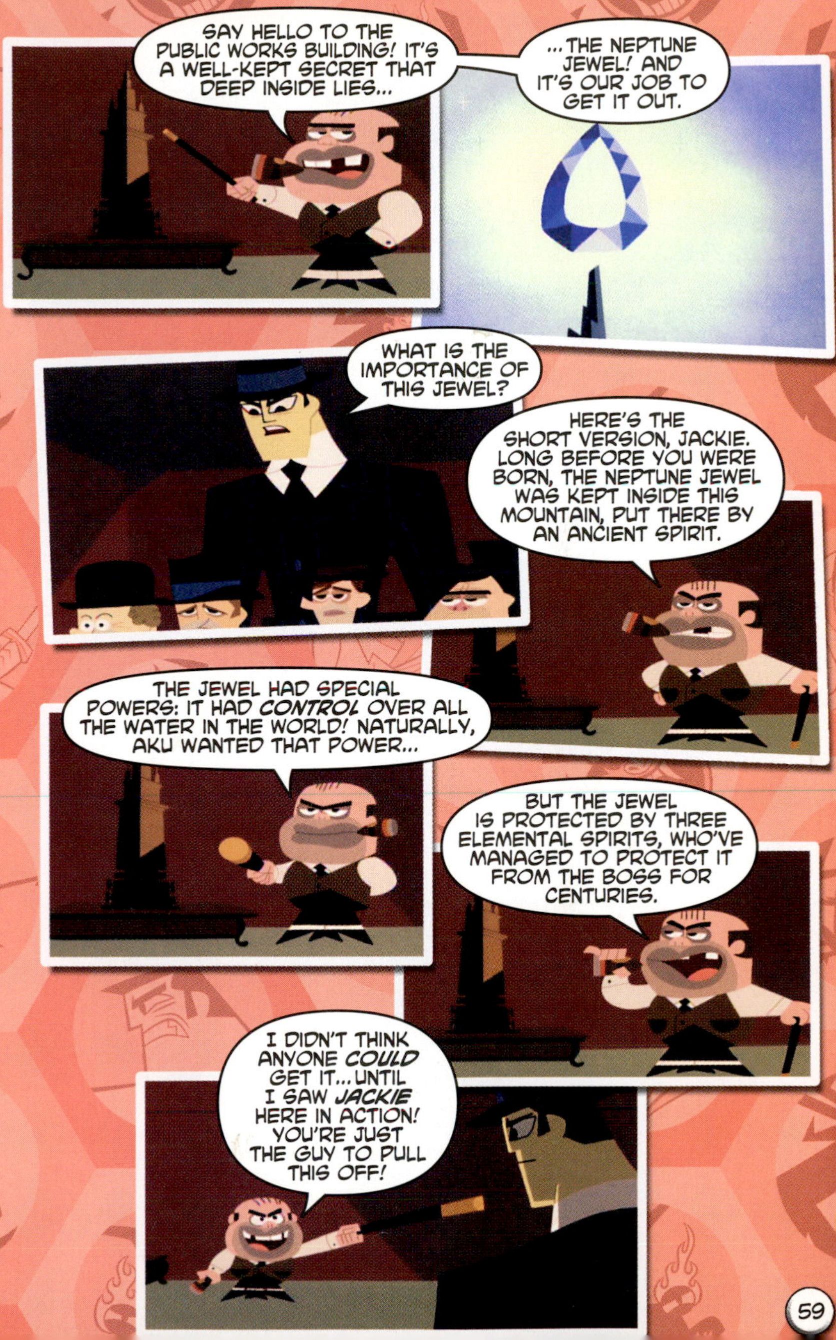

SAY HELLO TO THE PUBLIC WORKS BUILDING! IT'S A WELL-KEPT SECRET THAT DEEP INSIDE LIES...
...THE NEPTUNE JEWEL! AND IT'S OUR JOB TO GET IT OUT.
WHAT IS THE IMPORTANCE OF THIS JEWEL?
HERE'S THE SHORT VERSION, JACKIE. LONG BEFORE YOU WERE BORN, THE NEPTUNE JEWEL WAS KEPT INSIDE THIS MOUNTAIN, PUT THERE BY AN ANCIENT SPIRIT.
THE JEWEL HAD SPECIAL POWERS: IT HAD *CONTROL* OVER ALL THE WATER IN THE WORLD! NATURALLY, AKU WANTED THAT POWER...
BUT THE JEWEL IS PROTECTED BY THREE ELEMENTAL SPIRITS, WHO'VE MANAGED TO PROTECT IT FROM THE BOSS FOR CENTURIES.
I DIDN'T THINK ANYONE *COULD* GET IT... UNTIL I SAW *JACKIE* HERE IN ACTION! YOU'RE JUST THE GUY TO PULL THIS OFF!

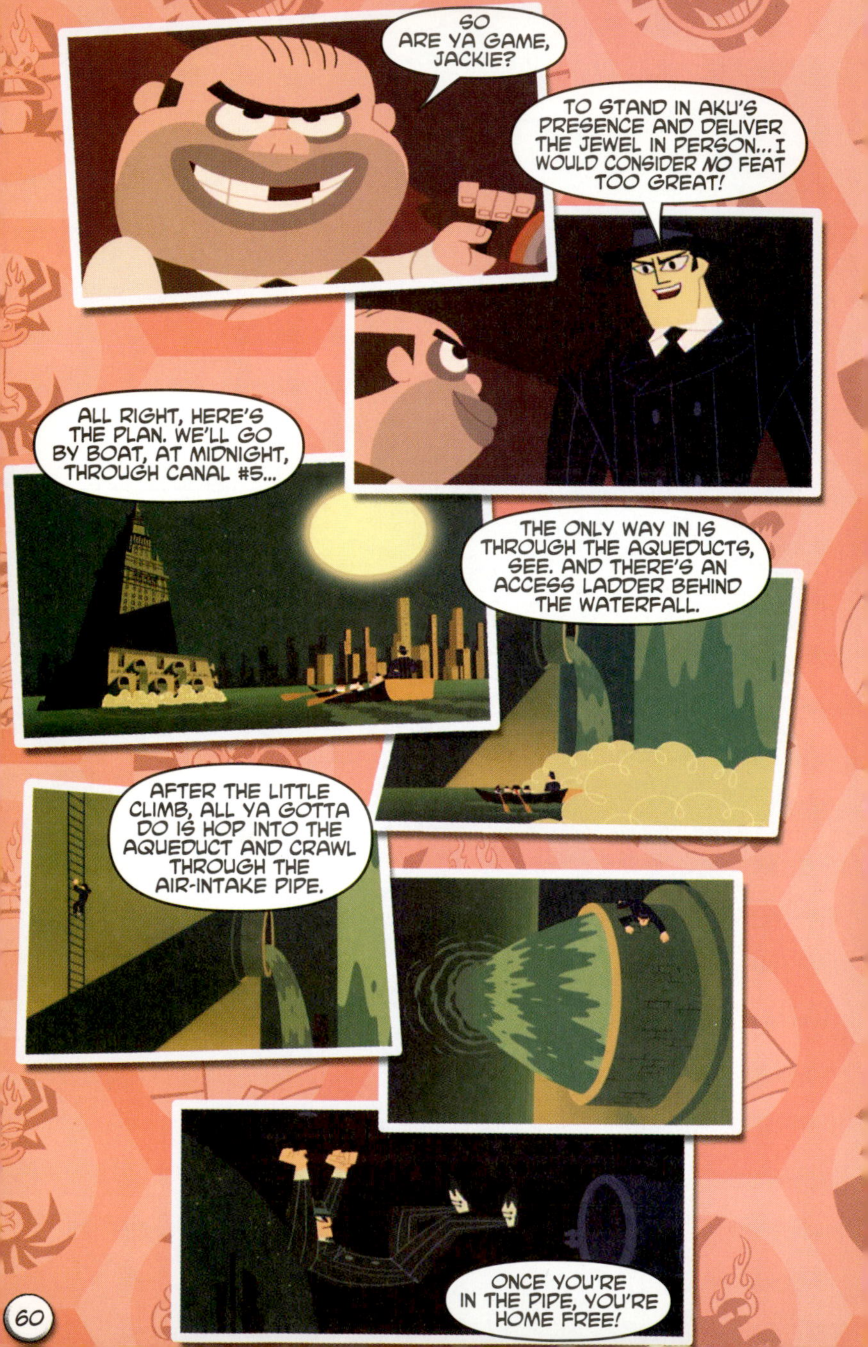
SO ARE YA GAME, JACKIE?
TO STAND IN AKU'S PRESENCE AND DELIVER THE JEWEL IN PERSON... I WOULD CONSIDER *NO* FEAT TOO GREAT!
ALL RIGHT, HERE'S THE PLAN. WE'LL GO BY BOAT, AT MIDNIGHT, THROUGH CANAL #5...
THE ONLY WAY IN IS THROUGH THE AQUEDUCTS, SEE. AND THERE'S AN ACCESS LADDER BEHIND THE WATERFALL.
AFTER THE LITTLE CLIMB, ALL YA GOTTA DO IS HOP INTO THE AQUEDUCT AND CRAWL THROUGH THE AIR-INTAKE PIPE.
ONCE YOU'RE IN THE PIPE, YOU'RE HOME FREE!

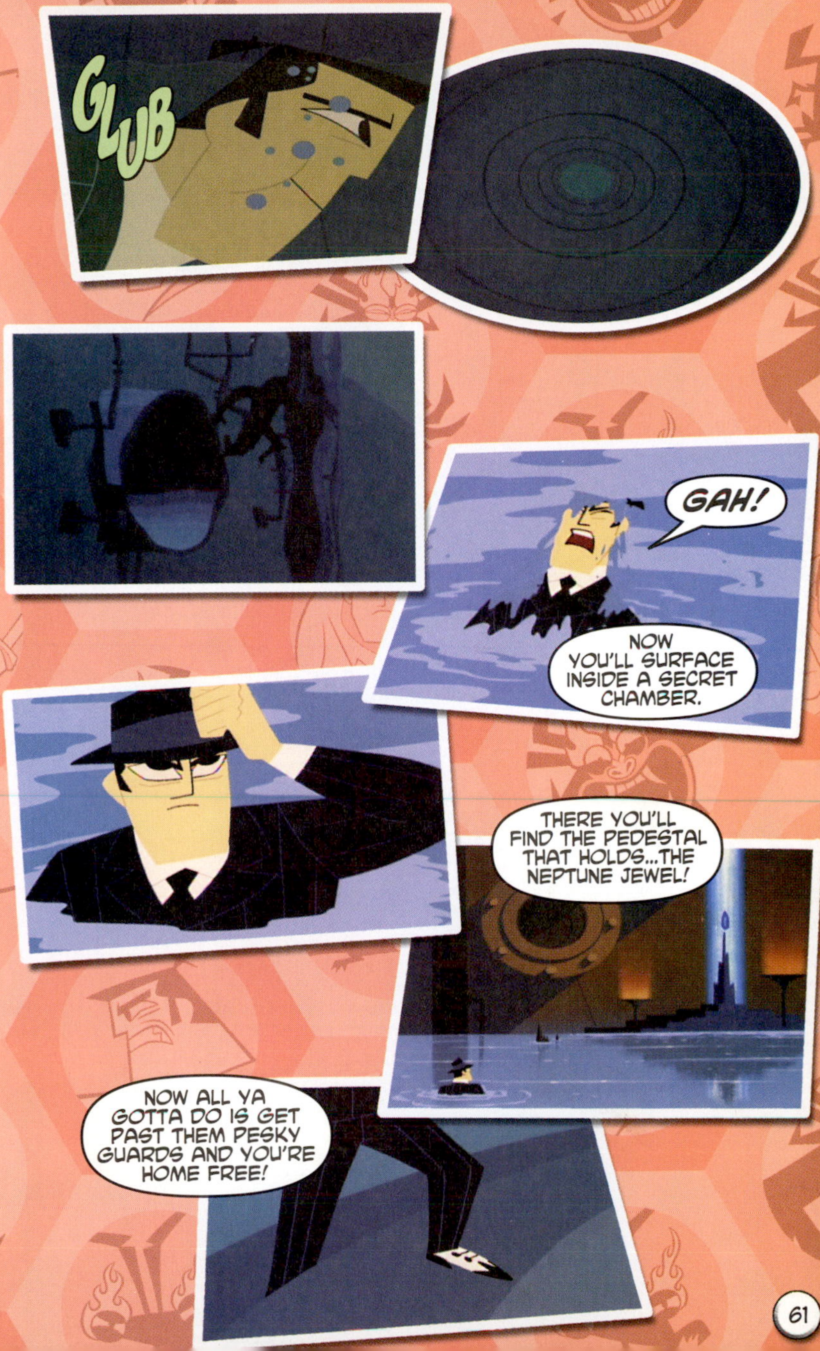
GLUB
GAH!
NOW YOU'LL SURFACE INSIDE A SECRET CHAMBER.
THERE YOU'LL FIND THE PEDESTAL THAT HOLDS...THE NEPTUNE JEWEL!
NOW ALL YA GOTTA DO IS GET PAST THEM PESKY GUARDS AND YOU'RE HOME FREE!

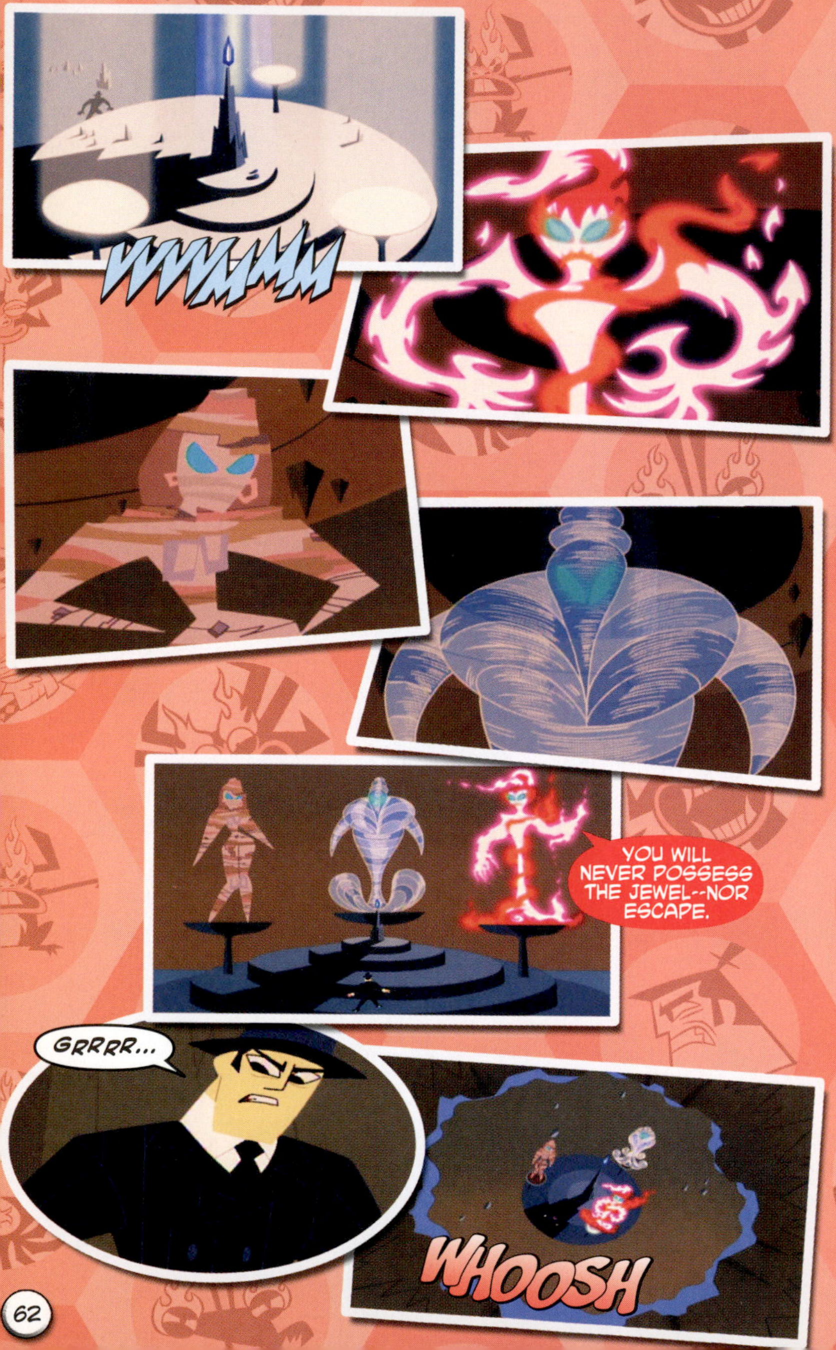
VVVMMM
YOU WILL NEVER POSSESS THE JEWEL--NOR ESCAPE.
GRRRR...
WHOOSH

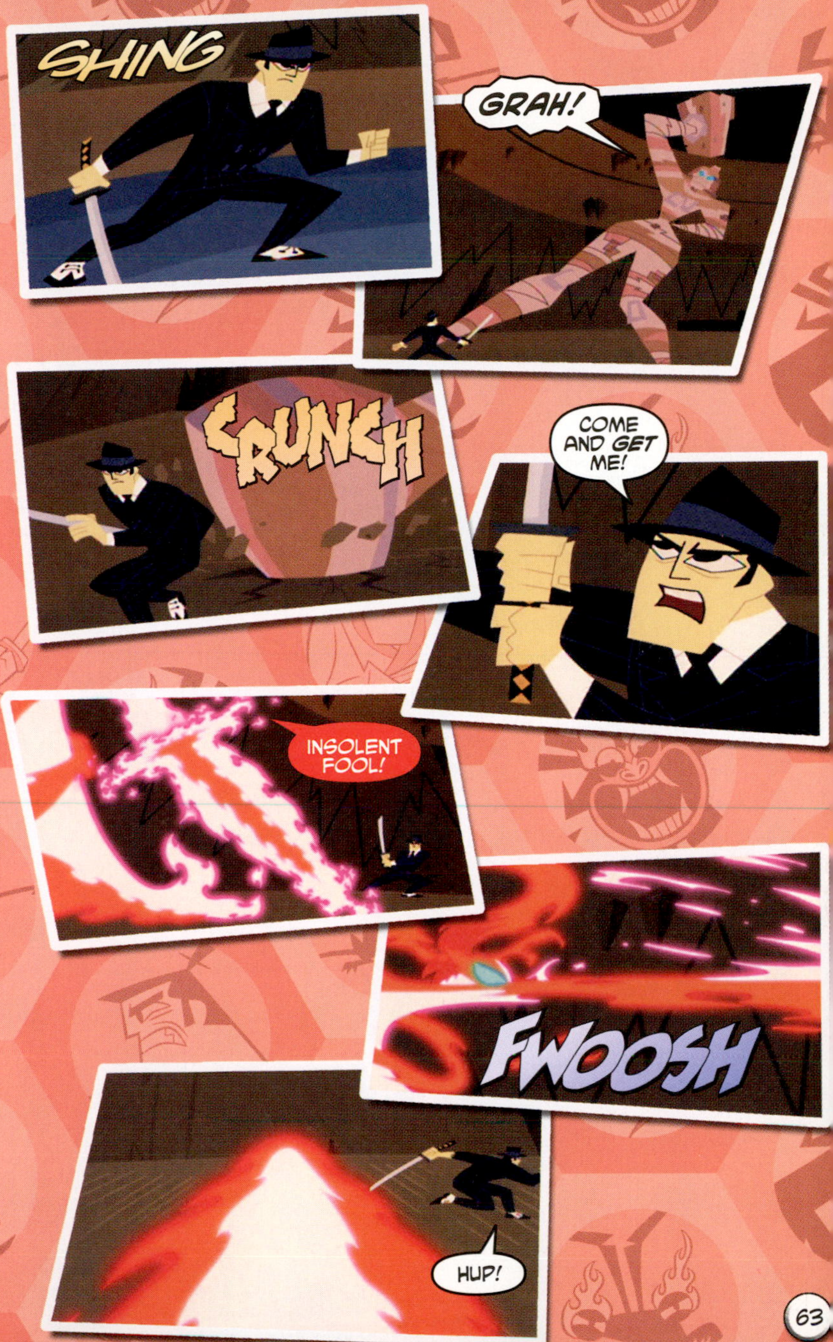
SHING
GRAH!
CRUNCH
COME AND GET ME!
INSOLENT FOOL!
FWOOSH
HUP!

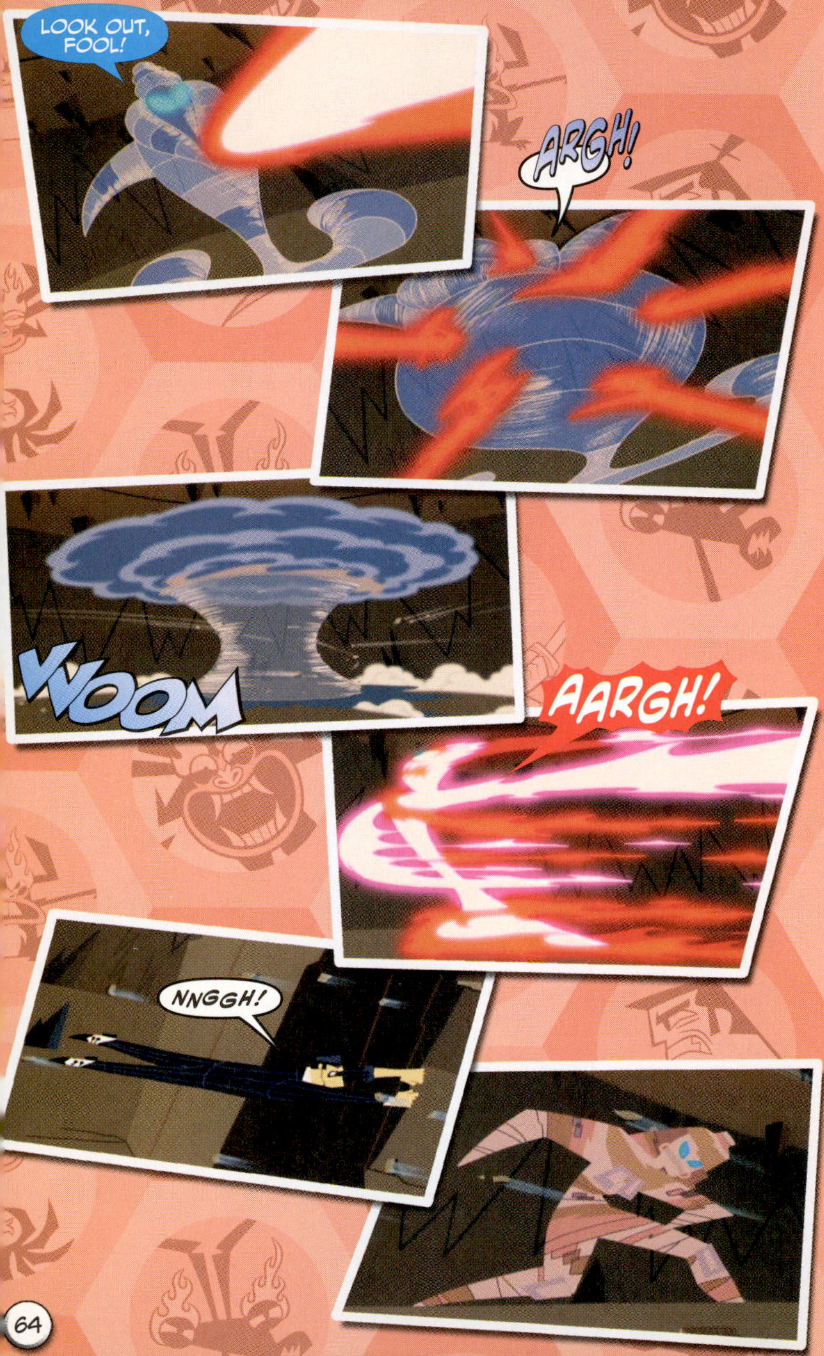
LOOK OUT, FOOL!
ARGH!
VWOOM
AARGH!
NNGGH!

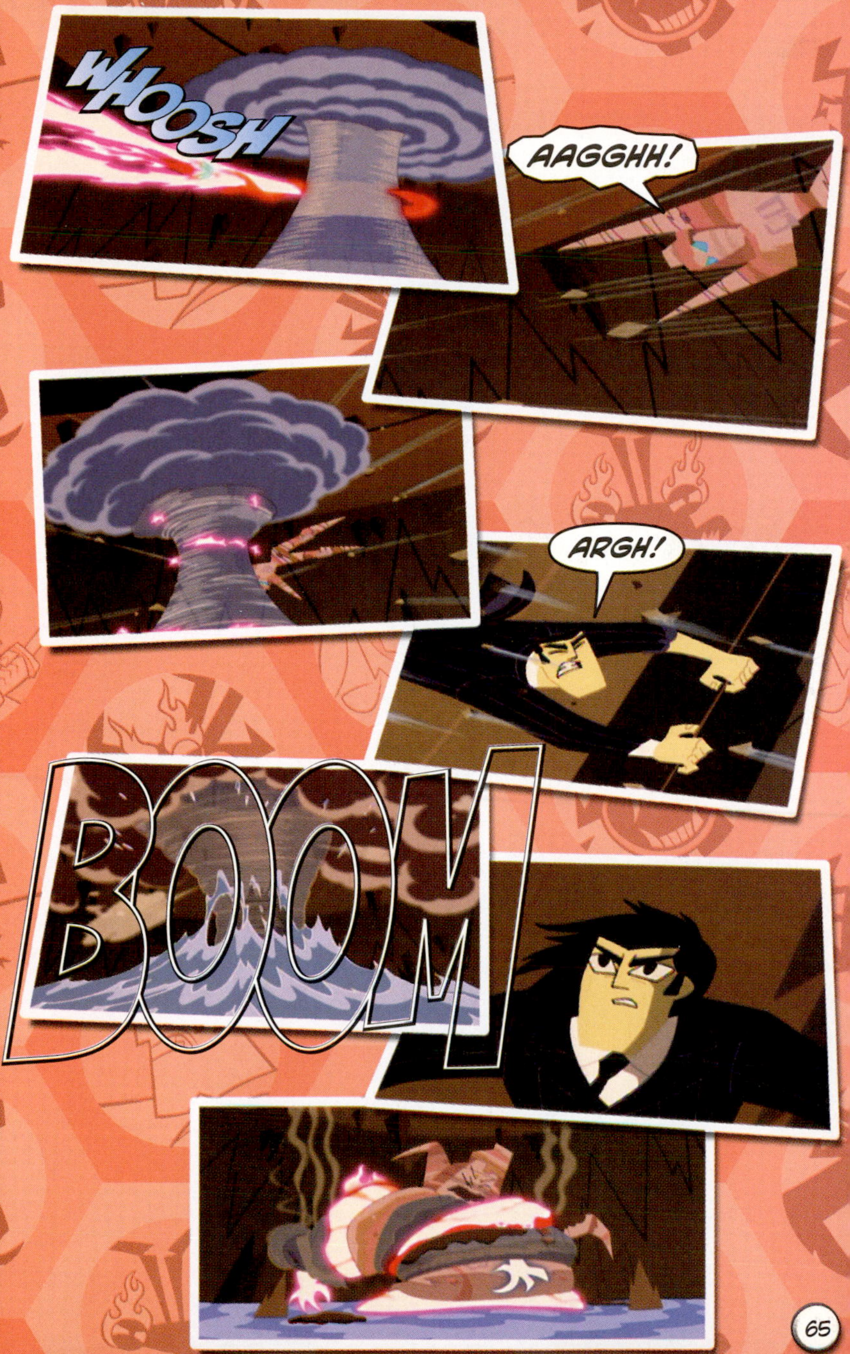
WHOOSH
AAGGHH!
ARGH!
BOOM

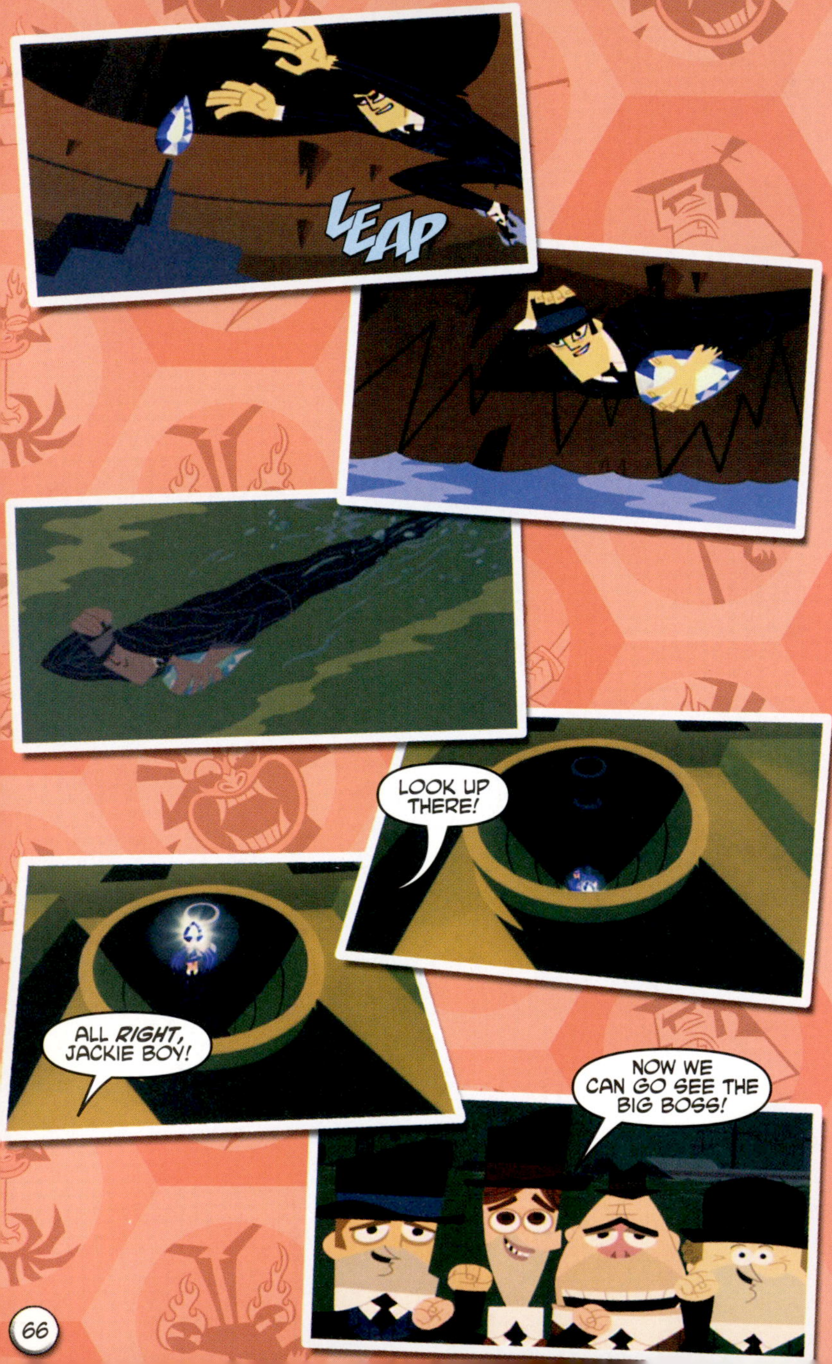
LEAP
LOOK UP THERE!
ALL RIGHT, JACKIE BOY!
NOW WE CAN GO SEE THE BIG BOSS!

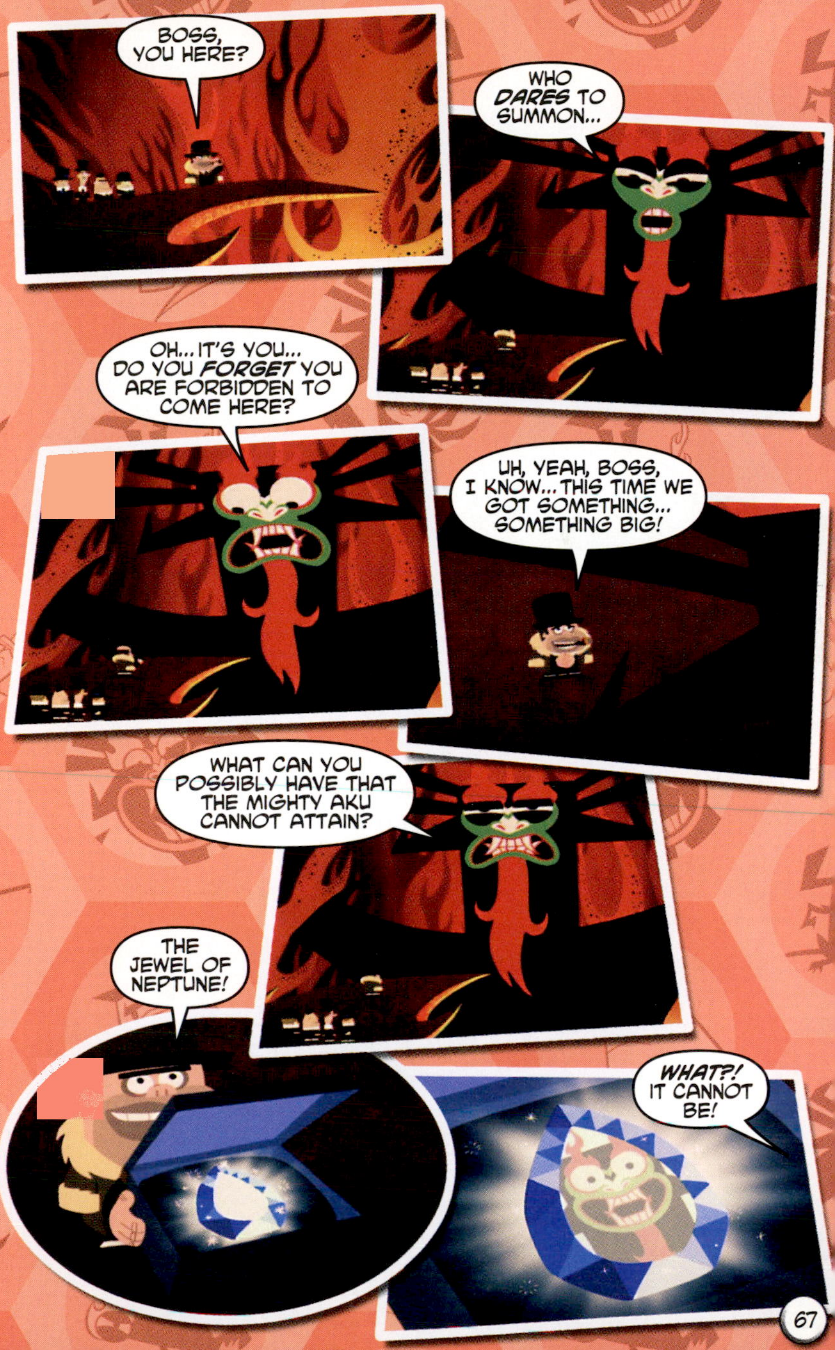
BOSS, YOU HERE?
WHO DARES TO SUMMON...
OH... IT'S YOU... DO YOU FORGET YOU ARE FORBIDDEN TO COME HERE?
UH, YEAH, BOSS, I KNOW... THIS TIME WE GOT SOMETHING... SOMETHING BIG!
WHAT CAN YOU POSSIBLY HAVE THAT THE MIGHTY AKU CANNOT ATTAIN?
THE JEWEL OF NEPTUNE!
WHAT?! IT CANNOT BE!

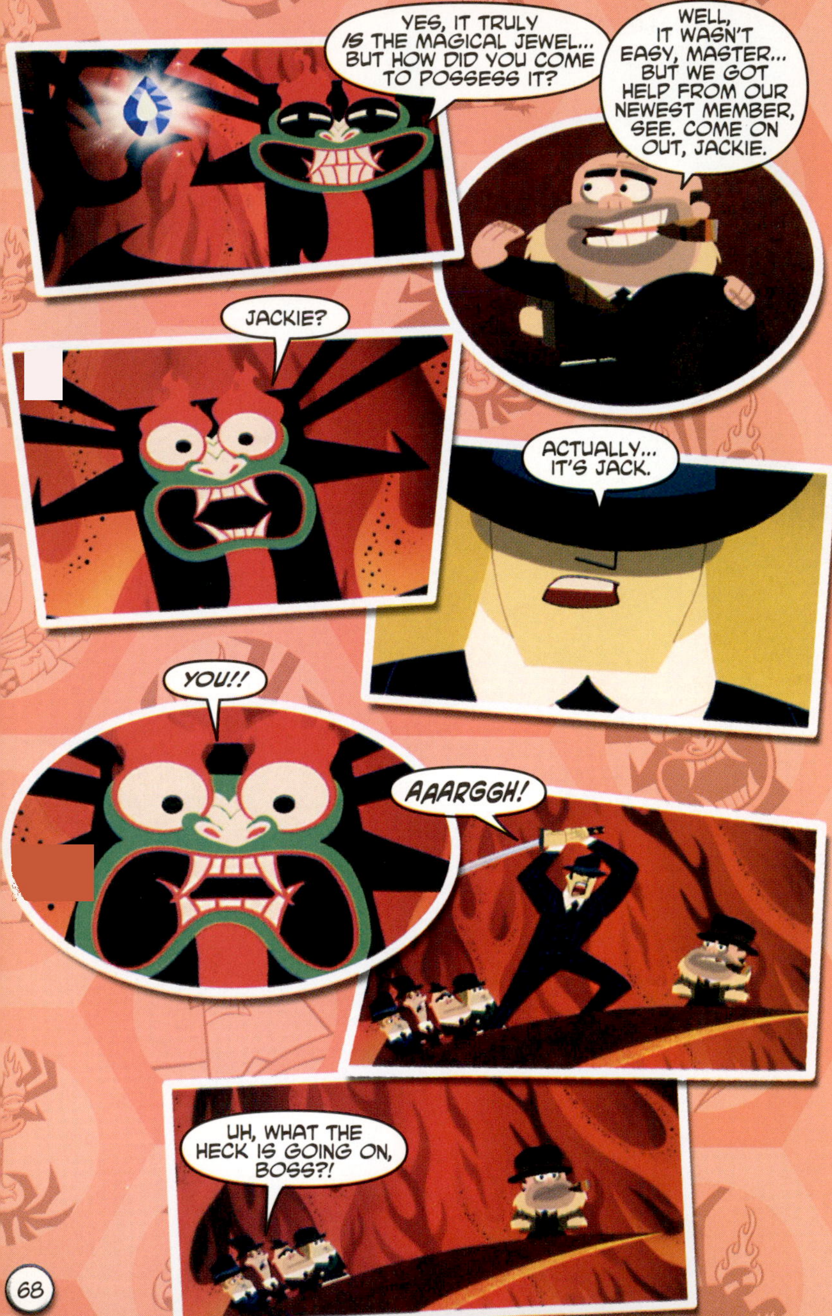
YES, IT TRULY IS THE MAGICAL JEWEL... BUT HOW DID YOU COME TO POSSESS IT?
WELL, IT WASN'T EASY, MASTER... BUT WE GOT HELP FROM OUR NEWEST MEMBER, SEE. COME ON OUT, JACKIE.
JACKIE?
ACTUALLY... IT'S JACK.
YOU!!
AAARGGH!
UH, WHAT THE HECK IS GOING ON, BOSS?!

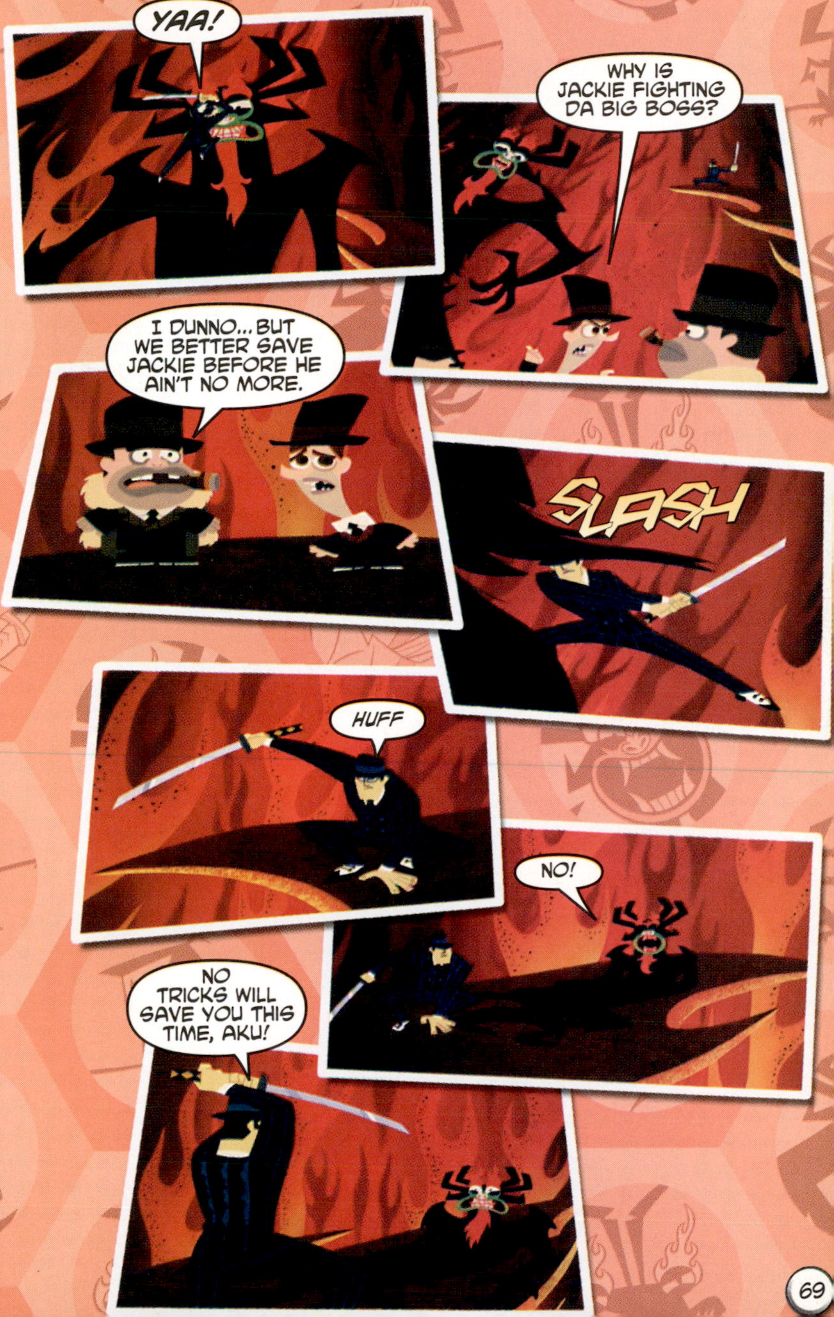
YAA!
WHY IS JACKIE FIGHTING DA BIG BOSS?
I DUNNO... BUT WE BETTER SAVE JACKIE BEFORE HE AIN'T NO MORE.
SLASH
HUFF
NO!
NO TRICKS WILL SAVE YOU THIS TIME, AKU!

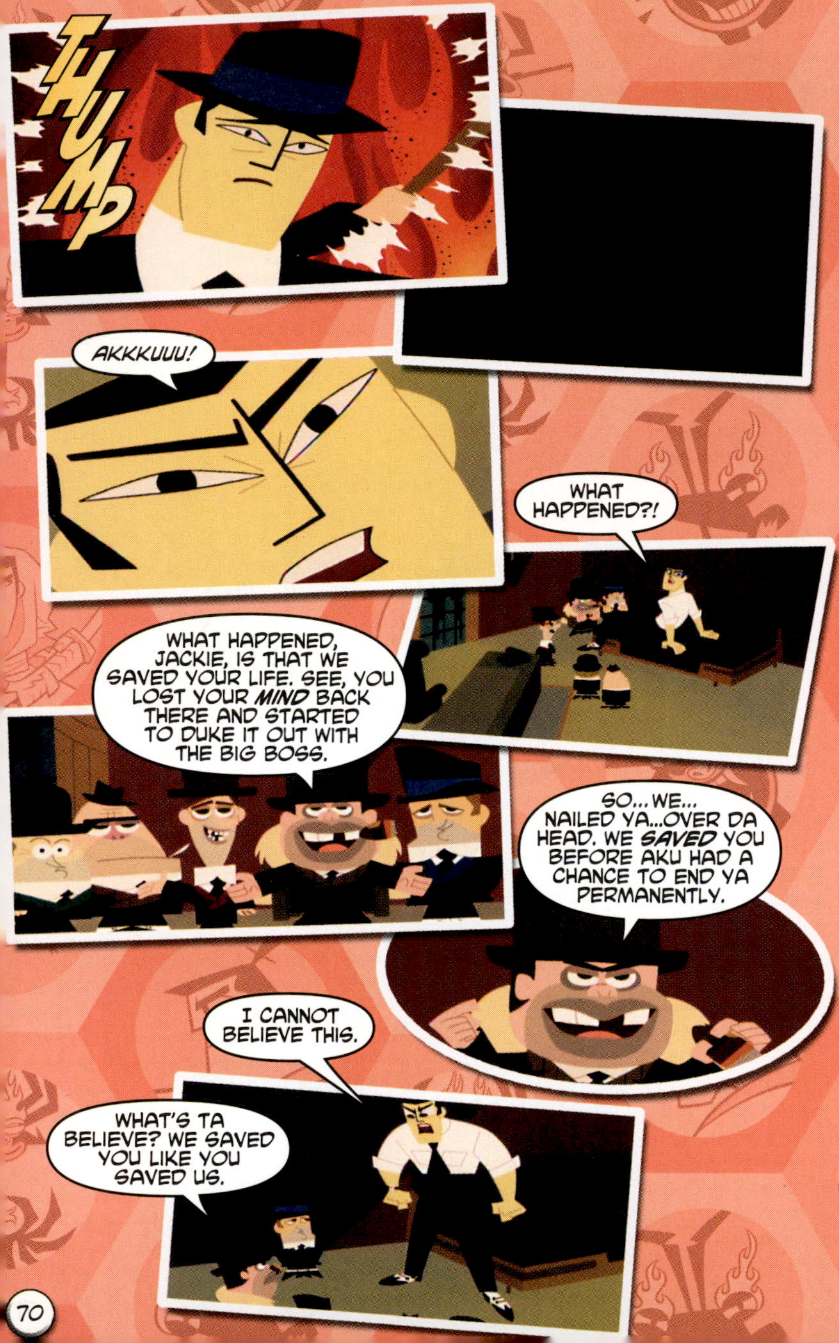
THUMP
AKKKUUU!
WHAT HAPPENED?!
WHAT HAPPENED, JACKIE, IS THAT WE SAVED YOUR LIFE. SEE, YOU LOST YOUR *MIND* BACK THERE AND STARTED TO DUKE IT OUT WITH THE BIG BOSS.
SO... WE... NAILED YA...OVER DA HEAD. WE *SAVED* YOU BEFORE AKU HAD A CHANCE TO END YA PERMANENTLY.
I CANNOT BELIEVE THIS.
WHAT'S TA BELIEVE? WE SAVED YOU LIKE YOU SAVED US.

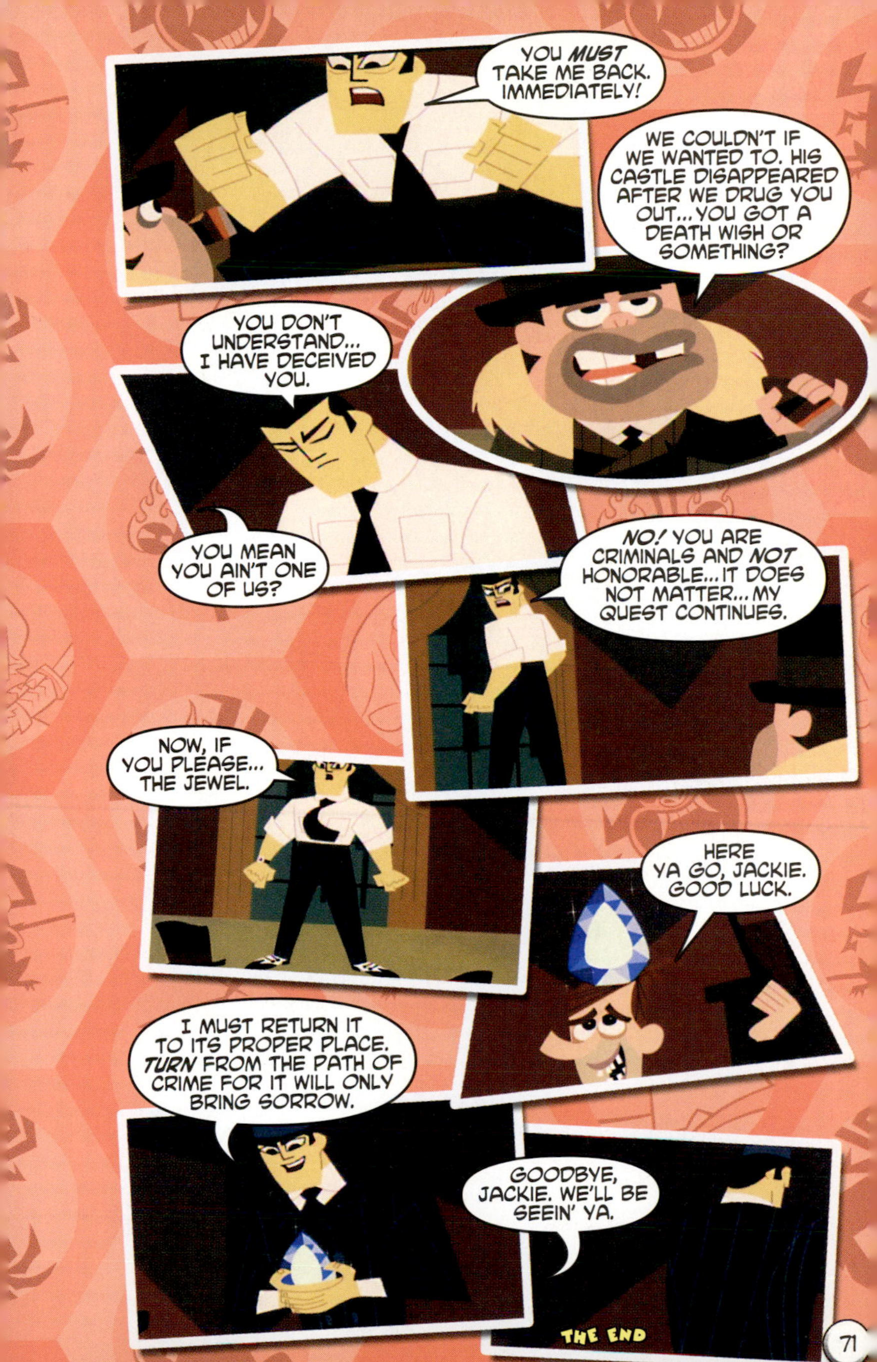
YOU *MUST* TAKE ME BACK. IMMEDIATELY!
WE COULDN'T IF WE WANTED TO. HIS CASTLE DISAPPEARED AFTER WE DRUG YOU OUT... YOU GOT A DEATH WISH OR SOMETHING?
YOU DON'T UNDERSTAND... I HAVE DECEIVED YOU.
YOU MEAN YOU AIN'T ONE OF US?
NO! YOU ARE CRIMINALS AND *NOT* HONORABLE... IT DOES NOT MATTER... MY QUEST CONTINUES.
NOW, IF YOU PLEASE... THE JEWEL.
HERE YA GO, JACKIE. GOOD LUCK.
I MUST RETURN IT TO ITS PROPER PLACE. *TURN* FROM THE PATH OF CRIME FOR IT WILL ONLY BRING SORROW.
GOODBYE, JACKIE. WE'LL BE SEEIN' YA.
THE END

The Grim Adventures of Billy & Mandy

"Tricycle of Terror"

Original Television Script Written by
Carl Greenblatt and Gord Zajac

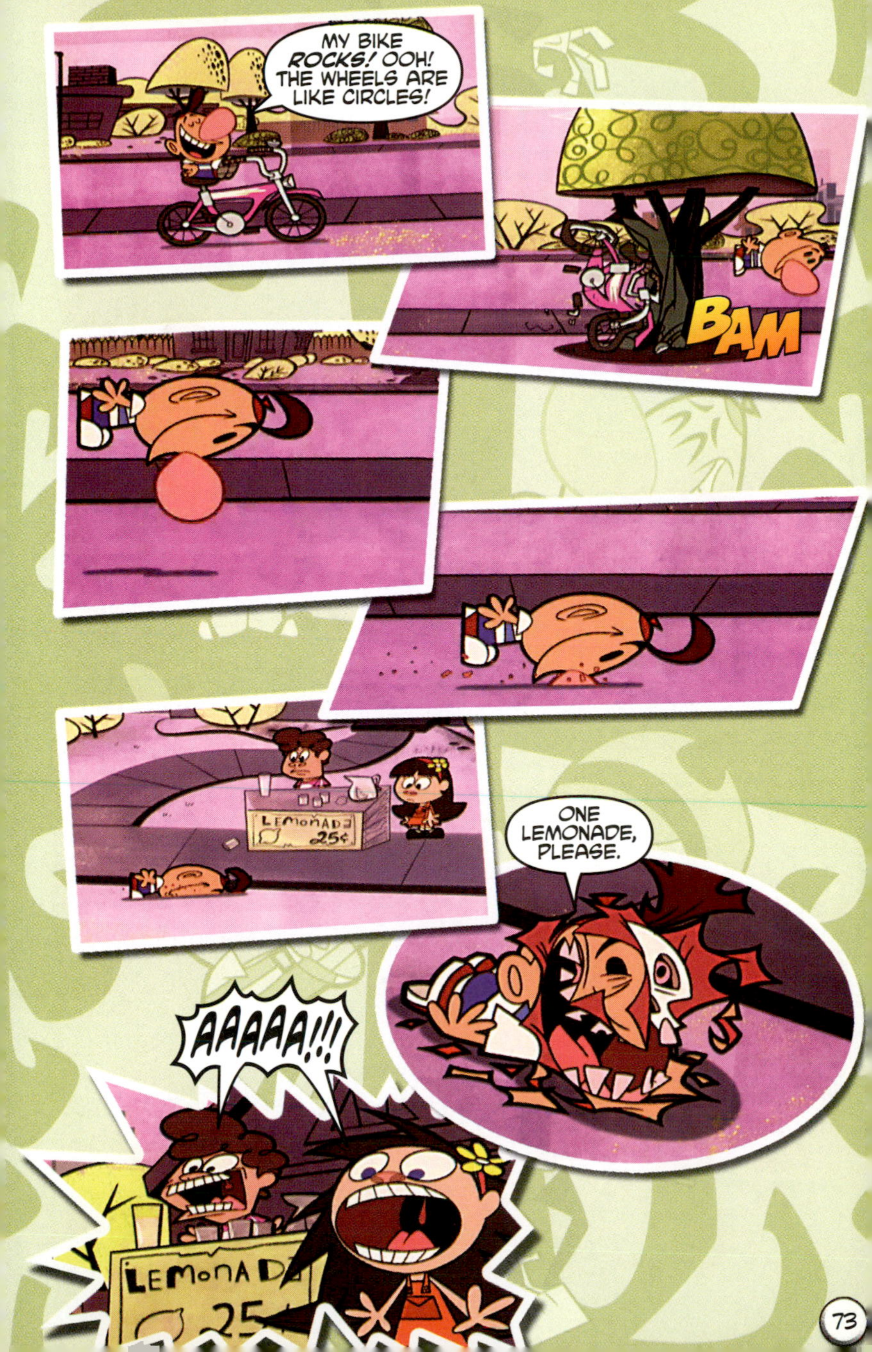
MY BIKE ROCKS! OOH! THE WHEELS ARE LIKE CIRCLES!
BAM
LEMONADE 25¢
ONE LEMONADE, PLEASE.
AAAAA!!!
LEMONAD

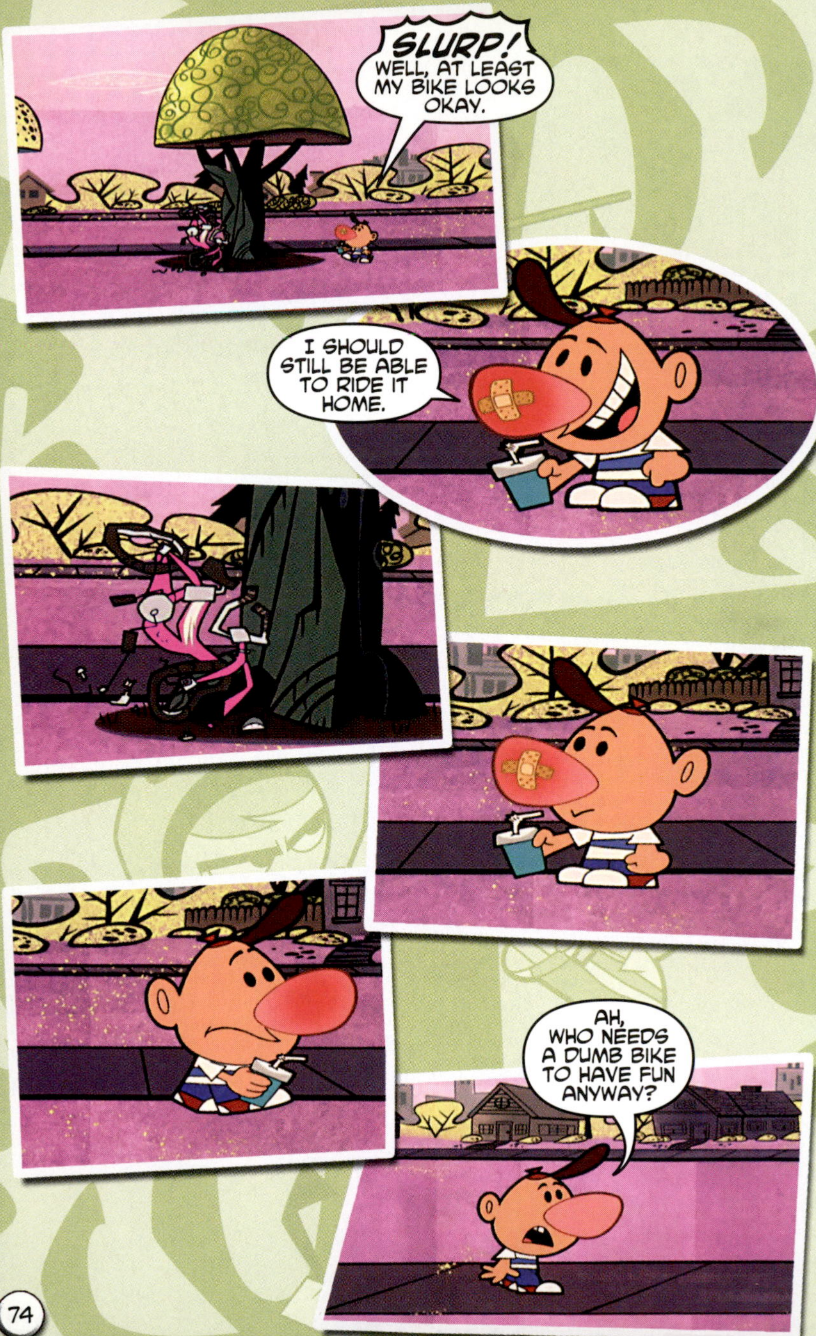
SLURP! WELL, AT LEAST MY BIKE LOOKS OKAY.
I SHOULD STILL BE ABLE TO RIDE IT HOME.
AH, WHO NEEDS A DUMB BIKE TO HAVE FUN ANYWAY?

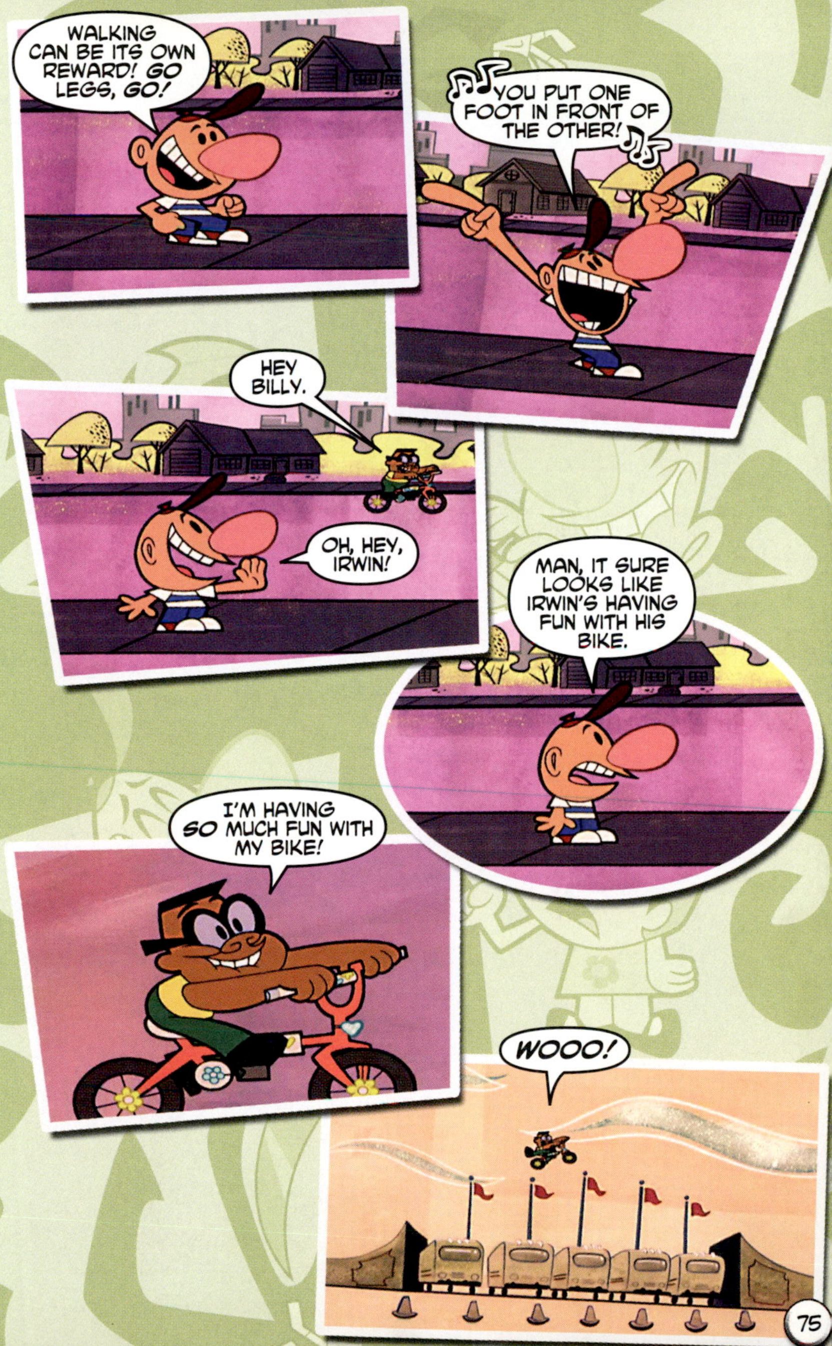
WALKING CAN BE ITS OWN REWARD! GO LEGS, GO!
YOU PUT ONE FOOT IN FRONT OF THE OTHER!
HEY BILLY.
OH, HEY, IRWIN!
MAN, IT SURE LOOKS LIKE IRWIN'S HAVING FUN WITH HIS BIKE.
I'M HAVING SO MUCH FUN WITH MY BIKE!
WOOO!

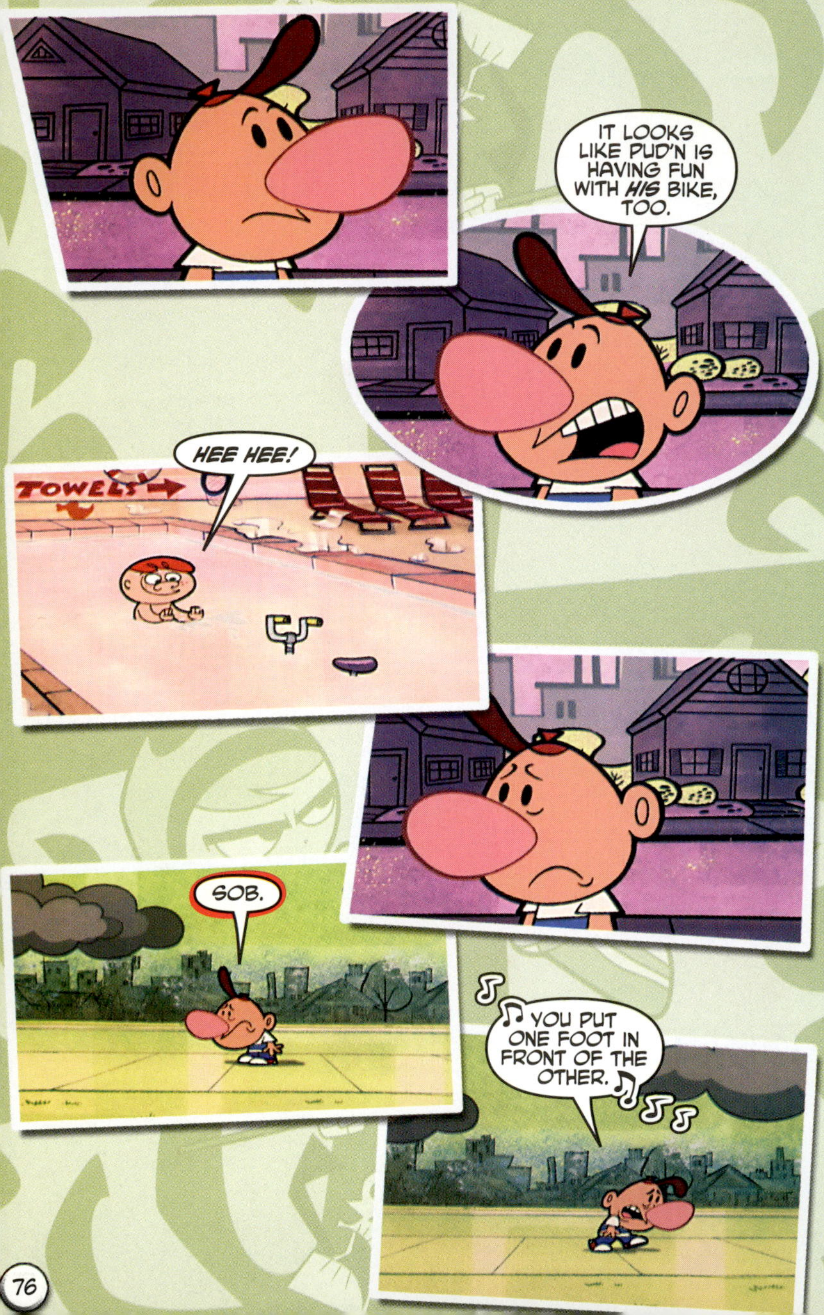
IT LOOKS LIKE PUD'N IS HAVING FUN WITH *HIS* BIKE, TOO.
TOWELS
HEE HEE!
SOB.
YOU PUT ONE FOOT IN FRONT OF THE OTHER.

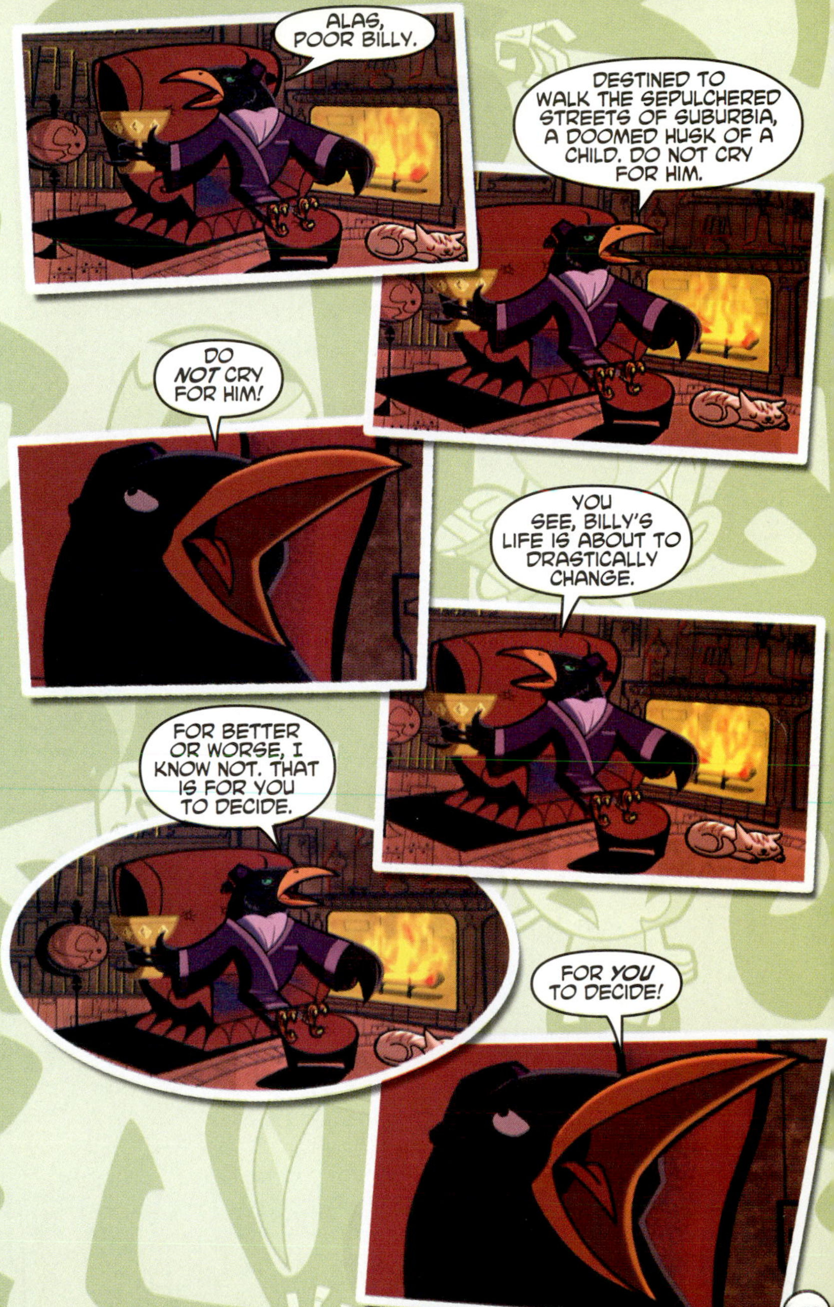
ALAS, POOR BILLY.
DESTINED TO WALK THE SEPULCHERED STREETS OF SUBURBIA, A DOOMED HUSK OF A CHILD. DO NOT CRY FOR HIM.
DO *NOT* CRY FOR HIM!
YOU SEE, BILLY'S LIFE IS ABOUT TO DRASTICALLY CHANGE.
FOR BETTER OR WORSE, I KNOW NOT. THAT IS FOR YOU TO DECIDE.
FOR *YOU* TO DECIDE!

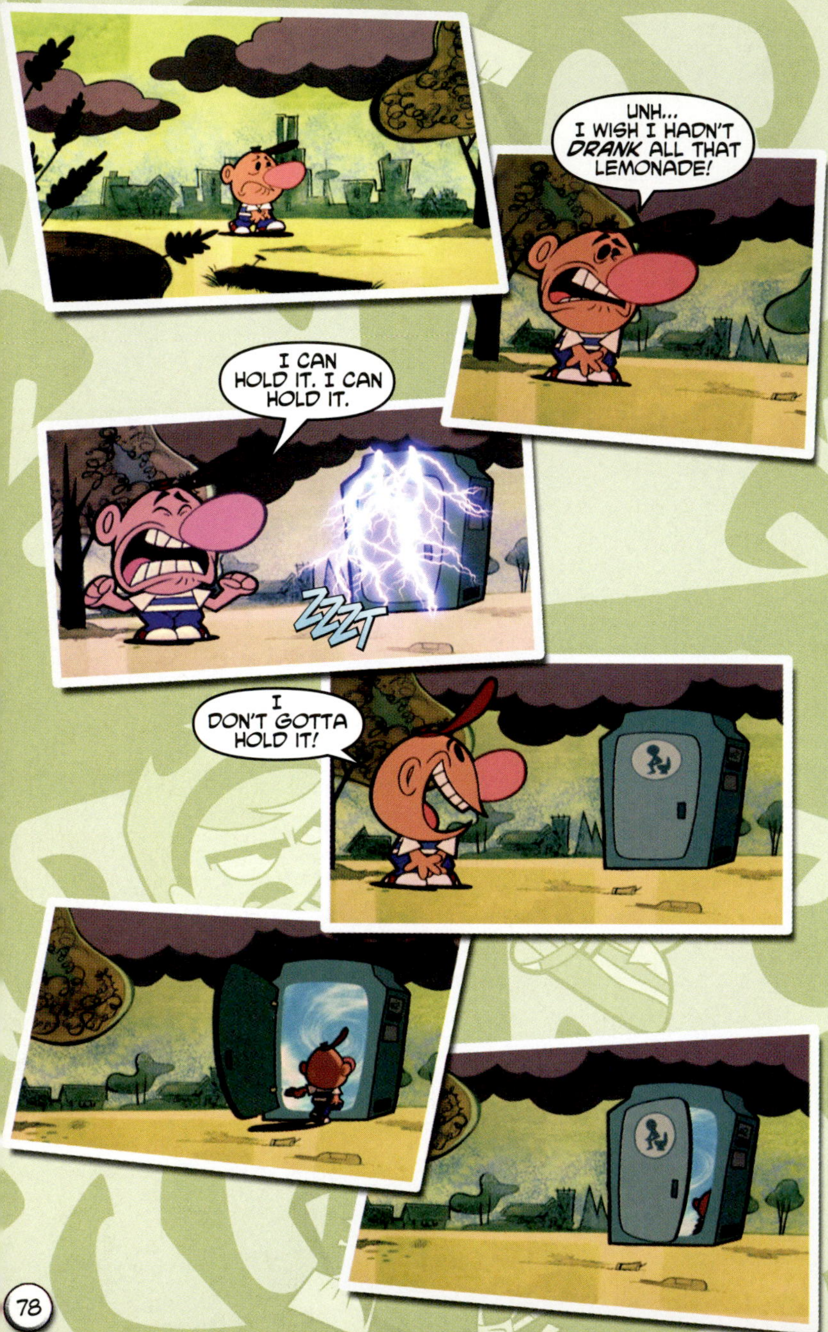
UNH... I WISH I HADN'T *DRANK* ALL THAT LEMONADE!
I CAN HOLD IT. I CAN HOLD IT.
ZZZT
I DON'T GOTTA HOLD IT!

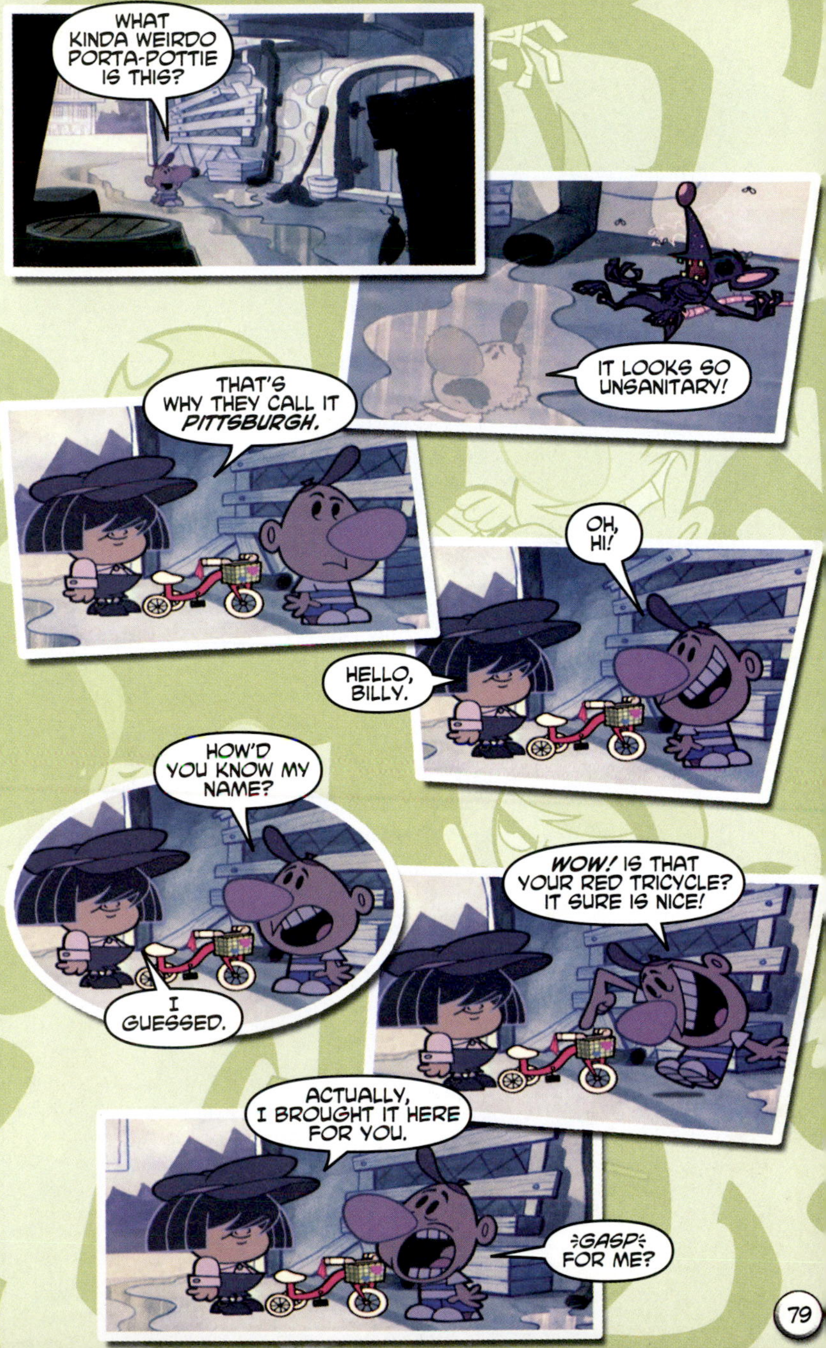
WHAT KINDA WEIRDO PORTA-POTTIE IS THIS?
IT LOOKS SO UNSANITARY!
THAT'S WHY THEY CALL IT *PITTSBURGH.*
OH, HI!
HELLO, BILLY.
HOW'D YOU KNOW MY NAME?
I GUESSED.
WOW! IS THAT YOUR RED TRICYCLE? IT SURE IS NICE!
ACTUALLY, I BROUGHT IT HERE FOR YOU.
GASP FOR ME?

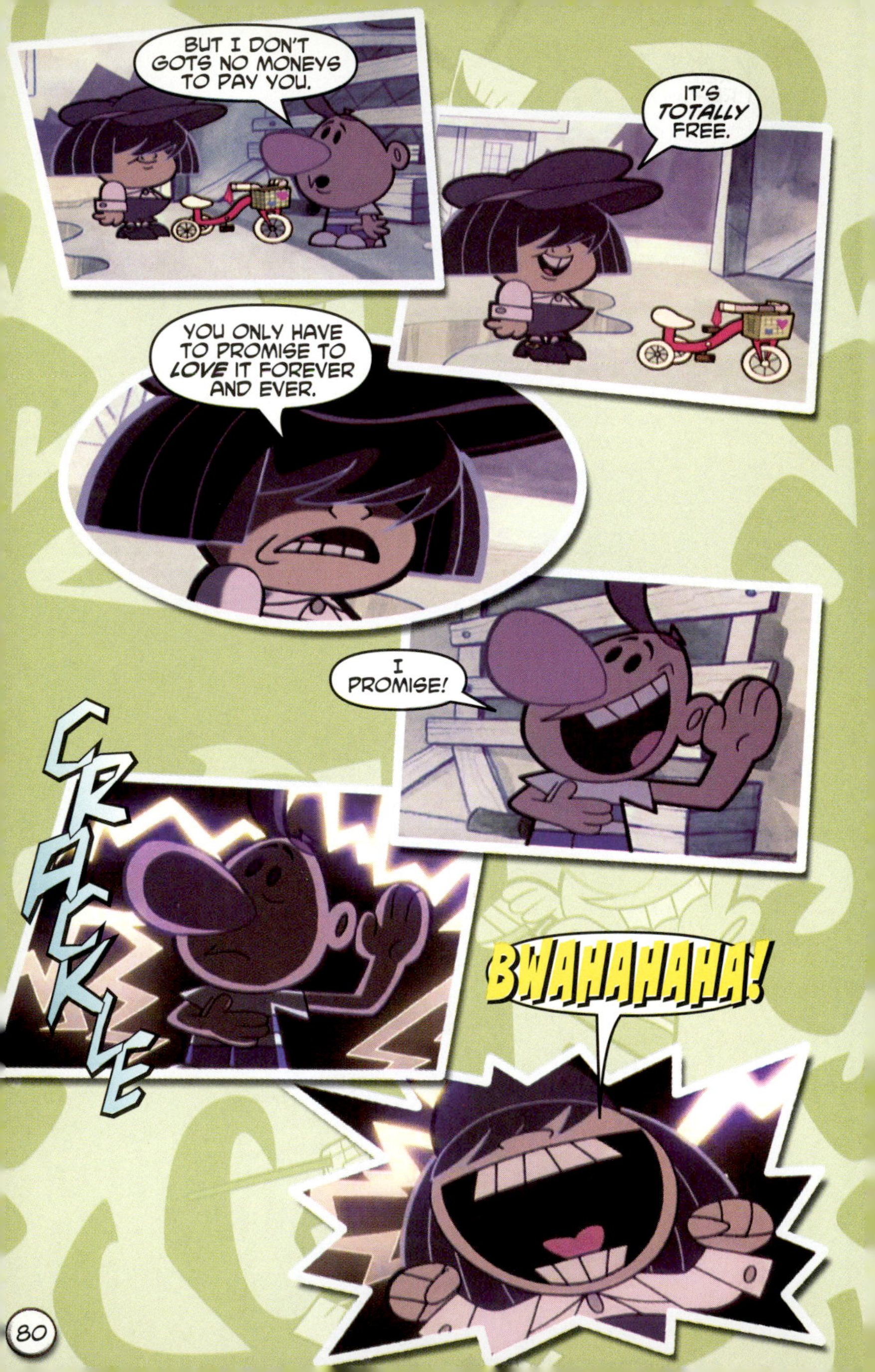

BUT I DON'T GOTS NO MONEYS TO PAY YOU.
IT'S TOTALLY FREE.
YOU ONLY HAVE TO PROMISE TO LOVE IT FOREVER AND EVER.
I PROMISE!
CRACKLE
BWAHAHAHA!

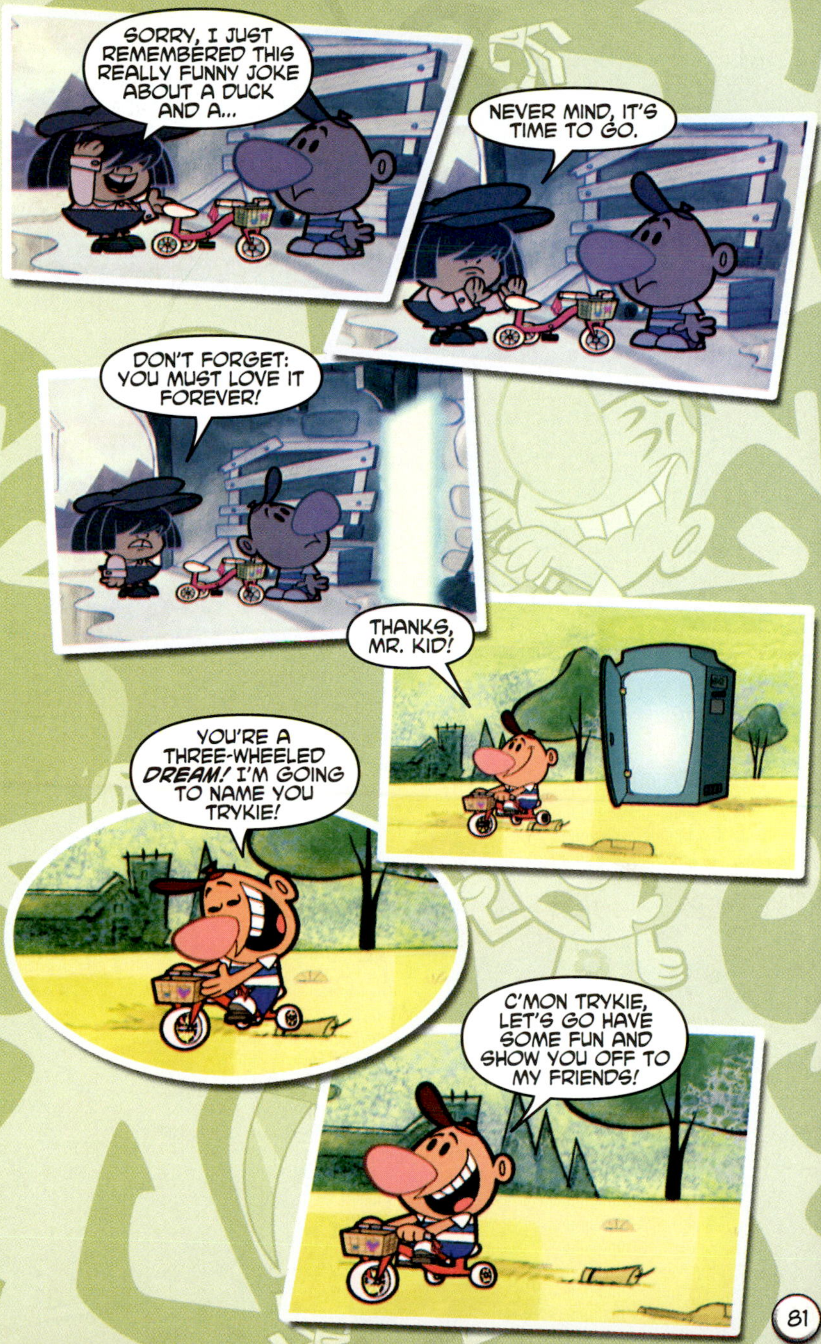
SORRY, I JUST REMEMBERED THIS REALLY FUNNY JOKE ABOUT A DUCK AND A...
NEVER MIND, IT'S TIME TO GO.
DON'T FORGET: YOU MUST LOVE IT FOREVER!
THANKS, MR. KID!
YOU'RE A THREE-WHEELED *DREAM!* I'M GOING TO NAME YOU TRYKIE!
C'MON TRYKIE, LET'S GO HAVE SOME FUN AND SHOW YOU OFF TO MY FRIENDS!

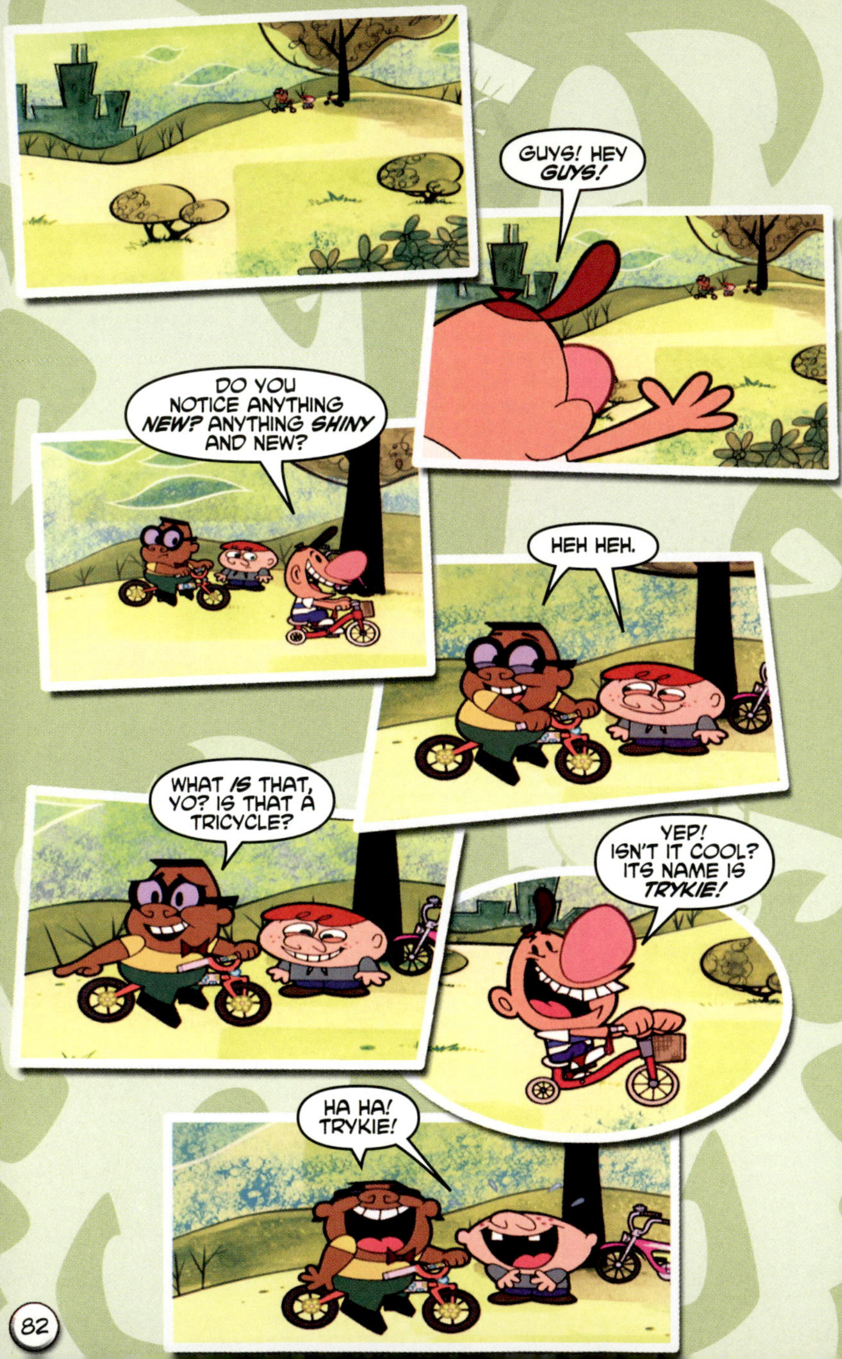
GUYS! HEY GUYS!
DO YOU NOTICE ANYTHING NEW? ANYTHING SHINY AND NEW?
HEH HEH.
WHAT IS THAT, YO? IS THAT A TRICYCLE?
YEP! ISN'T IT COOL? ITS NAME IS TRYKIE!
HA HA! TRYKIE!

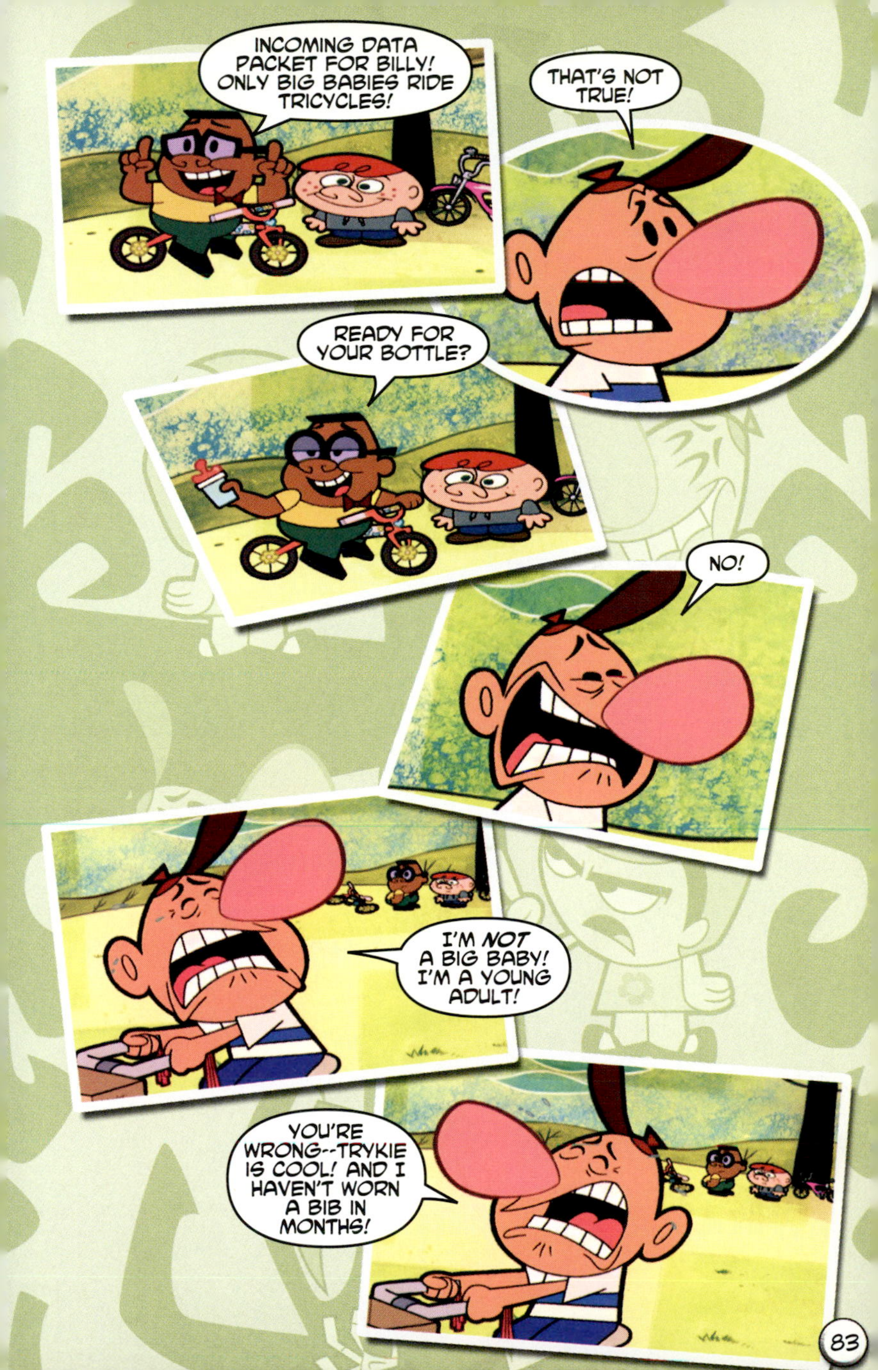
INCOMING DATA PACKET FOR BILLY! ONLY BIG BABIES RIDE TRICYCLES!
THAT'S NOT TRUE!
READY FOR YOUR BOTTLE?
NO!
I'M *NOT* A BIG BABY! I'M A YOUNG ADULT!
YOU'RE WRONG--TRYKIE IS COOL! AND I HAVEN'T WORN A BIB IN MONTHS!

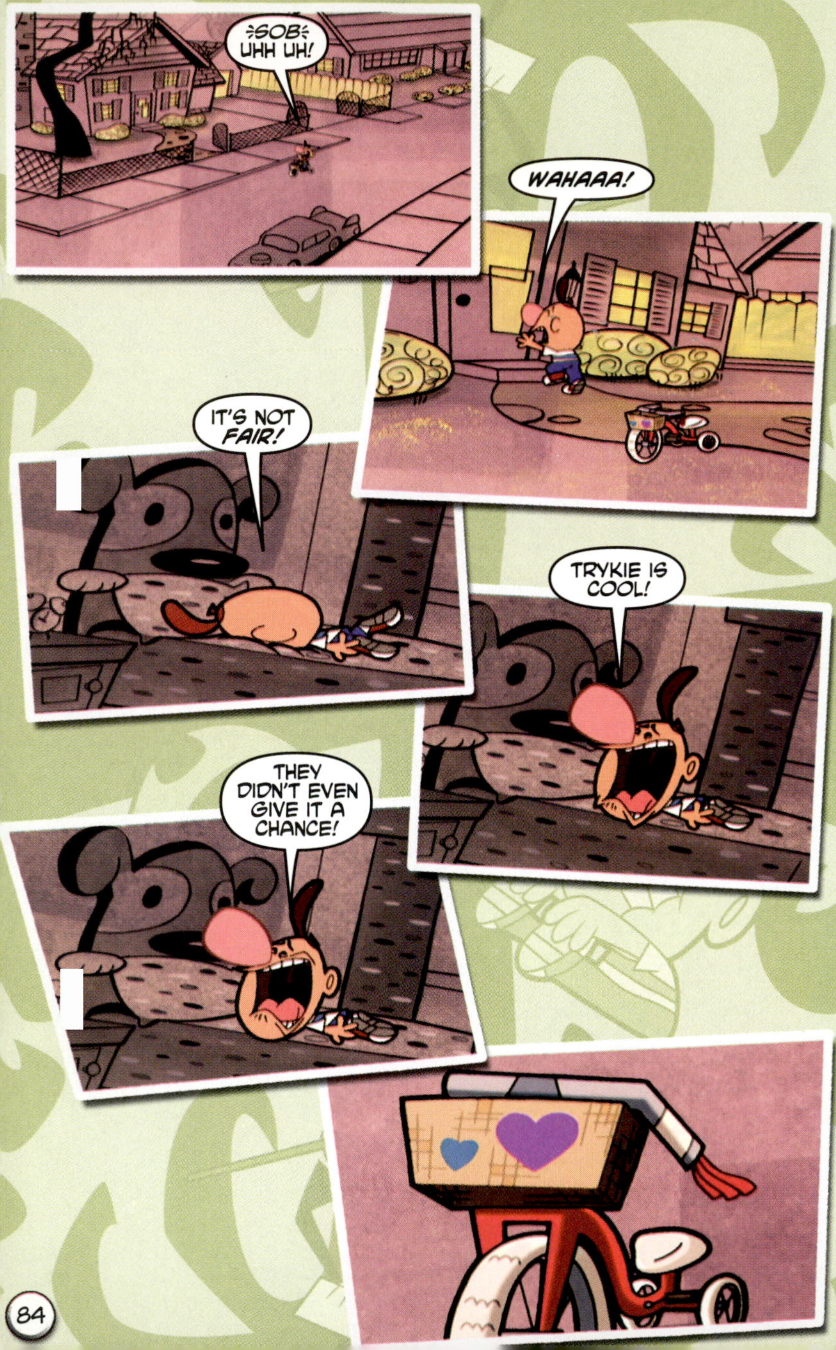
SOB UHH UH!
WAHAAA!
IT'S NOT FAIR!
TRYKIE IS COOL!
THEY DIDN'T EVEN GIVE IT A CHANCE!

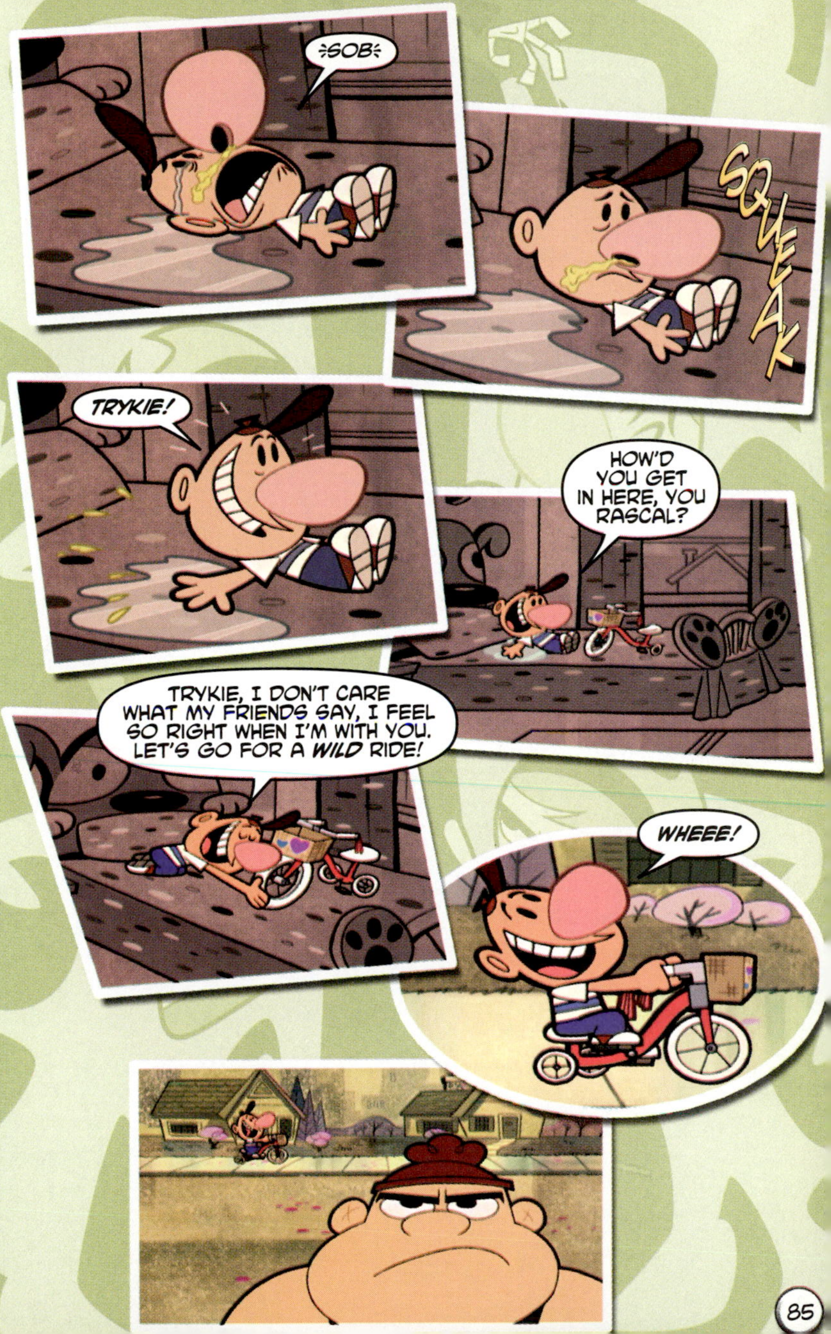

SOB
SQUEAK
TRYKIE!
HOW'D YOU GET IN HERE, YOU RASCAL?
TRYKIE, I DON'T CARE WHAT MY FRIENDS SAY, I FEEL SO RIGHT WHEN I'M WITH YOU. LET'S GO FOR A *WILD* RIDE!
WHEEE!

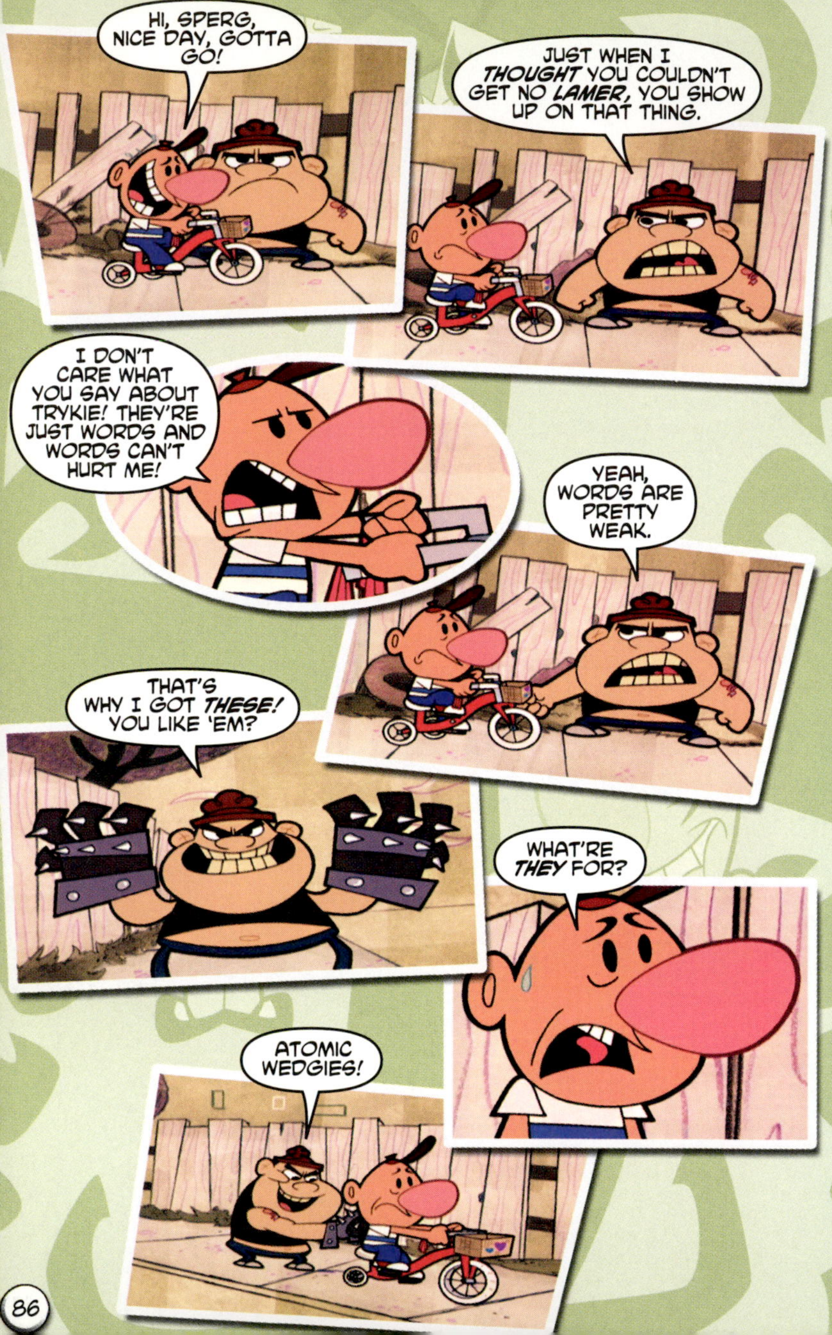
HI, SPERG, NICE DAY, GOTTA GO!
JUST WHEN I *THOUGHT* YOU COULDN'T GET NO *LAMER*, YOU SHOW UP ON THAT THING.
I DON'T CARE WHAT YOU SAY ABOUT TRYKIE! THEY'RE JUST WORDS AND WORDS CAN'T HURT ME!
YEAH, WORDS ARE PRETTY WEAK.
THAT'S WHY I GOT *THESE!* YOU LIKE 'EM?
WHAT'RE *THEY* FOR?
ATOMIC WEDGIES!

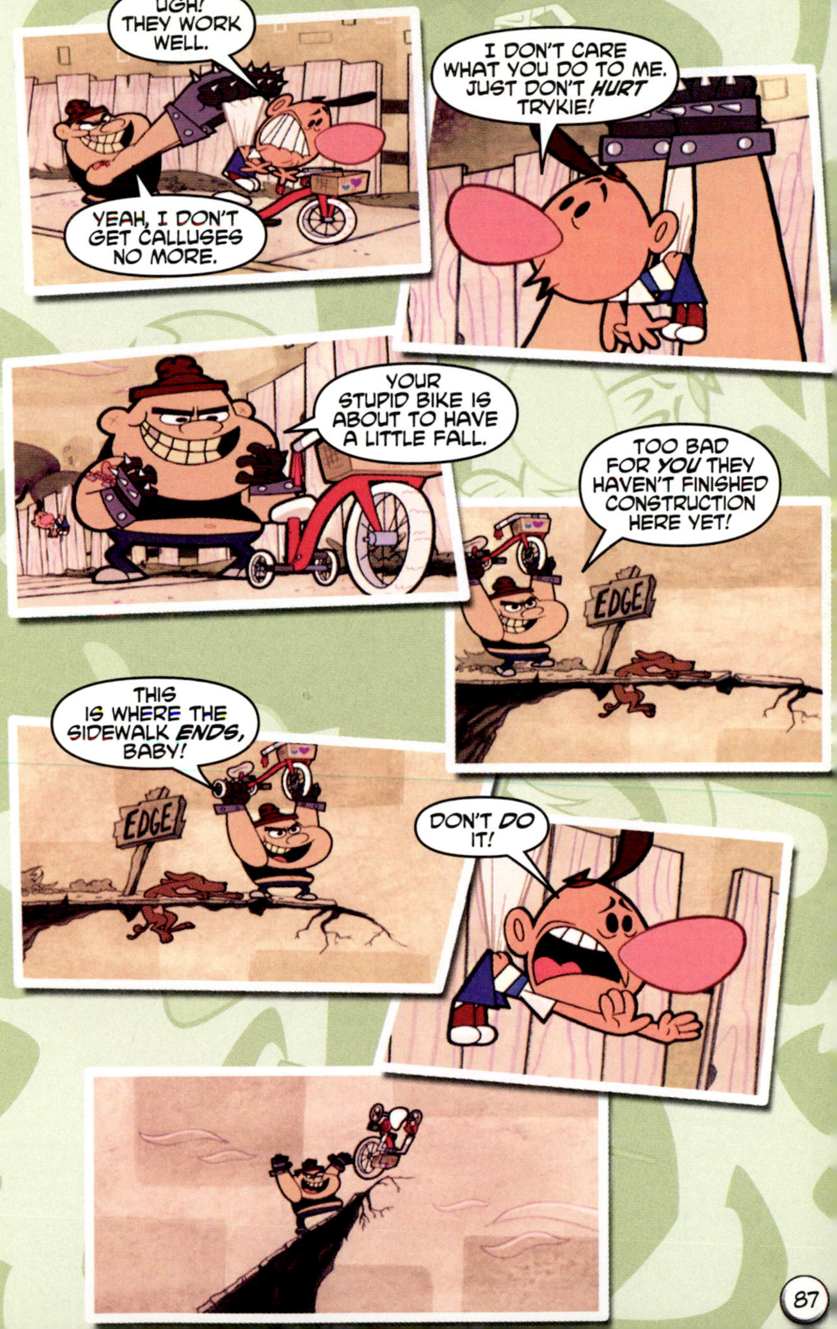
UGH! THEY WORK WELL.
YEAH, I DON'T GET CALLUSES NO MORE.
I DON'T CARE WHAT YOU DO TO ME. JUST DON'T *HURT* TRYKIE!
YOUR STUPID BIKE IS ABOUT TO HAVE A LITTLE FALL.
TOO BAD FOR *YOU* THEY HAVEN'T FINISHED CONSTRUCTION HERE YET!
EDGE
THIS IS WHERE THE SIDEWALK *ENDS*, BABY!
EDGE
DON'T *DO* IT!

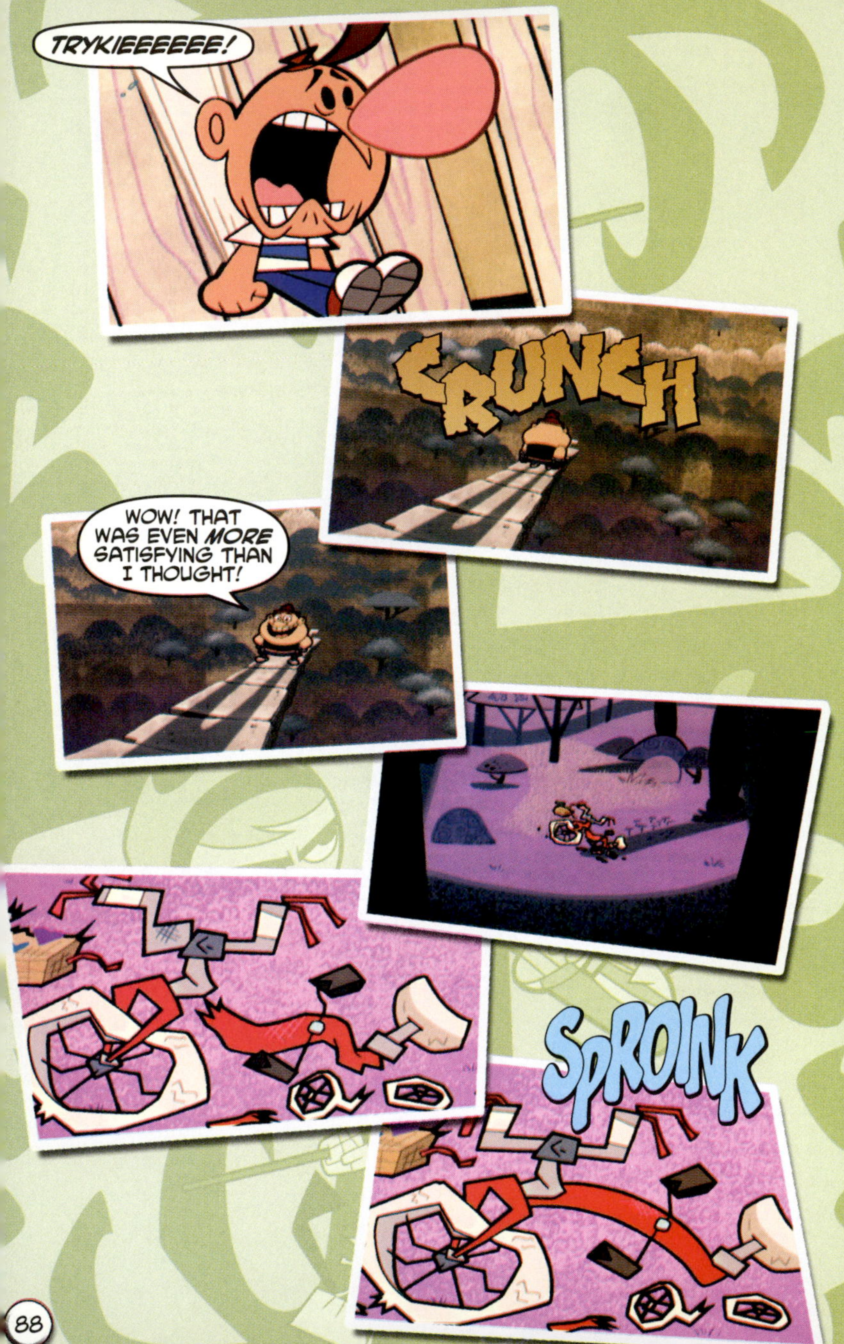
TRYKIEEEEEEE!
CRUNCH
WOW! THAT WAS EVEN *MORE* SATISFYING THAN I THOUGHT!
SPROINK

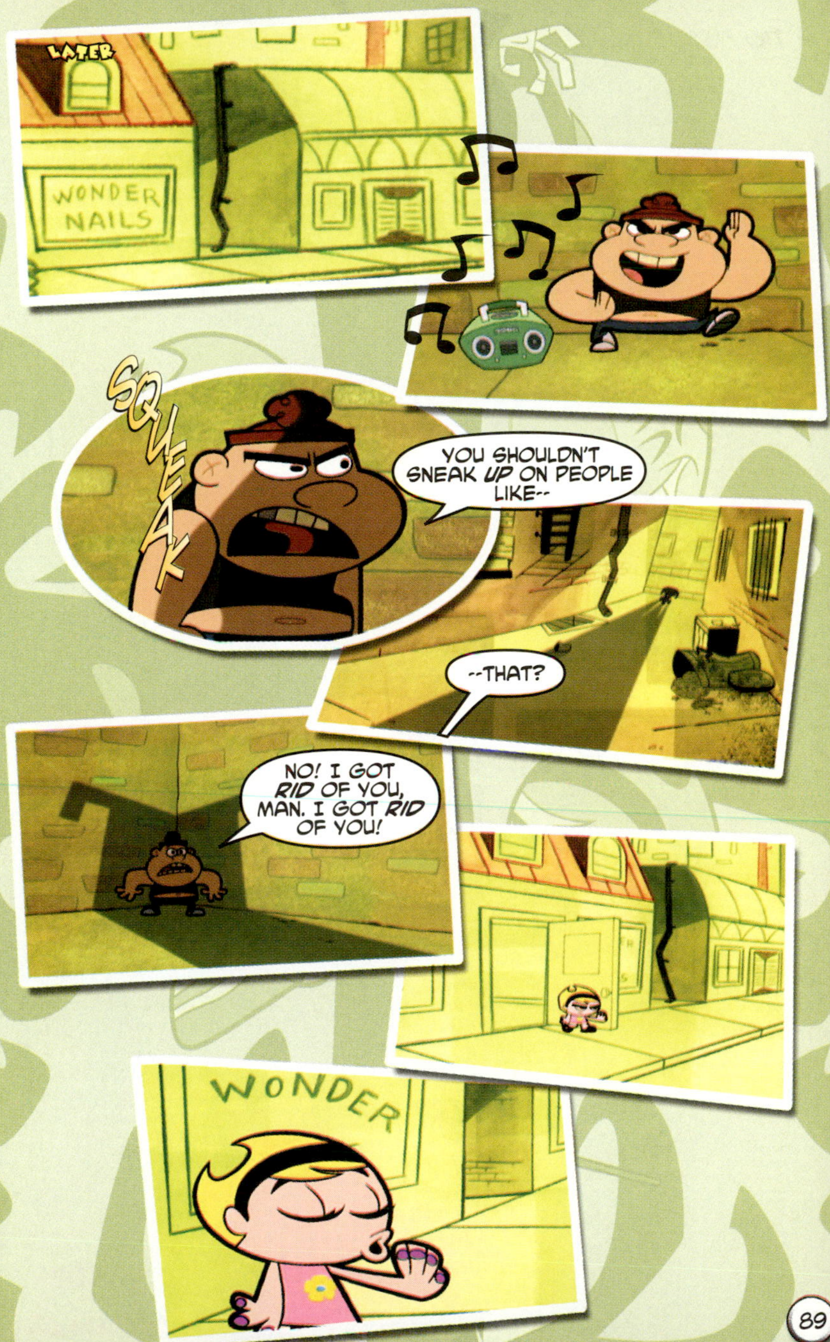
LATER
WONDER NAILS
SQUEAK
YOU SHOULDN'T SNEAK *UP* ON PEOPLE LIKE--
--THAT?
NO! I GOT *RID* OF YOU, MAN. I GOT *RID* OF YOU!
WONDER

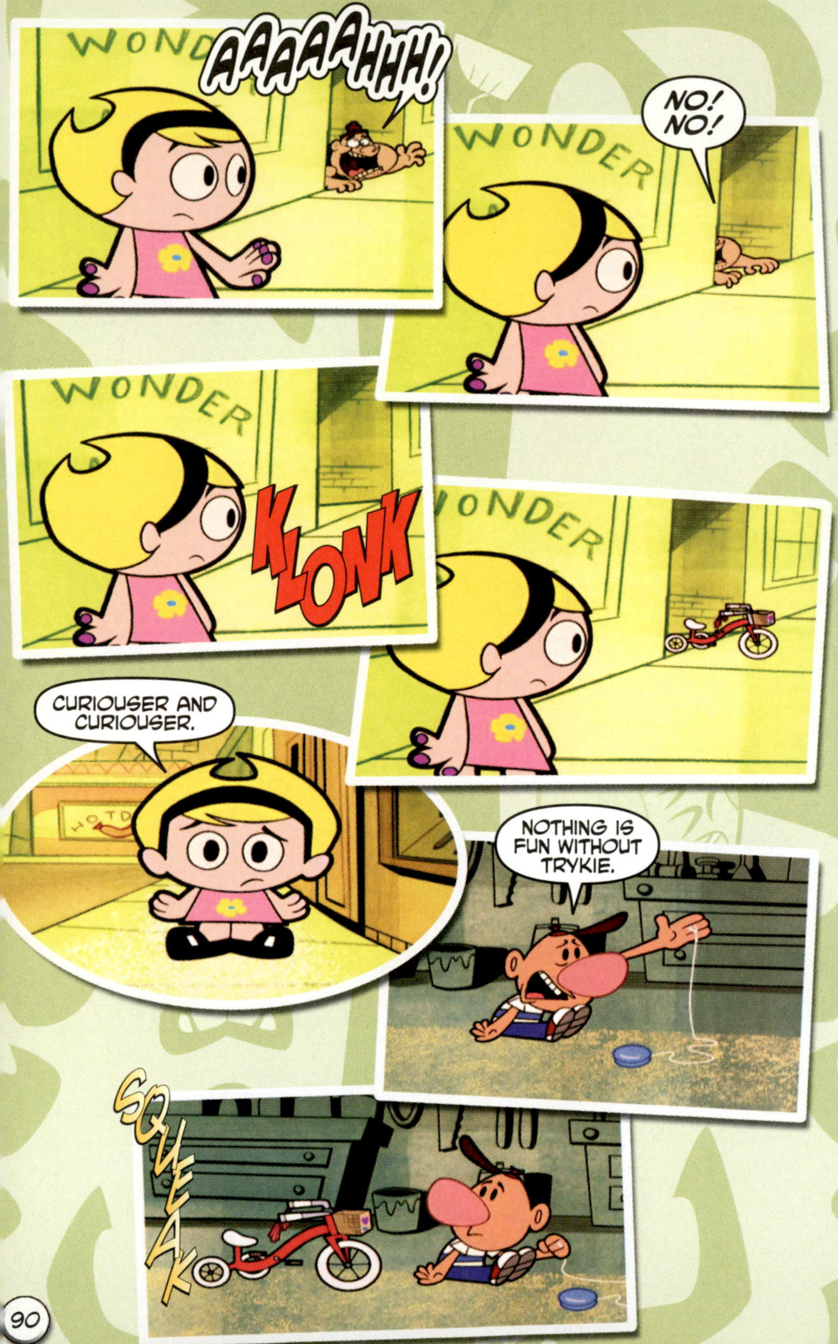
AAAAAHHH!
NO! NO!
KLONK
CURIOUSER AND CURIOUSER.
NOTHING IS FUN WITHOUT TRYKIE.
SQUEAK

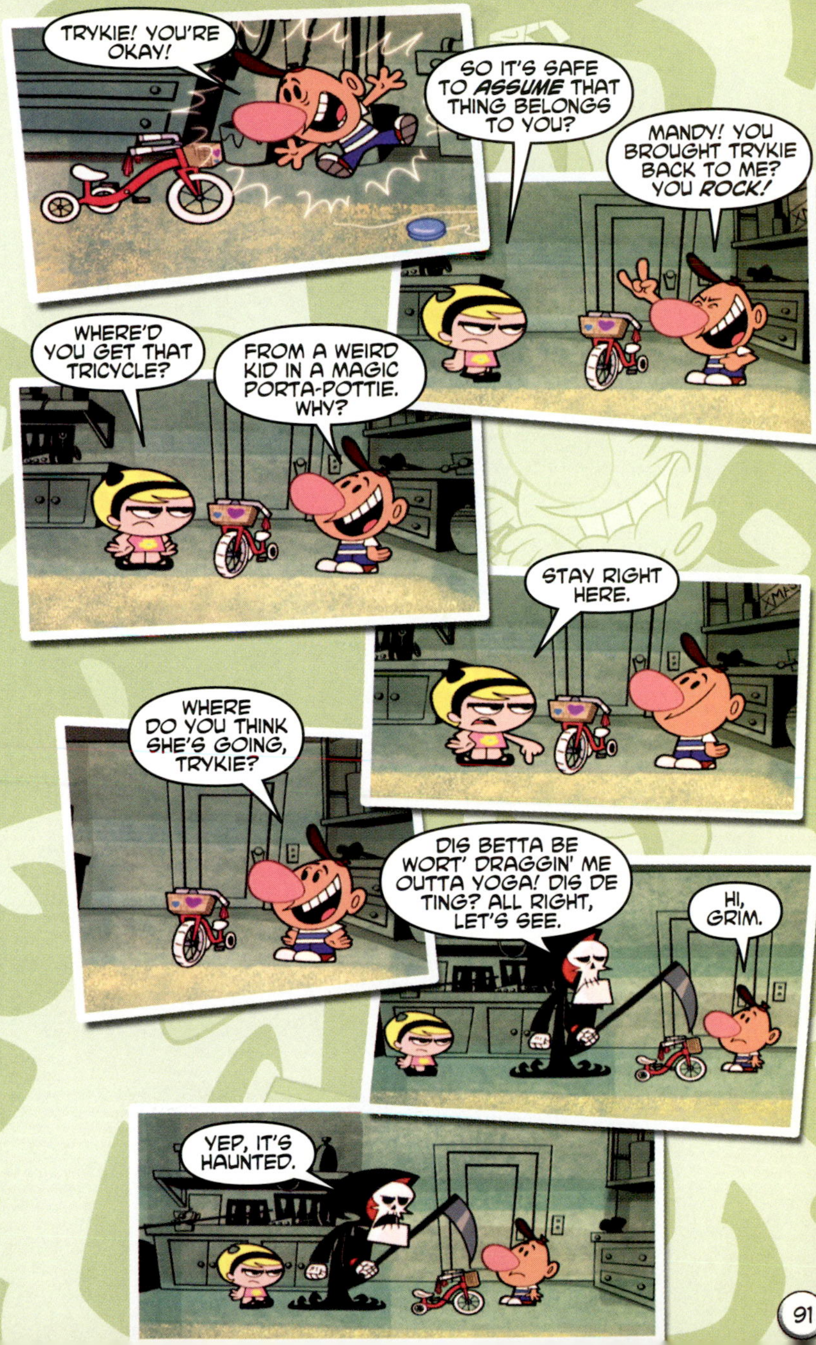
TRYKIE! YOU'RE OKAY!
SO IT'S SAFE TO ASSUME THAT THING BELONGS TO YOU?
MANDY! YOU BROUGHT TRYKIE BACK TO ME? YOU ROCK!
WHERE'D YOU GET THAT TRICYCLE?
FROM A WEIRD KID IN A MAGIC PORTA-POTTIE. WHY?
STAY RIGHT HERE.
WHERE DO YOU THINK SHE'S GOING, TRYKIE?
DIS BETTA BE WORT' DRAGGIN' ME OUTTA YOGA! DIS DE TING? ALL RIGHT, LET'S SEE.
HI, GRIM.
YEP, IT'S HAUNTED.

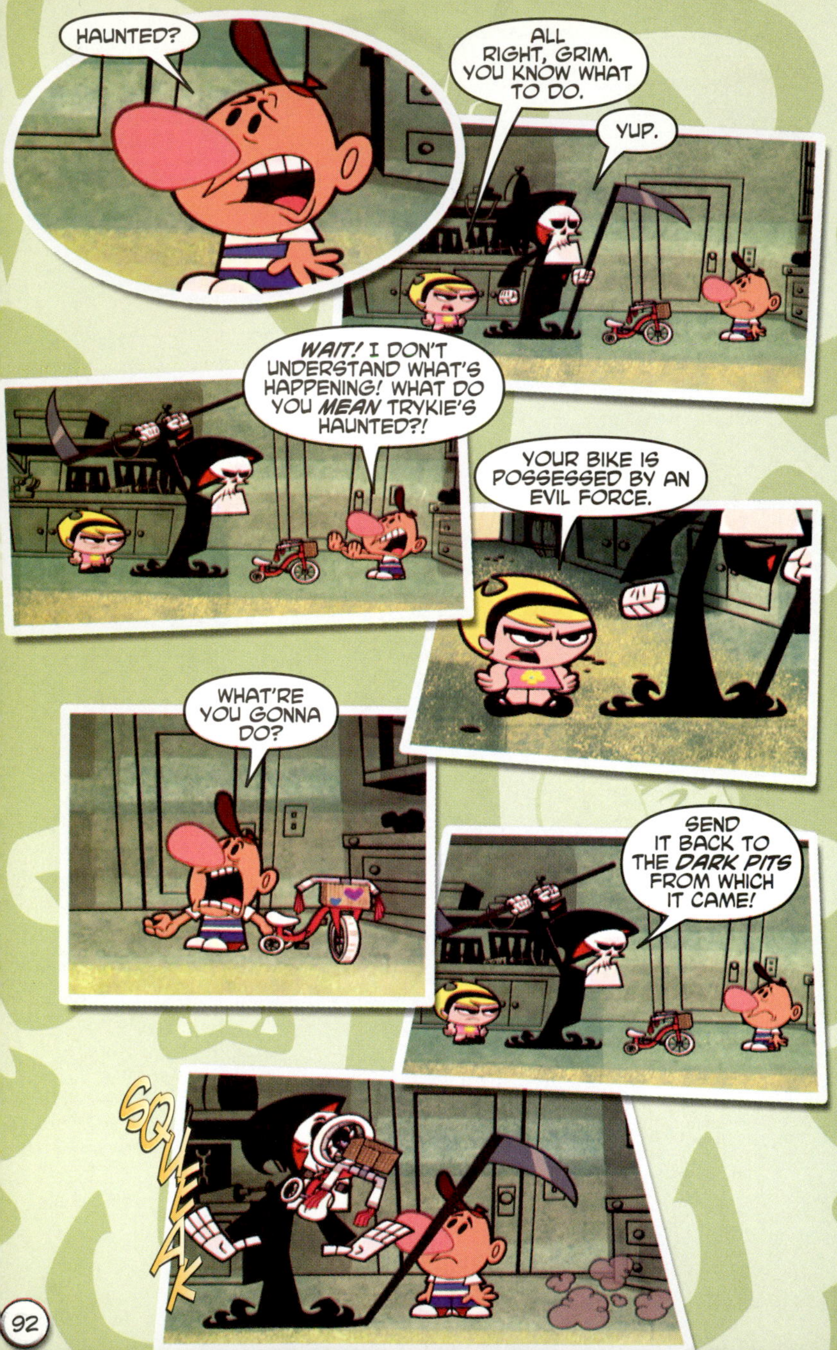
HAUNTED?
ALL RIGHT, GRIM. YOU KNOW WHAT TO DO.
YUP.
WAIT! I DON'T UNDERSTAND WHAT'S HAPPENING! WHAT DO YOU MEAN TRYKIE'S HAUNTED?!
YOUR BIKE IS POSSESSED BY AN EVIL FORCE.
WHAT'RE YOU GONNA DO?
SEND IT BACK TO THE DARK PITS FROM WHICH IT CAME!
SQUEAK

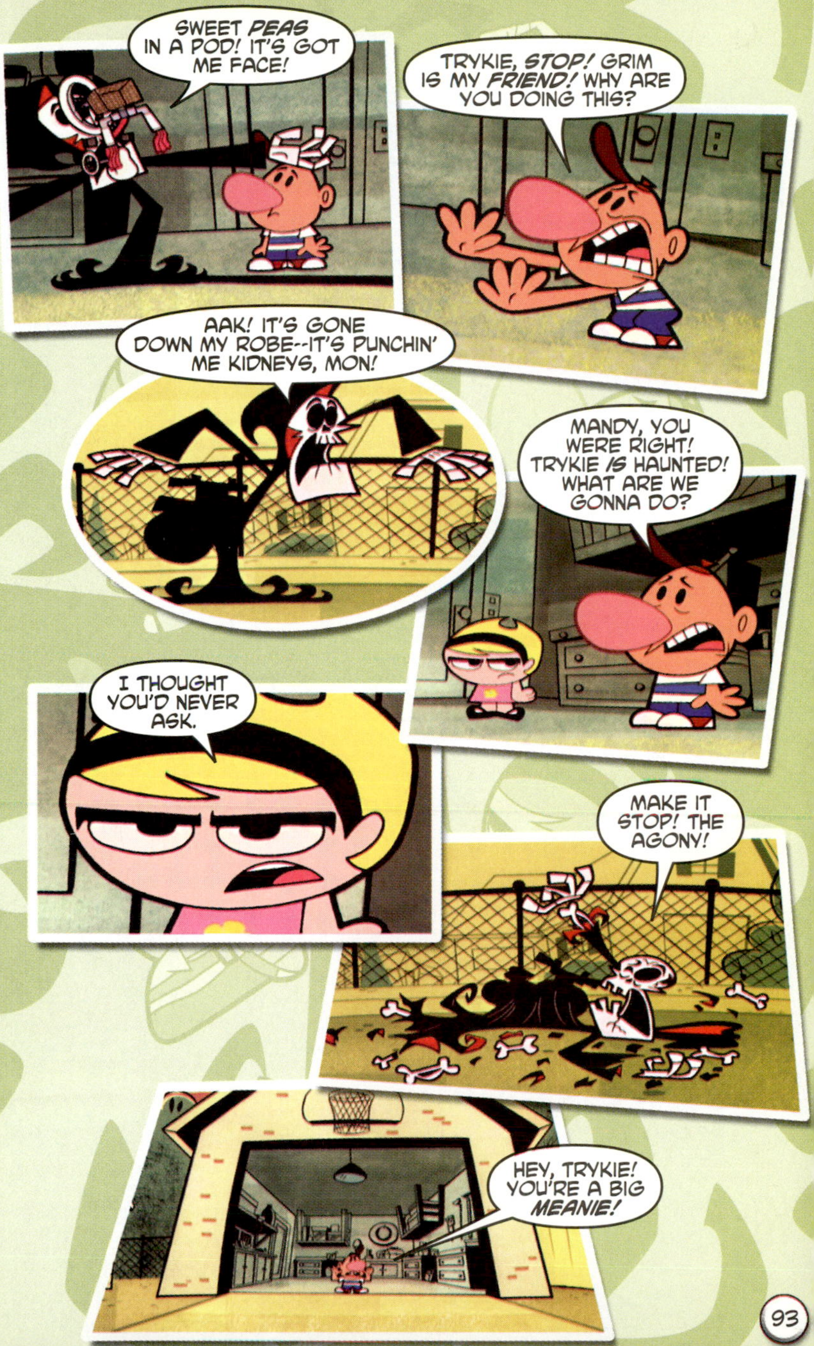

SWEET PEAS IN A POD! IT'S GOT ME FACE!
TRYKIE, STOP! GRIM IS MY FRIEND! WHY ARE YOU DOING THIS?
AAK! IT'S GONE DOWN MY ROBE--IT'S PUNCHIN' ME KIDNEYS, MON!
MANDY, YOU WERE RIGHT! TRYKIE IS HAUNTED! WHAT ARE WE GONNA DO?
I THOUGHT YOU'D NEVER ASK.
MAKE IT STOP! THE AGONY!
HEY, TRYKIE! YOU'RE A BIG MEANIE!

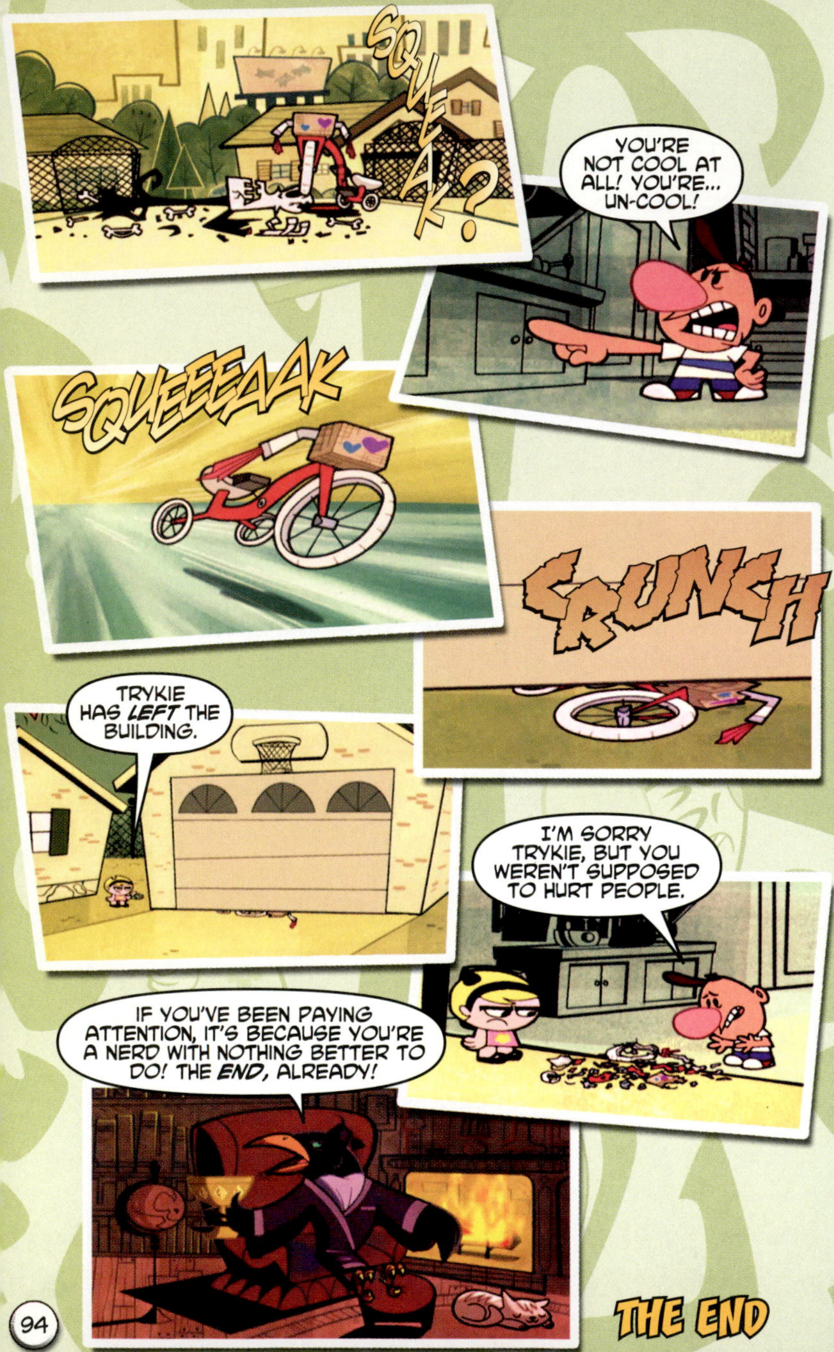
SQUEAK?
YOU'RE NOT COOL AT ALL! YOU'RE... UN-COOL!
SQUEEEAAK
CRUNCH
TRYKIE HAS *LEFT* THE BUILDING.
I'M SORRY TRYKIE, BUT YOU WEREN'T SUPPOSED TO HURT PEOPLE.
IF YOU'VE BEEN PAYING ATTENTION, IT'S BECAUSE YOU'RE A NERD WITH NOTHING BETTER TO DO! THE *END*, ALREADY!
THE END